Shadows of Gray

Murder Mystery Amateur Sleuth With A Past

Jodi Walter

THIRTEEN PAGES

Published by Thirteen Pages

ISBN 978-1-7387028-9-3 (softcover)

ISBN 978-1-7381594-0-6 (ebook)

ISBN 978-1-7381594-1-3 (audiobook)

1st edition 2024

To my son, who has shown me more strength in character than anyone else I have ever met. You grew up too fast and have become a wonderful young man who I am so very proud of. I look forward to watching you bloom into the amazing man I know you will be.

I love you,
Mom

CHAPTER 1

IT WAS ANOTHER AVERAGE Friday afternoon in the office, returning from a late lunch—reheated rice and spicy chicken with hot, black coffee. Not great for the digestive tract, but it was what he liked. Jed washed his hands, stared at his reflection in the mirror, then strolled mindlessly through the office, his feet finding the way as his mind drifted. The buzz of colleagues—some therapists, some social workers—busy with calls and clients that had come in right before their lunch breaks filtered under the doors, through the cracks, and around hinges before spilling out into the wide hallway.

Most of them never left their doors open. It'd been that way since he'd begun working there. It was understandable, though. During the days, his co-workers rarely had time to mingle, since they were focused on clients, both the ones who visited in office for in-person, individual and group sessions, and the ones who preferred the emotional distance offered by over-the-phone sessions.

Jed had his fair share of those clients; one had taken to calling at the same time each Friday for the past few months, and he was sure to call today, as always. Jed had a few in-office clients, too, but they tended to be post-rehab check-ins. Since he specialized in addiction treatment, Jed's patients struggled with rehab—and reintegration into the society after rehab—which meant a lot of them were members of the homeless community in the city. Generally, they were the type that would shy away from… no, wouldn't even consider coming into… his office to meet face-to-face.

The only reason he knew other people worked in this building were the brief moments when they all arrived to and left work, leaving behind a nod in hello here and a small wave there. Apart from those sparing interactions, the only reminder of their presence were the whispers of their calls and conversations as he passed by each day, to and from lunch.

Back in his office, Jed sank into his seat, eyes settling on a tree across the street. He let his thoughts take him somewhere up in the clouds that hung above the tree, miles away in the vast, open space of somewhere, and let time drift by for a while. The sun was pouring in through the glass panes that separated his small office from the outside, but it didn't make him feel warm and cheerful like it did most people.

He sighed. Leaning even further against his chair and throwing his feet up onto the desk, he thought of the week he'd endured. Nothing out of the ordinary had happened. He'd been to work every day, gone home in the evenings, went to the gym, and even, sometimes, into the running trails to exercise at night. Hell, he'd managed to make himself a homecooked meal three nights out of seven. Just the usual.

Damn.

It'd been the most boring week ever, but it'd felt so stressful—like the world was caving in on him with each step. He needed to take up journalling again.

It'd been a long week—a long *life*. Maybe too long, but he squashed that thought and refocused on the sunlight that spread across the rug and over the desk in front of him. He couldn't wait to disappear off the work radar and hide at home for the weekend. He needed a break from everyone and their problems. He needed a break from *his* problems. Jed enjoyed the work, that was certain. But the fresh 'save the world' energy he felt every Monday slowly faded as the week dragged on, until on Fridays, he, sometimes, wanted to hang up on his callers. He never did, though. He cared too much about their wellbeing to put them in jeopardy.

The phone rang.

Ah. There was the call he'd been anticipating all afternoon. It was an hour late.

"Hello?" He relaxed back into his chair after picking up the receiver.

"Hey man. Got caught up in a fight earlier this afternoon. Needed some bandages so I had to go trade at the store to get 'em," the voice explained. "But uh, yes. Here I am."

"A fight, Max?" Jed stifled any trace of surprise in his voice. "Wanna tell me about that? And what were you trading?"

The young man laughed, a genuine guffaw, like the question amused him. Jed didn't smile.

"Come on Mr. G you know what we trade. And they don't call me Mad Max in these streets for nothing. I be tearing these mo'fuckas up. I can't let 'em play me like I'm a punk."

Jed ignored Max's attempt to evade his question. "How did the fight start?"

Max sighed.

"Aw man, don't talk to me in that tone. Man, I'on like that. I feel like a kid or something."

"You're seventeen, Max. According to the law, you *are* a kid. But I'm not trying to patronize you. I'm just… concerned."

Jed knew that Max didn't respond to stern tones and force. The boy was too hard-headed for that strategy and wasn't pretending to be a hard-edged criminal. He *was* a hard-edged criminal.

"Tell me what happened," he pressed.

"I was on my block, y'know, where I stay at. And I was making some *tea,* y'know what I'm saying, Mr. G? Couple a guys run up on me from behind. They thought I ain't see 'em coming." Max laughed when he said that, coughing for a minute before getting back to the story.

On his end of the line, Jed was making short notes, connecting the dots in today's adventure to those unanswered questions he'd been left with from the previous stories the boy had told him.

"So, I let the dumb mo'fuckas run up, but I dodge to the side like *BOW*, and then I tripped the first one as he was coming past, and he fell out the edge of the window ledge where I been sitting, and he hit the ground like *BOOM*. And the other one swung round to swing at me, and I seen he had a knife, so I dodged like *BAP* and pushed him in the side out the window, too."

Jed found himself smiling as Max told him the story of his victory, able to picture the kid as he used animated gestures on the other end of the phone. He pinched the bridge of his nose. This kid was nuts, but Jed liked him.

"But thing is when he swung at me, he cut me on my hand cuz I was dodging."

"Were you able to dress the wound?"

"Yeah, man. I went up by the grocery in my hood. They have a lil trade system, y'know what I'm saying? Yeah so, I got a couple stuff, and I dressed it up, you feel me? Just another victory badge to the collection man."

"Where are the two guys that attacked you?"

Max burst out laughing.

"Where are they? Their bodies be down at that there morgue that's on your street, my guy."

"You know where my street is? Why don't you come see me sometime?" Jed asked, diverting attention away from the major confession Max had just made. But he made a note.

Their bodies be down at that there morgue that's on your street, my guy.

He would have to check the morgue records this week to see who the two young men were. It wasn't the first, or second, time Max had reported being attacked. That's why Jed was so worried about him. He wanted him to go to rehab and get off the streets. Badly—more than he wanted to feel better himself.

"Nawwwww," Max dragged. "I can't do that. You nice folks won't tolerate a guy like me in y'all fancy building."

The kid hid it well, but Jed knew he wanted to come. He knew Max wanted to change his life into something better.

"I know you know me better than that, Max. But thank you for calling today. Is something on your mind? Or did you just want to do the weekly catch up?"

The line sat silent for a few heartbeats.

"I um, I called my mom like you suggested last week. We talked for a while; she wants to see me in person. To talk."

"You did a good job reaching out to her. She must have been worried, and I can understand why she wants to see you."

"Yeah. She wants to see me next week. I don't know what to do. I want to see her, but…"

Jed heard the rest of the sentence play through his mind as clearly as though Max had said it aloud.

"You don't want seeing her to make you feel… some sort of guilt? Or obligation to go back right away?"

Max hesitated again.

"Yeah. I want to go back but I—I'm just not ready. There's so much to process through, man—so much I been through on the streets, so much I'd leave behind."

So much I'd leave behind, echoed through Jed's mind.

"What's one thing you're struggling to let go of? That's stopping you from coming back?" he asked.

"Um, I got a girl out here. We just started out, but… I see myself with her, y'know? And she feels the same. If I leave this part of town, I can't come back. Them boys will kill me any chance they get—you know they're already trying to. I'on got no phone. I'on got no way to contact her if I leave."

Jed sat up straight in his chair, his eyes resting on the office door without seeing it. "Take her with you."

The line was silent.

"How? I don't got no house, no job, where would she stay at? I'on want her to be in danger or uncomfortable, and it would have to be somewhere up to scratch… because she'll be thinking that she coulda stayed home, and she'll leave."

"Call your mom and tell her you'll see her. I think it'll do you both well. Leave the other part to me. There are some state-funded housing options for rehabilitating youth and the homeless. They're hard to come by, but I'll do some looking and digging to see what I can do."

"Y-you would do that for me, Mr. G? I'on wanna be no burden on you, man."

With a huff and a grin, Jed said, "I would do that for you. And I will."

Jed was looking at his phone, at the timer he'd started right when Max called. Nine minutes on the clock.

"I'll call her."

"Good. Your time is running out, isn't it?"

"Yeah," Max answered. Jed could hear the sadness in the boy's voice, though he tried to hide it.

"Next time we talk, I'll have a way you can fix that time limit, too."

Max laughed. "I hope they're paying you good, man. You really out here tryna help me. I gotta run. I needa talk to my girl about what you said."

"Be safe, Maxwell."

On the other end of the line, far from Jed's office, the boy hesitated. He looked down at the concrete, feeling warmth spread through his chest. Nobody ever called him by his full name. And there was certainly nobody telling him to be safe with such obvious care in their voice, either. He closed his eyes.

"I will. They won't get me." He finally answered.

When they'd ended the call, Jed realized he wasn't so sure he could believe that. Max seemed confident. He was sure-footed, quick-witted, and a fast learner. He'd only been on the streets for a couple of years, and he'd already made his way to the top of the food chain in his section of town, with a reputation that spilled over into the rest of the city. That wasn't good. He was a walking target, and he needed to get out of there, now, before one of his attackers proved successful. Jed wondered how he'd managed to thwart them all.

How did he always see it coming? How did he always have a way of escaping their traps? It didn't make sense if he thought about it like a counselor, but he knew well the adaptability and foresight that one had to develop when on the streets and involved with the wrong crowd.

When he'd first met Max, it had been the board of the juvenile detention facility he had been incarcerated in that had reached out to Jed. The officer, Tony, who had worked closest to Max had seen something in the teenager that had made him eager to get him in contact with an addiction therapist.

The officer had described his motivation for getting Max into contact with a therapist as a 'spark of life'—look in the kid's eyes that made Tony sure Max wanted more out of life than just drugs. He wasn't hardened like the rest of kids in the program, and Tony had told Jed that he didn't think Max was doing drugs for the hell of it, but because of something else that he might be able to work through with a therapist. Tony had hoped the kid would reintegrate into society.

Max hadn't appreciated it in the beginning—at all—and it had taken a while before he and Jed had built a genuine connection. In the beginning of their therapeutic relationship, Max had outright refused to come into the office and had dictated that he would only do this 'lame therapy thing' on his terms, by calling in. Jed had agreed. Calling in was better than refusing to talk. Over time, Max had lowered his guard but still hadn't been willing to open up about his situation.

9

It was one day two months ago that they had finally reached that breakthrough. Jed knew that no two clients were the same. With Max's journey, it was the consistency that seemed to get through to him—the fact that Jed was always present, calm, and attentive when they spoke each week. In the beginning, Max had sometimes hung up at four minutes in, sometimes right away. But as he continued to call each week, whether because he was curious about addiction therapy, or he was bored, the calls got longer and longer. Then, one day when Jed asked Max how he was doing, the teenager sighed, *We're all a little fucked up man.*

For Jed, getting clients to the point of starting recovery required more than just talking to them and covertly bullying them into signing up for rehab. It had a lot more to do with understanding why they were resisting so he could breakthrough that barrier with them.

Jed sighed as he stared out the window into the street again. He eventually signed off his work systems before closing the lid of his laptop. It was five in the afternoon—quitting time. He had a dinner meeting planned at seven. Standing, Jed tucked his laptop into his workbag and ran through the plan in his mind for the fiftieth time since he'd woken up. *Go to work, get home, shower, change, get to the restaurant on time, get back home, breathe easy for the rest of the weekend.*

The prospect of getting home, showered, and changed was task enough. He'd weighed the option of spending a little extra time at work and showing up to the restaurant as he was, but that idea made his stomach churn. It would only be appropriate to meet up with friends that way—they wouldn't mind how tired he was or that he hadn't changed to freshen up.

But first impressions were important to him, especially when it came to women. He was going to be working with this woman for the foreseeable future, since the nature of their partnership was permanent, instead of case-by-case collaborations like he had been doing with the police department as an investigative therapist. His work with the department in the past had been to help during court cases once crimes were solved. This new partnership was a pilot program that had just been created.

So, the least he could do was put some effort into his appearance the first time he met his new partner, even if he looked like death when she saw him the second time. He picked up his bag and headed out of his office, down the lonely hallway. He wondered whether his co-workers had real lives outside of their jobs. No matter how late he stayed after work officially ended, the calls still seeped into the hallway as he passed, and the lights were on under the doors. He knew that life well.

Jed burst out onto the windy street, breathing the acrid air deep and settling into his walk. It was something he didn't have to think about much—the result of months of walking the same route. Sometimes, he'd walk into his apartment and wonder if he really had just walked all the way home without noticing any of the people he passed or the stores that had flash sales or the stalls he could have stopped to buy food at.

Often, as he stepped into his apartment, he tried to remember his walk home and always came up with a vivid recollection of what had transpired in his mind. He'd ruled his surface level obliviousness down to just being comfortable with his commuting routine.

This evening, however, his consciousness was fully present. As he passed the hot dog stand a block down, where a crowd of people could be seen gathered around, money in hand, waiting to grab, pay, and go, his feet slowed. His stomach rumbled, and conceding, Jed joined the throng, five-dollar bill between his fingers. He'd never bought from this stand before, but every evening and every morning when he walked by, without fail, there was a crowd of people with their hands outstretched. There was no harm in buying a hotdog on a Friday evening.

When it was his turn, the man behind the stall asked gruffly, "Pork or chicken?"

The sign on the stall read: $2 for pork, $1.50 for chicken.

"Both."

The guy looked up at him for a second as his hands worked the grill.

"Toppings?"

"Everything you've got."

The crowd had dispersed, and he was the only one left. The gruff looking guy grunted.

"Alright, big guy. Here you go."

Jed looked at his outstretched hand and swallowed. This was the biggest hot dog he'd ever seen. It was massive, spilling over with two sausages, cheese, mayo, relish, ketchup, and some other sprinklings he couldn't identify off the bat. He took it, handed his five over, and turned to head down the road again, at his usual pace. A block later, he tucked the last piece of the delicacy into his mouth and nodded to himself. He'd seriously been missing out. He definitely had to visit that stall more often.

A little further down the road, Jed stopped at an AT&T store to buy a new phone. Not for himself, no, but for Max. The measly ten-minute time slot the kid had to call in each week wasn't nearly enough to get through everything they needed to in his sessions. He called from a payphone near the building he stayed at, and according to him, it was the only one around he had unthreatened access to. The others were in dark alleyways and deep corners where anything could lie in wait for him. *Not that I'm scared, or can't fend for myself,* he'd added. *But leaving your back open to these streets to be attacked ain't no sense.*

That thought had stuck with Jed since Max had first said it about a month ago. Now, every, week he waited with more anxiety than he'd like to admit for the phone to ring at exactly four thirty-five. Max called around the same time every week, only ten minutes allotted by the payphone for each number that dialed. Jed shook his head as he thought that the system needed to be upgraded.

The door to the shop clanged shut behind him as Jed walked back out onto the street. He'd bought the phone. Now he just needed to figure out how to get it to Max.

At home, he tossed his bag onto the sofa and headed straight for the shower. Sixty minutes. He had an hour before he had to meet Christie at table eleven at The Revolve. He'd made the reservations; he couldn't afford to be late.

"So, when did you transfer here?" he asked as they waited for their food to arrive.

He'd made it on time. By some stroke of divine luck, he'd actually managed to arrive early—before his dinner date had. He'd been able to claim their table and wait for her to arrive, as a gentleman should. That vantage, of course, came with the added benefit of seeing her before she could see him. And what a first impression she made.

He'd watched her enter, her purse daintily on her arm, the soft pink satin that slid across her skin shimmering under the golden light inside the restaurant. She searched for a moment, and then their eyes met. He'd been almost dumbfounded as she approached and watched the same expression of awe filter onto the face of every man she walked by. As Jed stood to greet her, and as she smiled, he swallowed. Their quick embrace left his mind swimming in her scent from where his nose had pressed into her hair. Sweet, fresh roses with a dark, spicy afterthought; he wondered if she would have the personality to match her scent.

Christie sat across from him, looking more beautiful than he'd seen a woman look in a very long time. Her hair was down around her shoulders in curls that floated about her cheeks, making her look youthful and full of energy. The strands were a shade of brown reminiscent of milky coffee, with what looked like threads of gold woven among them. She smiled, a tinge of embarrassment in her eyes, and he realized he was staring.

"Well, I was asked to transfer a few years ago when the crime rate started going up around here." She answered.

She was looking right at him, and he felt his neck grow warm with a bit of embarrassed heat. Had she realized he'd been staring at her? Jed hoped he hadn't made her uncomfortable—or made himself look stupid so soon.

"I was told you were the best in your city," he prompted, hoping to hear more about her experience.

"I'm the best wherever I go." She tucked her hair behind her right ear. "Eight years of experience and decades of wisdom passed down from my father."

Another smile graced her lips, but this one didn't reach her eyes.

He nodded. They had already ordered drinks—Massepo's red wine for Christie, Lyre's rosa negroni for Jed. He'd taken extra care in his restaurant selection to check for non-alcoholic drink options that were actually good. Fortunately, this place had a wide range of options, including his favorite, Lyre's. He watched her take a sip from her wine glass.

"Experience in the field is definitely important, but the insight of those who have gone ahead of us in the profession is indispensable," he commented.

She nodded, her gaze moving across his features, not knowing where to settle. He was as tall, dark, and mysterious as they came, Christie realized. Handsome, too, with brown hair arranged to perfection, biceps straining against the material that encased them, and brown eyes that locked on her.

They had exchanged outfit colors, agreeing to wear something pale pink to the restaurant meeting to make finding each other easier. When she'd stepped through the door, butterflies in her belly, Christie hadn't expected to find herself sitting across from a man like this. With the way Chief Lucas had described his wealth of experience, and his dedication to his career, she'd been expecting someone much older—not a brooding thirty-something, relaxed in his seat, looking across the table at her with a masculine intensity she was unused to. She swallowed, remembering to speak.

"It is. I would never have gotten this far in my career if not for my dad. Being an officer of the law is in my blood, I fear."

They both laughed at that, and she looked down at the tablecloth for a second, a hundred options running through her mind for how she could divert the topic away from her father and family.

"What brought you into your field?" she asked, peering inquisitively at his calm expression.

"A fascination with the human mind and how many problems it gets us into." Jed smiled. "Diffusing triggers and helping people heal is one of my favorite parts of the job."

She nodded.

"That makes sense. I see why we were paired together."

His brow raised. "Would you like to fill me in on this juicy tidbit you seem to have discovered?"

She laughed, and his eyes twinkled across the table.

"Well, I hear you've got the best results in the game. Best meets best. We're a perfect match."

"We definitely are. I'm looking forward to solving some crimes with you."

He raised his glass in a toast, and she clinked hers against it.

"To crime solving."

CHAPTER 2

JED WAS WALKING HOME again, feet barely touching the ground from all the spring in his step. He'd enjoyed dinner more than he had expected to.

He recalled the phone call that had brought Christie into his life. Getting a call on a Wednesday after work from the NYPD was usually a request to come in to handle some case or other, but this time it had been the police chief on the other end of the line, not the administrative assistant he'd grown used to speaking with. Chief Lucas had, ever so gruffly, reminded Jed about the partnership the department had initiated a few months back when he had initially joined forces with them as an investigative therapist. The paperwork and communications had finally come through, and Chief Lucas had been calling to let him know that he would be meeting his partner that Friday.

She's the best we've got, Gray. We trust that you two will make an incredible team and finally put a dent in the crime upsurgence in the city. I'm counting on you to bring a new perspective to the mental health issues and opioid crisis we are consistently dealing with. We've put every resource we have into making sure you two will have everything you might need. There's a lot riding on this partnership. Make us proud—no pressure.

No pressure. Yeah, right. Even the chief had laughed before he'd continued.

You're also the best we've got. I'm confident in you both, and even more confident in this partnership.

Christie had echoed that sentiment. *I'm the best wherever I go.* That kind of confidence was exactly what solved crime and brought about rehabilitation in hardened criminals. Not only was it an explicit indication of how much she believed in herself, but it was an indication of just how much she valued her work, her experience, her skillsets, and her colleagues. Being the best wasn't just about numbers, the percentages of crimes solved versus assigned cases that most investigators got absorbed into. It was about who you were serving and protecting, or more specifically, repairing the breech in the gap where you had failed to protect and honoring the victims of crime by solving their cases and bringing justice to the perpetrators. Defending the fallen, that's what it was about.

He looked both ways before jogging across the street and falling into a simple walking rhythm again. Walking was therapeutic, especially as a New Yorker. You didn't need to think about it. You didn't need to wonder where to go. You just walked. You'd get there, eventually.

That thought made Jed think back to Christie, as she'd entered the restaurant. She was beautiful. Five foot seven, and at least twenty-eight was what he'd guess. She'd come right on the hour, walking in like she owned the place, glossy lips pouting a little as she'd looked around. Chief Lucas had given them each other's contacts, and Jed had gone out of his way to schedule a meeting on neutral territory, away from both their homes and immediate workplaces.

He remembered how cheery and sweet she'd sounded when she'd picked up the phone on Wednesday night. He'd been just as caught off guard then as he had been today when he saw her for the first time.

As he made his way down the street past coffee shops and bookstores, all closed for the night, Jed passed a homeless man who stretched out a hand to him as he went by, asking for spare change. Jed didn't make a wide berth away from the begging man the way most New Yorkers did. Instead, he just nodded to him and walked on by. He had stopped and talked to this man on several occasions during the daylight hours when it was safer to do so, and he made a mental note to bring him some change in the morning.

Jed had given him a coffee and sandwich the last time he saw him and had a conversation with him to see what he could do to connect the man with any resources he might need. He thought his name was Allan, a man who had fallen on some hard times in the last year and had recently lost his wife. Jed heard the man sigh, his shoulders sagging against the wall behind him in defeat. A pang of guilt and sadness flowed through him, and he sighed himself. He didn't have spare change right now, and neither did he want to dig into his pockets, search for his wallet and dig around in it, standing on a dark roadway where anything could go wrong.

There is no wisdom in leaving your back open to these rocky roads. He pressed on, reaching home a few minutes later and sinking gratefully into his bed after taking another much-needed shower. His bed felt like bliss. It was his favorite part of the apartment, his refuge when he was feeling tired, when he was stressed, when he was unhappy, when he just wanted to relax… it was his favorite place to be.

When he'd just gotten out of college and struck out on his own, in his first apartment, Jed had tossed two hundred dollars on a random mattress he'd found on clearance at a big box store. That had been a mistake. It had never been truly comfortable. Actually, he had paid the price for his hasty, nonchalant buy with many sleepless nights and suffered aches and pains when he did wake up from whatever morsel of sleep he could get.

Now that he was older and wiser, he knew well that a good mattress was one of the most important investments one could make. If one third of your life is spent asleep, you might as well sleep in style and utmost comfort.

Now that he was home and had successfully gotten through his business dinner, the tingling uncertainty that had been resting just below the surface of his emotions had faded. He wasn't nervous anymore. It had been the last-minute call from Chief Lucas and rushed dinner arrangements that had made him so uneasy this past week, kept him so exhausted though he hadn't done anything outside of his normal, daily routine. Wake up, hit the gym, walk to work, work, walk home from work, sleep.

Routine. It was the air he breathed, the thread that kept the parts of him bound together tightly so that he could function well.

Jed looked up at the ceiling and smiled to himself, laughing off how nervous he had been before dinner. She was sweet, though, and their meeting had gone surprisingly well. None of his worrying had been worth it, because the two of them clicked just as easily as they had clinked glasses. Their conversation had never dulled or faded through all five courses of dinner.

He loved a woman he could have an easy-going conversation with. They'd talked about everything from family, to work, to education, to hobbies, and to recent cases that had been solved by the department. In the morning, the first item on his to-do list was to thank her for showing up to dinner, then to get his laundry done. His laundry—that definitely needed to be taken care of.

As he slipped into sleep, the faint blaring of a siren sounded through the New York City night.

The shrill ringing of the phone cut through his peaceful dreams of being lakeside, naked, relaxing under the trees and the gentle breeze. As he struggled to sit up and gain his bearings, Jed wondered what the matter could possibly be. It was a Saturday morning, barely sunrise, and the only people who usually rang his direct line were his mom and his aunt and uncle—though the last two were only occasional. The 'Private Caller' that flashed across his screen as he reached for the phone made something turn in his stomach.

"Hello, this is Jed Gray."

"Jed, this is Christie. I'm afraid there's been some bad news. I need you down at the station—stat."

He sat, staring down at his sheets, the sun barely peeking through the curtains that separated his bedroom from the outside world. That was all she'd said to him before hanging up. He hadn't even gotten the chance to ask what was going on, or to say 'okay' in response. Jed swung his legs over the side of the bed and sighed heavily as he got up to get ready. He had a sinking feeling that today was not going to be the laundry and relaxation day he had planned.

Arriving at the police station only required his usual short walk, but when Jed walked in, he felt exhausted as soon as he saw everyone's grim faces. Even the front desk admin, usually smiling ear to ear as she greeted him, was busy on calls—or so she tried to seem. He could glean from her lowered eyes that she just didn't want to look at him.

He made his way through to his partner's office, which he had learned was on the second floor, while running through the list of things that had happened this week. On Monday, he had left work late, on Tuesday, he'd arrived to work late, on Wednesday, Chief Lucas had called and he'd gotten into contact with Christie. Jed pressed the button for the second floor in the elevator, folding his arms across his chest as the doors closed.

On Thursday, he'd gone through the day perfectly. It was his Friday that had deviated from the usual. Max had called late, he'd stopped to buy the best hotdog he'd ever had, bought a phone he still didn't know what to do with, and gone to dinner with the woman he was about to meet, yet again.

Why did this meeting feel so precarious? Like he was walking on thin ice or had already crossed some invisible line? They hadn't planned to meet until the next week, but now here he was, knocking on the door to her office.

"Come in."

He did, entering and pulling the door shut behind him.

"Don't close it," Christie waved a hand to stop him. "We're going down to the interview room to review some evidence."

"Evidence? Evidence for what?"

She still hadn't looked up at him. She was shuffling papers around on her desk and sifting through a file folder that looked cleaner, fresher than all the others there. He didn't like where this seemed to be heading.

25

"New case. You'll get the details in a second, when we're in the interview room. Trying to follow correct protocol." She paused. "I'm in a weird position right now."

Jed's brows furrowed. She walked past him to the door and gestured for him to follow. Withholding information until they got into the interview room was strange behavior for a detective, unless that was how she handled all her cases. The interview was for criminal suspects and victims, not for partners on a case.

When the heavy, soundproof door closed behind them, Christie sighed, sinking into one of the chairs at the only desk in the room. He followed her lead, sitting before crossing his arms again.

"What is going on?" he pressed. "Why are you handling me like I'm a suspect on a case?"

Her expression never wavered. "That would be because you are a suspect on a case. There was a murder on 55th last night, at around nine pm."

Jed's brows pulled together. What was she getting at?

"Do you remember where you were at nine pm last night, Mr. Gray?"

His eyes narrowed. "There's no need for me to respond. You're going to tell me, aren't you? Get it over with."

His tone had hardened, and Christie resisted the urge to sigh. She hated to do this; she really did. Christie hadn't even gotten home properly before she'd received the call that someone had hacked a homeless person to death on

55th avenue. According to an eyewitness who preferred not to have their identity released or anything recorded, they'd seen Jed walking down that stretch a few minutes before the screaming and grunting had started but hadn't seen where he had gone. By the time they heard the commotion, the witness had moved away from the window for too long to be sure.

Now Christie was sitting across from her investigative partner, a man she'd only met last night. Even so, she knew he hadn't done it. She was sure. But she was bound by protocol.

"You were seen on 55th Ave at eight fifty-three in the evening yesterday. At two minutes past nine, there were sounds of violence and struggling heard there. You are the primary suspect at this time."

Jed didn't bother to speak. His lips were pressed into a line.

"We've acquired CCTV footage of 55th and the avenues connected to it, and we're going to go over the footage together. The footage was delivered to me a few minutes before you arrived. I was waiting for you to arrive before I watched it."

Jed sat silently as Christie picked up a small, black remote that had been hiding underneath her folder and pointed it toward the screen on the wall across from them. She pressed the play button.

And there he was, in all his glory, walking down 55th, entering from the left side of the screen and walking across it, though the footage was a little blurry. He could easily recognize himself, with his hands deep in his pockets, lost in thought, not even seeming to be paying attention to where he was going. Then he passed the homeless man, who had had his arm stretched out, and he saw the man sink back when Jed walked past. He could see his own shoulders slump a little in the video and remembered how he'd sighed. Then, the footage showed him turning down a side road, on the far right of the screen, and he faded from view.

They kept watching the screen in silence, and he watched the clock on the bottom left of the screen as the seconds changed, then minutes, until it got to a minute past nine. From the left, another figure came walking down the street, moving swiftly, like they were in a hurry. As they got closer to the homeless man, they suddenly veered off their path, toward him, pulling what looked like a long knife from their pocket and plunging it into the guy, over and over again until he finally slumped over.

The small, middle-aged homeless man had put up a brave fight while he could, Jed noted as he watched the gruesome scene unfold. In the end, though, he was no match for the glinting blade that kept coming at him from above. Jed was glad that there was no audio in the video. He didn't know if he'd be able to handle this if he'd heard the man screaming, likely pleading for his life.

That could have been him getting stabbed, he suddenly thought. What if he had stopped to search for some change like he always tried to do when he came across the less fortunate? He cringed to think that his back could have been the target of that oncoming blade.

Christie turned back to face him, pausing the video. Her tone was softer now.

"Now that we've reviewed the evidence, and your name has been cleared, we can start working, *partner*."

Her emphasis on 'partner' wasn't lost on Jed, and he nodded, eyes level with hers as she opened the folder. Since her call earlier, he had been feeling more like a criminal than like her partner.

"I'm sorry for pulling you out of bed so soon, on such short notice," she began. "I would have waited, but policy and protocol demand contact as soon as possible. I wouldn't want a negligence strike on my profile. That would have put both of us in trouble."

He nodded.

"You're mad at me?"

His silence didn't break.

"You're no longer being interrogated, Gray. Say something."

Jed spread a stiff smile across his face and shook his head. His features held an expression, an emotion that she couldn't identify. "There's nothing to be said."

"Yeah, you're mad at me."

His lips melted into a grin then, and the tension in her body eased just a bit. That smile was genuine. She watched him shake his head again before he looked back to her, re-connecting their gazes.

"I'm not mad. Just… thinking. That could have been me on the end of that blade." He glanced at the screen again. "I'd been thinking about stopping and offering him some change if I could find any. But something made me walk by. I've spoken to the guy a few times, tried to get him some help. Good guy, just a lot of bad luck. His name is Allan… he has no next of kin. His wife died of cancer a few years ago, and that seems to be what started his spiral into drug addiction and eventually led to him living on the streets."

Something made him walk by… more like *someone*. Christie's eyes widened, and a sick feeling flooded through her. Her brows pulled together, not liking the hunch she got about the potential angles of this case. He didn't see. He was looking up at the screen again.

"I'm glad I didn't stop. That would have been…" He trailed off.

She didn't respond.

"So, what do we have so far?"

Christie cleared her throat. "An eyewitness report, the weapon that was found at the scene, two suspects—one of which has been cleared—basic suspect profile, and the identity of the deceased."

He nodded. "So essentially, we have nothing."

She grinned. "Nothing, for now."

CHAPTER 3

A KNOCK CAME AT his door, and Jed paused, his hands hovering over his keyboard. He'd been looking at housing options that were available across the city to see what he could find for Max and his girlfriend. So far, only shared housing options were turning up. He glanced at the time. He wasn't expecting a client.

"Come in," he called.

Monday had come quickly, and he was already back in the office, sorting through the weekly pile of court cases, documentation, and rehabilitation reports. Saturday, by the time he made it home, he'd been absolutely exhausted. When he walked into his apartment at seven after a long day of going back and forth over initial clues and a play-by-play of the murder, his feet ached, his body felt sore and itchy, and all he had wanted to do was stand in the shower and let the hot water burn the memories of the day away.

It was when he'd tossed his phone and backpack onto the kitchen island that he'd breathed a hefty sigh of relief that rose from the tips of his toes and spread right through him. Apartments with washers & dryers were not at all common in

31

New York, but Jed had never been happier that he lived in an apartment that offered that luxury. His two-month housing search had paid off.

Jed watched the knob on his office door turn, and his brows pulled together when a tall, blonde-haired man dressed to the nines entered the room. Jed rose to his feet.

"Hey ya! It's Jed, is it?" the blonde shook his hand firmly, and Jed nodded slowly. "I'm Hugh," he continued. "I'm your next-door neighbor." The man pointed to the wall next to Jed's desk.

This man worked here? Jed couldn't help noticing his well-manicured nails and the watch he was wearing. He was only slightly shorter than Jed was, with blue eyes that looked almost green in the bright room and blonde hair that was slicked back to perfection. If Jed had passed him on the street, he would have thought Hugh was a lawyer.

"Nice to meet you, neighbor," Hugh added.

Hugh smiled, and Jed nodded.

"Well, what can I do for you?" he prompted.

Jed had little time for idle talking—he was already behind on the tasks he had left for the day. Besides, he was always wary of strangers, especially men, and the way Hugh was looking around the office intently made him even more uncomfortable with this strange man in his space. In new social situations, Jed was usually an introvert and preferred solitude over new, uncomfortable interactions.

"Oh! I just thought I'd introduce myself. I recently got placed on this floor, so I've been introducing myself to everyone, day by day, office by office. I'm in social work. What department are you in?"

"Addiction therapy," Jed answered.

Hugh nodded as though it made complete sense to him and then smiled.

"It's not very active on this floor, is it?"

Jed shook his head. Hugh winked and added, "They aren't a very lively bunch, bless their hearts. It's as lively as a morgue on this floor."

They both laughed at that, Jed's thoughts moving to the case. Though he'd been working on other cases and spent the morning sifting through the trenches of abuse and neglect cases, thoughts of Friday night never left his mind. They lingered right behind his eyes. When he closed them, Jed could see himself walking down the street again, passing the tired man sitting in the corner, and hear the man's despairing sigh as another person walked by without trying to help him.

"I heard there was a murder a couple days ago," Hugh mentioned as though he had just remembered the fact.

Jed looked at him. Was this man a mind reader?

"It was a homeless man, too, I heard. It's so sad. He had nowhere to run to."

Jed nodded. "It's very sad. I wish we had a housing solution for them."

Hugh nodded in agreement. "They really need to be taken off the streets. The homeless population is growing. I'm afraid it's getting out of hand."

New York needed to implement rehabilitation centers that were willing and equipped to handle the free entry and exit of those who needed help. As it was now, the only way to get on a rehab path was to commit some sort of crime, get a recommendation from a licensed counselor or behavioral therapist, or sign up and pay for it yourself—the latter two, the homeless didn't have the know-how or access to accomplish. On top of that, all the free walk-in shelters were always at capacity, turning away those that need access every single day.

They needed something simple. Something that was accessible.

"Well, I hope they find the culprit soon," Hugh quipped, standing and turning toward the door. "There's no room for somebody like that to just be waltzing around, free of consequences."

Jed nodded in agreement as the door closed, and then he was alone. He moved back to his desk, sitting once more in front of his computer. He looked at the door. That had been kind of… nice. He unlocked his computer and got back to his work.

"How have the initial investigations been going? Anything interesting coming up?" he asked Christie over the phone.

It was Jed's lunch break, and he'd already eaten his plate of rice and chicken breast. On the other end of the line, his partner sighed.

"I do have some ideas I wanted to discuss with you, yeah. Initial tests and reports, some items recovered from the scene... the body."

He nodded, eyes on the afternoon sun that was bearing down outside.

"I could come over and take a look at it with you." He took a sip of his water.

She hummed in agreement.

Jed coughed, the water slipping into the wrong section of his throat as he swallowed and tried to speak at the same time. Christie giggled. Water had spilled all over him.

"I'm at the station. Can you come now?"

He pinched the bridge of his nose, sighing heavily before taking a deep breath. She laughed again.

"Gray, are you alright over there?"

"I'm fine. I just spilled some water all over myself and choked on air, is all."

She kept laughing, and a smile tugged at his lips. He reluctantly gave in to it. "I'll drop by the station in a few minutes."

After he had hung up, Jed sighed to himself in the large room. Now he was soaked through from what should have been his refreshing, afternoon drink of water—and he was embarrassed. Way to go, Gray. He huffed as he closed out his work tabs and saved his files, then changed into a spare dress shirt he had at the office for court dates or messes, like this one.

Closing the door to his office with extra care, Jed turned down the hallway and headed for the elevator. He'd been satisfied with his lunch a few minutes ago, but now that he was leaving work, he was craving a hotdog with all the bells and whistles on it. Jed could get two and take one to the office for Christie—if he could stop himself from eating them both on the journey there. He chuckled at that thought as he headed out onto the street, watching people mill about in the afternoon sun.

There were couples holding hands, kids begging their parents to go into toy and gaming stores, and teenagers with chunky headphones on, blasting some pop music or other, probably depressed, with their annoyed-looking parents standing beside them.

"I want two hotdogs this time—everything on them."

The man nodded and grinned, hands working the grill with a skill that had probably taken years to acquire.

"You new around here?" he asked, peering at Jed from under the blue, stained baseball cap he wore.

Jed grinned. The man was likely asking because he'd never seen him at his stall before, and now here he was ordering more food than everyone else did when they came.

"Nope. I walk by here every day."

"Really?" The man paused, looking straight at Jed for a minute. "Nah. You must be new around here."

Jed laughed.

"I work a couple blocks up, and I live a couple blocks down." Jed shrugged.

The cheese came oozing out of the bottle as the man layered it on before dipping into his tub of onions and relish and piling on a hefty serving of each. Jed's mouth began to water.

"I'm Jamie. Everybody knows me round these parts."

Jed nodded, still staring at the hotdog in Jamie's hands. The vendor was now adding pickles.

"I know. Your stall is always full, no matter what time I pass by."

Jamie laughed, handing the first hotdog to him and beginning to assemble the second.

"Yeah, well, what can I say, y'know? The people treat me and my little stall well."

Jed nodded, stretching his hand to pay the man as he collected his second piece of precious cargo.

"I'm Jed. And yes, you'll be seeing me more and more frequently. I don't know what you put into these, but it's got me good."

Jamie's laugh was deep and rich, and Jed grinned as he turned to head off down the road.

"The truth is," Christie was saying, "that I'm not sure what to make of what we have so far."

She tapped her finger on her cheek, her brows knit together as she thought. Jed's eyes raked over her as he entered the room. She'd started talking about the case as soon as he'd opened the door to her office. Her hair was brushed back into a low ponytail, and those navy pants fit so snugly on her frame that he could see every curve outlined under the soft material.

She turned to him, about to say something else as her ponytail swished to the side.

"I—"

She paused.

"Is that for… me?"

Jed couldn't help the grin that slid onto his face.

"You insult me. You think I'd walk in with two giant hotdogs and eat both of them myself?"

She flushed, scratching at her ear with her free hand. In the other hand was the same brown file, folded open. She had been reading through it when he'd walked in. Christie put the folder down and walked over to where he was standing at the door. He lowered the hotdog to her, and she bit down on her lip.

"Oh my God, this is huge!"

He grinned, watching her take the giant bundle and assess it with her eyes.

"It is huge. And it's absolutely scrumptious. I had it for the first time last Friday, and I wanted you to try it today."

She gazed up at him with those perfect hazel eyes, and his throat constricted around the rest of the words he'd been planning to say.

"That's so sweet of you!" she exclaimed, now looking down at the hotdog. "The smell is making me hungry. Let's sit down right away."

Jed laughed as she turned to scurry toward the desk in the center of the room where he met her on Saturday when he first arrived at the station. He noticed her hips sway as she walked away, the jingling sound of the handcuffs attached to her belt catching his attention. He smirked.

"Came prepared, huh?"

She didn't miss a beat.

"You know I'm always ready."

It was the wink and the sly grin on her lips that made his chest grow warm. Christie sat, sliding the papers away from her to avoid getting gooey cheese and spicy mayo all over them.

"Okay, here goes."

He grinned as she went to take her first bite. She struggled to figure out how to eat it, no matter how wide she opened her mouth. Christie managed it eventually, though, and he waited, eager to hear what she thought. She chewed once, her eyes widening.

"Oh my God!" she exclaimed around the mouthful of sausage and cheese.

Satisfaction oozed from Jed as he bit into his own hotdog. They were still steaming, like they'd just come off the grill even though the stand was a seven-minute walk from the station. That was because he'd basically run all the way here so she could try it while it was still warm. He smiled again as he watched her concentrate on getting a second bite.

"Is it good?" he asked, teasingly, as she struggled to chew the giant piece she'd bitten.

Christie flushed, beginning to laugh at herself. Jed's eyes twinkled as he watched her. She was so beautiful when she laughed.

"It is!" she chimed as she nodded. "It is *so* good."

"I'm glad you're enjoying it. I thought it might help take your mind off the case for a while."

Her eyes softened. "Thank you, Jed. That's really sweet of you."

He smiled. "You're welcome, but is it working?"

"It definitely is." Christie grinned around a mouthful of cheese.

The two finished eating in silence. After the hotdogs had disappeared into their bellies, Christie sighed. Jed cocked his head to the side, watching her focus shift back to work. She reached across the table to pick up her folder again, and Jed noticed her lips press together.

"Alright," he said. "Lay it on me."

"We haven't established a motive for the killing. There is a profile—or, at least, a sort of vague description—of the killer, and we could get an even more detailed profile, but the CCTV footage on that street doesn't support cropped viewing angles." Jed realized Christie sounded particularly annoyed by that detail.

He leaned back in his chair as Christie laid out the crime scene photos across the table while she explained what she had found so far.

She read from the paper before her. "The eyewitness doesn't have anything else to offer… we've cleared your name, and the autopsy came back exactly as expected. 'Allan Cartwright, age sixty-two—death by shock and hemorrhage as a result of repeated, sharp force trauma. Suspect sustained twenty-three stab wounds—three to the neck and shoulders, one to the face, and nineteen to the chest and abdominal area.'"

Jed swallowed. His heart had fallen into his stomach. She looked over at him.

"So far, we have two leads, and one piece of evidence—the knife at the scene."

He nodded.

"We've had an anonymous report to check out a potential connection to a local businessman's involvement in this case, and another anonymous report with a connection to someone who works with the homeless population."

That made Jed's ears perk up.

"Apparently, this businessman has some sort of very outspoken vendetta against homeless people. He's a developer with an interest in expanding his business and doing construction in some parts of the city where there are abandoned buildings and run-down infrastructure."

Christie tapped her finger against the desk while she paused, looking down at her notes. Jed's mind went to Max's side of town right away. He wondered if Max might know anything about this entire ordeal, or if he had heard what was happening. He probably had. Word traveled fast in this city, especially in the underground. Not that he could ask him. That would create a conflict of interest, and it was just downright unethical to cross the lines like that. Addiction therapy and investigative therapy were separate disciplines, and Jed intended to keep them that way. The only way he'd ever know if Max knew anything about the case was if the boy brought it up himself.

"Name?"

Startled, Christie looked up from the paper.

"Sorry, I got lost in thought for a second. His name is Thiago Carrillo. I was thinking. Even if a businessman hated the homeless, would he risk bloodying his hands, his business and livelihood—hell, his whole life—on one murder?"

"Who says it was meant to be just one?"

She blinked at him.

Jed continued. "We have no idea whether this was an isolated event, if the killer is mentally unstable—you saw how the person veered off their projected path and suddenly sprang into attack mode. It's not like they'd been walking toward the homeless man to begin with. We don't know if they're planning to do more of these sporadic attacks, and like you mentioned, we still don't know what the motive was. We have nothing in that regard."

She nodded, seeing where he was going with the thought. "So, if it does play out to be more than one murder of the same sort, then Thiago would be a sure suspect instead of a vague one?"

"Yes. At that point, we'd be able to bring him in for a talk. Right now, it's unlikely that he did it himself. But that brings me to the other part of this."

Christie's brows pulled together. "The other part?"

Jed nodded, taking a sip of his water, and tried to get comfortable in his chair. The material was hard and worn, and his forearms itched where they rested on top of the armrests. He wondered why the force didn't invest in more comfortable seating in their offices. Even the walls were drab and depressing.

"You made an excellent point when you asked why a businessman would risk it all on one lousy murder—*not* that I'm belittling the value of Allan's life..."

She nodded.

"But a man that's concerned about developments and building new construction in run-down areas in the city has the means to hire his dirty work out. I'm certain he's not on site from nine to five, carrying bricks and mortar and mixing cement."

Christie's eyes lit up, and she chimed in. "So even if it was an isolated murder, he could still be behind it, but it might be that it wouldn't be his DNA at the crime scene!"

Jed nodded, a small smile coming to his face as she reached for her pen and began furiously writing down what they had just discussed.

"He's a strong suspect either way," Jed ceded. "So, he's still in the running."

She was still making notes, nodding at what he was saying as she wrote.

"What made the anonymous reporter mention him? What's the vendetta?"

She looked up from her paper. "Apparently, he always runs into trouble securing development rights for certain spaces that have gone derelict because the state is in favor of those homeless people having the space. Since so many of them live there and form communities in those spaces, if Carrillo got the go ahead, all those homeless would migrate into the heart of the city. We're having that migration as it is already, so the state thinks those derelict spaces should remain—for now. At least until they 'figure something out,'" she finished, using air quotes at the end.

"Hm," Jed pondered. "And he's likely not very happy that the state favors homeless people, which are a nuisance to him, over his plans for development."

Nodding, Christie continued. "I was told that he is very arrogant when it comes to his business—and that he hates the idea that the state keeps rejecting his project proposals. According to what I heard, Carrillo believes he's doing the city a favor by offering to fix those spaces."

"A paid favor," Jed commented under his breath.

Christie's lips pressing into a line. "He lost around twenty-five million dollars in profit in the last quarter, alone, because of denied projects."

Jed's brows shot up. "The rationale is certainly there to get rid of the problem on his own, then. Wow."

"Yeah," she sighed. "The motive is certainly there. Most would kill for far less than that."

They both sat quietly for a while, her looking down at the notes she'd just written, and Jed thinking through their conversation.

Finally, Jed broke the silence. "What's the other lead?"

"His name is John Whitman. He's reportedly very close to and always interacting with the homeless people around the city."

She paused, and Jed cocked his head to the side again.

"But?" he prompted.

She sighed, rubbing a hand across her forehead.

"I checked him out this morning. He was at work when it happened, but he got into a pretty gnarly altercation with a homeless man a week prior. They got into an argument while he was handing out care packages. The guy must have said something Whitman didn't like, and they ended up in a fight.

Also, I have a team looking to see if we can connect Allan to either Carrillo or Whitman."

Jed watched Christie pinch the bridge of her nose before summing up what she had said. "So, what we really have is the video recording and times of the incident, the profile of the killer, an autopsy report that confirms what we already know, one lead, and the murder weapon collected from the site."

She nodded. "Yes. That is what we have. For now. We are waiting on the forensics from the scene and the murder weapon. In the meantime, I'll do some deep diving into our records and search for any other previous murders that match the profile of these recent ones to see if the suspect has done this before. And most importantly, we have Whitman coming in tomorrow for an interview."

CHAPTER 4

JOHN WHITMAN WAS ENTERING the interview room. He was limping slightly, Jed noticed, like he'd sustained an injury to his left leg that had never fully healed. The man was sixty-five years old and just under six feet tall, with slight balding and a receding hairline.

He sat down when prompted by Christie and smiled pleasantly. Jed watched him keenly from his position in the observation room, where the one-sided glass afforded him the perk of being an invisible spectator.

"Thank you for coming in, Mr. Whitman," Christie began.

John nodded and smiled. "I'm happy to help as best as I can." He spoke slowly, like saying each word took careful effort.

"We understand that you've been working with the homeless people of our city a great deal in the past years."

Whitman's features seemed to light up.

"Yes, I like to lend a hand. I make care packages and give them out to the poor. You know how hard it is to survive and stay afloat in a city like this. Even at my age, after establishing myself over the years, it can get difficult for me. A lot of the men on the streets are my age, or only a little younger. I hate to watch them struggle."

"That's very kind of you." Christie smiled at him. "Not very many people even notice the less fortunate, yet you go out of your way to help them."

Whitman smiled again and nodded along as Christie spoke. He looked very pleased with himself.

"Are you familiar with Allan Cartwright?"

"Oh, yes. I have talked with him frequently. Sad story. He lost his wife to cancer a few years back. He fell into a pretty severe depression after that. I try to visit him weekly and bring him some food to make sure he is okay."

"Do you know of anyone that would have a problem or issue with Allan?"

"Not that I can think of."

"Anyone that is overly aggressive that Allan could have met? You know, a 'wrong place at the wrong time' type of thing?"

"Not really. People on the streets generally respect each other's spaces and tolerate one another."

"It is really commendable, the work you do with the less fortunate. Do you get along with them well?" Christie sounded genuinely interested and curious—like she admired the man's efforts. Jed was impressed.

"Yes, we always get along very well. I talk with them, and they talk with me. We're all equals, you know?"

Christie nodded along like Whitman's ideals were, and always had been, her own.

"Is that why you got into a physical fight with a homeless man on 56th Street this past week and knocked him over? Because you get along so well all the time?"

Jed expected the man to be mortified when he was caught in his lie, but he watched Whitman narrow his eyes and glare at Christie instead. The switch into anger was so seamless that it slightly startled Jed. No surprise, or even fear, entered his features. He'd gone from cheery and pleasant to cold and filled with rage.

"That was an isolated event."

Christie nodded understandingly.

"What about the run-in you had six months ago on 49th Street? Was that an isolated event, too? You bashing his head in?"

Now, Whitman refused to speak.

"Where were you on the evening of September 16th at nine pm, Mr. Whitman?"

"I was at work. I take on the night shift most days."

"And where do you work?"

"I work at a twenty-four-hour pharmacy."

His responses were short and snappy now. Suddenly, John Whitman didn't seem to want to talk anymore. Jed listened to Christie continue to ask questions for a while until she suddenly smiled brightly.

"Is there anything else you want to tell me, Mr. Whitman? Since you get along with all the homeless people, you must have heard someone mention something. Well, maybe you wouldn't have heard anything from the two you assaulted, but all the rest like you, right?"

With his lips pressed together, John rose to his feet, fists tight at his sides.

"I have had enough of this. Good day to you, Detective."

After he had gone, Jed joined Christie in the room, where she stood gazing down at the papers in front of her.

"I'll have an officer stop by his work to double check on whether he was there at the time of the murder," Christie said, as Jed approached her.

"That'll be valuable."

Christie nodded, finally looking up. "Did you see the way he got angry as soon as he realized he was a suspect and not just a friendly interview?"

Jed chuckled. "I didn't know detectives conducted friendly interviews."

Christie snorted and then shook her head.

"I didn't know either. But that must have been what he was thinking, what with his cheery attitude and good reports of what he's done for the homeless. Maybe he thought his smile could throw me off the scent."

Jed grinned. "Nobody throws Christie Jamison off the scent, huh?"

Christie smiled in return. "Nobody."

CHAPTER 5

JED WAS WALKING HOME after the interview. He'd avoided walking home in the late evenings since he'd almost been the victim of a murder the week before, but here he was, walking down the dark streets of New York, yet again. He'd taken a different route this time, opting to walk through a busier part of town before turning onto a side road that led to his apartment.

As he walked, Jed mused over how, whenever he spent time with Christie, time seemed to get away from him. He couldn't understand it. He'd left work for the police station at twelve-thirty in the afternoon, so how was it now ten at night?

All they'd done was sit and talk through the case, the Whitman interview, and then talk some more. Where had the time gone?

The city was alive around him, and all the streetlights, building lights, and car lights made his head hurt. He missed the countryside. He missed the lake, its cold water on his skin. And the tall trees that wind whistled through every morning and evening. He missed the lake house with its solid oak floors and open balconies and the way the sun streamed in through the wall of glass that faced toward the water at sunset. Most of all, Jed missed the silence. Out in the countryside, there were no cars honking, no trains rattling underfoot, no people laughing and screaming on every corner, no lights except the stars. It was the only place he felt peace. It was his safe space.

The whirring of a bike pulled him out of his reverie as it whizzed past him on the pavement, and Jed shook his head. He needed to take some time off from work and go home—his real home. As he turned down a darker, less traversed side street, he came face to face with the thoughts he'd been trying to avoid.

He was used to handling crimes and cases that turned the stomach, cases of abuse that could pull screams of agony out of even the hardest of hearts. But this one was different. Because though he'd been involved in and with cases that had been emotionally hard on him, he'd never almost been the target, himself. He'd never missed the knife's blade by quite the narrow margin he had this time. Two more minutes, he thought. Just two more minutes in the restaurant with Christie, and he'd have been passing Allan on the side of the street at the same time as the killer.

And who knew if the madman would have turned on him, too? Jed had seen how arbitrarily, as if on second thought, the killer had swerved over to Allan and pulled the knife. What if he'd been walking by right then and had witnessed the attack? Jed knew he would have stepped in and tried to help Allan.

And if nothing else, that would have been his undoing. Or, the killer would have swerved toward him instead, and the dagger's blade would have pierced his flesh.

A wave of guilt overcame him as he walked. He was going further and further into the dark alley, and if there was anything waiting for him, lurking in the darkness, it was too late for him to run. He couldn't help but feel guilty for walking away now. Initially, it had been *I should have stopped to give him money.* He'd passed Allan on many evenings and knew the man had simply fallen on hard times. It was easy to fall on hard times, especially in a city like this where the cost-of-living was sky high and the income levels were never increasing to match the rising inflation. Add to that, losing a loved one the way Allan had, and all the odds were stacked against him.

Jed sighed. Now that he'd seen the CCTV footage of Allan being attacked, and so brutally murdered for what seemed like no reason, he wished he'd been there to help. Even if he would have sustained some sort of injury, Jed would have fared better than the older man. A lump of sadness and angry tears blocked his throat as he tried to swallow.

Once he made it safely onto the adjoining street at the end of the alleyway, he quickened his steps. He hurried past closed cafes and a bookstore with darkened windows, passing by another homeless man who was standing next to a garbage can that was blazing. The man held his arms out to it to warm them.

Jed's heart grew even heavier. Homelessness was such a big problem in America, and in New York, it seemed rampant. It was a concern that was close to his heart—very close. But it was a much bigger a problem than he could tackle alone, so for now, all he could do was commit to solving Allan's case and do his best to help wherever he could.

He nodded to the old guy he passed, and the man grunted a greeting, beady eyes watching Jed as he walked by. The man held a cigarette between his lips, and his ragged clothing and the gaping holes in his shoes were a stark contrast to the pride and determination Jed saw in his eyes. It was hard to hazard a guess as to how old he was. People aged so much quicker on the streets.

Once in his apartment, Jed released a pent-up breath. He was safe. Shoes and socks were removed at the door and stowed away, keys were placed in the bowl on the counter, and his bag was thrown on the sofa. Jed took his clothes off, and into the scorching-hot shower he went. The routine every night was the same—except that nothing was the same these days. He'd been thrown into a loop of uncertainty and confusion, and he needed some time to catch his breath and refocus. He had even been missing the gym, which usually helped clear his mind at the end of the day. Jed always tried to do this three times a week, but all he'd had time for this week was a morning run before work. He reminded himself that he needed to get back into his gym routine next week.

He trudged out to the kitchen again after pulling on sweats and leaving his chest bare, pulling the cabinets open to survey his options. There was cereal—three kinds—and pasta and potatoes, too. He was starving, and his belly rumbled over and over as he stood, frozen with indecision. Eventually, he pulled the pasta from the cupboard, and the rest of the ingredients from the fridge that he would need to make a quick pasta. As Jed grabbed the cheese, he noticed a tub of ice cream higher up, in the freezer, that he'd bought two grocery trips ago, still sitting there, patiently waiting. A pang of guilt seared through him.

There were so many people on the street right this minute who hadn't eaten all day and had nothing to eat before they laid their heads to rest on the hard, filthy streets of the city that never slept. He pulled the tub out, too. He was having ice cream for dessert.

No sooner had he finished eating and put the dishes in the sink than his phone rang. His heart sank. The clock on the wall read eleven forty-nine. The Caller-ID read 'Christie'.

"Hello?"

The other end of the line was silent for a second, until a sigh filtered through.

"Jed, I'm afraid we have another murder on our hands."

He felt like his heart might fall through his feet. No. It couldn't be. Another homeless person had fallen victim, just like they'd all but predicted in their session earlier in the day—the same way the first murder had happened right after they'd toasted to crime solving as a unit.

"Another homeless person?" he asked, almost not wanting to hear the answer.

"Yes. And guess who the primary suspect is this time?"

Her voice had softened, and he closed his eyes.

"Let me guess. It's me."

I need you in the office first thing in the morning. He walked into the station's main reception area, yet again. He figured that, like last time, everyone else had already heard what happened and would avoid him, but the receptionist called him as soon as he walked in, much.

"Mr. Gray!"

His steps slowed, and he turned to look over at her.

"Yes? Can I do something for you?"

She flushed a little, and he realized she was embarrassed.

"I-I wanted to apologize. Word travels fast, y'know, and I guess I assumed the wrong thing the first time around. But we all know you were cleared, and we're confident in you, just the same."

Jed nodded, eyes moistening a little. "And this time around?"

She gave him a small smile. "I know you'll be cleared this time, too."

In the office, Christie was already waiting for him.

"Hey, Jed!" She waved as he entered.

He paused where he was, narrowing his eyes. His reception today was very different than the first time he had met her in her office.

"What? No silent treatment and formalities this time?" he asked.

She glared at him. "Well, I guess I had that coming."

He joined her at the table, making himself as comfortable as he possibly could in the hardbacked chair. He watched her fidget for a second.

"I'm sorry I doubted you so terribly the first time."

His brow raised. What was going on here? "Did you guys have a company meeting to discuss this or something?"

She looked confused and batted her eyelashes at him.

"What?"

"Everyone's either been apologizing outright or smiling apologetically to me since I got here. Am I the department's laughingstock?"

Christie flinched, and his anger faded immediately. He was being harsh. She didn't deserve that. It was protocol to treat all suspects like suspects, no matter how close they were to you. He knew that well. But it had stung. Stung badly.

"We didn't have a meeting about you. I haven't discussed this or you with anyone but you, and no one is laughing at you. So, no."

They looked at each other in silence for a few moments until she sighed.

"You are the primary suspect in this, the second murder in less than a week, yes. You have also been cleared of both. *This* time, there was both CCTV *and* a crop lens. We have an even better shot of the act, from a better angle, and in brighter surroundings."

Jed merely listened.

"The profile we have for the second murder matches the profile of the killer for the first."

Jed's ears perked up.

"So, it was the same person?" he asked incredulously.

"It was," she said.

He dropped his head into his hands and groaned. Things were worse than he'd imagined. It was bad enough that it could have accidentally been him that got attacked in the case of the first murder, but now, it was starting to seem like this person was following him and trying to frame the murders on him intentionally.

"His name was Warren, and he was forty-five. Do you want to see the video?" she asked when he failed to respond.

"Yes."

Christie pressed the button, and the video started. The homeless man was in view right away, standing next to the trash can. Small flames were visible over his shoulder as he stood with his back to the camera, his arms outstretched over the fire. Jed came into view, entering the frame from the left. He watched the recorded version of himself nod to the man and could almost hear the man's grunt as he nodded back. Then, Jed disappeared out of the frame on the right.

It was so quiet inside the room that Jed could hear his heartbeat in his ears. It didn't help that the recordings had no audio. He glanced over at Christie. Her eyes were glued to the screen. His own gaze turned back to it. The clock at the bottom of the screen climbed to ten thirty. Five minutes had passed since he'd exited the frame. No one else had walked down the street. Finally, from the left, a hooded figure entered. Warren was sitting next to the dying flames in the trashcan.

The attack was quicker, surer this time than he had been with Allan. In a flash, a long, glinting blade was pulled and raised high into the air as the hooded man lunged toward Warren. There was a scuffle as Warren tried to overpower his attacker, but it was short lived. Again and again, the knife was raised into the air, and Jed could see that it was coated in blood as it did. The blade no longer glinted.

The video ended, and Jed's exhale filled the room. Christie turned to look at him.

"That was pretty gnarly," she admitted, picking up her pen and beginning to write.

Jed's response was another exhale. "I notice the scuffle was longer, and more violent, this time." He took a sip of water from his bottle to cool himself down. Watching videos like that one made him queasy.

"I noticed that too. Like it was more work to overpower Warren than it had to overpower Allan."

"Allan was older, and in a frailer condition than Warren," Jed added, watching Christie write.

She nodded.

"Do you see the other pattern here?" he asked.

Christie looked up, a question forming on her brow.

"This person is either after me or trying to frame me."

She blinked.

"What are the chances of a murderer attacking two home-less men right after I walk by them, *twice* in a row?" he demanded of her.

"I did think of that when I called you earlier." She sighed. "I knew you realized the pattern as well when you guessed it was you that was the primary suspect yet again."

"While I was walking home last night is when the thought came to me. What if they had been after me. But I didn't have enough reason to believe it. Now, though, after last night, it's starting to seem more and more like the case."

"Well, it happened on—"

"I know where it happened," he interjected. "I was there. I nodded to the homeless guy when I passed. I was hoping he would make it back into society someday."

Christie didn't know what to say. She watched Jed run a hand through his hair, pushing it out of his face as he exhaled heavily. She started writing again, a lump forming in her throat. What if the killer was really after Jed? The thought made her head swim.

"If he's after you, why do you think he hasn't already made a move to attack you?"

Jed looked up at her.

She nudged him and went on. "He seems to know you well enough to identify you and follow you while you're walking on the road late at night. If what he's after is your life, why does he keep giving away his chance and attacking other people in your place? And why the homeless?"

The anxiety that was raging through his head dimmed long enough for Jed to think logically and evaluate what she was saying. She was right.

"That makes sense," he finally admitted.

She looked up from the notes she was making and nodded.

"Thank you," he added.

Her brow raised, pen pausing where it was poised over the page to write. "What for?"

"Diffusing my anxiety with logical thought. You're right. If he was after me, he'd have made an attack on my person the first time. That street had been both dark and deserted—more so than the path I took this time."

She nodded, smiling. "Of course. I'm happy to help."

Jed looked off into space for a while, lost in thought. "If he isn't trying to attack me, then it follows that he's trying to frame me."

Christie agreed, "I can see how the two might connect."

Jed watched her go back to writing, her head down and hair in a ponytail—the way she always wore it for work. He longed to see it down around her face again. He longed to sit across from her at a dinner table again.

"Do you think that he knows where you live? Since he appears to follow you?"

His heart lurched at her question, and he closed his eyes for a moment.

"I would hope not. But, in the grand scheme of how things are playing out, it's not impossible. He does run off in the opposite direction after he commits the act, though, and the weapon at the crime scene was the same kind of dagger as in the last crime scene."

She nodded, waiting for Jed to continue his thought.

"What was the official cause of death this time?"

Christie spread the murder scene photos across the table for Jed to view, then she flipped to the previous page of the folder.

"Warren Wint, age forty-five—death by hemorrhage as a result of repeated sharp force trauma. Suspect sustained a total of twenty stab wounds—five to the neck and shoulders, three to the face, and twelve to the chest and abdominal area."

He closed his eyes and breathed deeply. *Three to the face.*

"Facial wounds are usually a sign that the perpetrator wants to make the victim unidentifiable, right?"

"Usually yes," she answered, tapping the pen against her cheek. "Sometimes, there are more sophisticated reasons. Perhaps the murderer wants to send some kind of cryptic message by marring the face of their victims."

Jed nodded. Criminals were always eager to prove themselves smart and powerful. It was a consequence of an inflated ego and a grandiose sense of self—a twisted worldview that was far more common than the average person realized.

Christie continued, "In this case, perhaps our killer is trying to say that these homeless people are nobodies? That we shouldn't even bother to investigate because they're a waste of space and city resources?"

He looked across the table at her. "I think that's it. That's exactly what he's trying to say."

They both thought in silence for a few minutes, taking stock of what they knew, what pieces of the puzzle were missing, and what they needed to do to figure it all out.

"I think that the stab wounds to the face tie into the motive—the motive we don't know yet," Jed added.

Christie sighed, reaching behind her to the nape of her neck. He watched her remove the elastic that held her hair in place, and as it fell around her face, he smiled. She raised a brow.

"Why are you smiling?"

"Your hair. I love how it frames your face."

Her eyes softened. "Oh. Thank you," she answered.

Now she was smiling, too.

"Nothing's checked out in my look into our records of serial killers. There have been five in the last seven years—three are dead, two of those killed in police raids, one by gang violence, and the other two are currently incarcerated. I went as far as calling the prisons to make sure they hadn't escaped, and we just… didn't know about it. No other recent murderers fit our profile."

"That would be very unlikely," Jed offered.

"It would." She closed the folder. "But nothing beats making absolutely certain."

"I guess that means we're looking at a new serial killer profile being created in real time." Jed pinched the bridge of his nose.

"That's exactly what it is." As though an afterthought, Christie's head popped up, and she said, "There's two more things. I asked an officer to check Whitman's alibi, and it came back as a lie. His workplace has a record of him going on a forty-five-minute walk at eight-thirty pm."

Jed leaned forward. "And if he went on a forty-five-minute walk at that time, his being away from work coincides with the time of the murder."

"Exactly. So, Whitman is still very much a suspect in this case, and now with the second murder taking place with the same pattern, we need to speak with Carrillo as soon as possible. We have him coming in tomorrow for an interview. He also has the means and a motive to have these men killed."

Jed let the new information settle into his mind for a few moments as Christie reviewed her notes. The room was quiet for a minute.

"Now that we've covered mostly everything about this case, I have some other news for you."

"Oh?" Jed leaned further forward in his chair, elbows on the tabletop. "What's up?"

"I spoke to the Chief yesterday, after I got wind of the second murder, and he suggested you wear a body cam—both for your protection and to eliminate the need to formally clear your name if this keeps happening. I'm not sure how you'd feel about doing that."

Jed looked down at the desk, thinking over what Christie had just said.

"I agree that it makes sense, and it would decrease the chances of this maniac trashing my reputation completely," he started. A sly smile slipped onto his lips. "As my partner, I presume you're going to have primary access to the camera's live stream?"

She nodded, her cheeks coloring. He nodded in turn.

"I'll do it. As long as you promise not to watch me while I'm in the shower."

"Jed!" Christie exclaimed as she laughed.

He chuckled, running a hand through his hair again. "Then we won't have a problem."

Now, her cheeks even more flushed. She hadn't realized she could potentially watch him shower if he wore a body cam all the time—not that she would watch him at his most vulnerable moments. That was a huge violation of privacy and trust, even if she did want to see what was hiding under the loose clothing he always wore.

Jed and Christie went over the list of questions she was planning to ask Carrillo in the interview today. Actually, it was Jed that was looking over the questions. Interviews were police and detective work, not the work of investigative therapists.

He half-read as he also watched Christie set up the room ahead of the suspect's arrival. There was not much to do—just tidy up the space and arrange the chairs so that she could face the suspect directly.

They hadn't spoken much since he had arrived, and Jed put it down to the fact that they were doing another interview today. He watched her move around the room a few more times, looking the details over, making sure that everything was in place. He wasn't sure what she was working towards achieving with the few pieces of furniture in the room, but he was content to just watch her work.

After she was satisfied, Christie turned to him, and he looked up at her over the edge of the paper in front of him when he felt her attention moved to him.

"Ready?" he asked.

She nodded, stuffing her hands into her pockets. "Just waiting for him to arrive."

"So, it's gonna be a long day of work. Have you eaten breakfast and lunch today, Detective?"

"I had a light lunch," she said.

Jed nodded, having anticipated that response. He could understand. Interviewing suspects in murder cases was not something to be taken lightly; it definitely was not a walk in the park. It was a stressful environment, with suspects who were largely unpredictable. There was always the need for caution in these circumstances.

Jed's attention was torn away from her as another police officer entered the room. The man nodded to them both before handing a few papers to Christie, turning, and leaving.

She stared down at them for a few moments before sighing and raising her head to look back at Jed.

"Let's get this show on the road."

Once again in the observation room, behind the one-sided glass that let him view the interrogation, unnoticed, Jed watched Thiago Carrillo walk into the room. He was the developer that the department had received an anonymous tip about, the businessman with a vendetta against the homeless people that the city favored over his development proposals.

Carrillo was only a little taller than Christie was, around five-foot-ten, and had a stocky build with a beer belly poking out in front of him as he walked. He took his seat when she invited him to, and Jed looked down at the profile in his hand as Christie began the conversation.

"Good afternoon, Mr. Carrillo. How are you doing today?"

The man huffed, barely looking at Christie.

"I'm fine. I don't have much time for this silly investigation, so you can cut the small talk and get into the questions."

Jed's eyes narrowed at the man's attitude. The person who had given them the anonymous tip about Carrillo's business and his arrogant attitude was right on the money so far.

"Small talk? Is that what you call asking someone how they're doing today?"

"Yes. That is exactly what that is."

"Very well, let's move on. What exactly is it that you do for work?"

Carrillo slanted Christie a nasty look.

"The police force really should hire some competent people. You invite me in for an interview about some bloody murder case, and you don't even know what I do for work?" His voice rattled with anger. "I'm a businessman. I run Carrillo Contracting and Development."

He puffed out his chest as he mentioned the name of his business, and Jed wanted to snort.

From the three-piece suit, Rolex, and wide-rimmed glasses Carrillo was wearing, Jed could gauge that he was coming right from work. He wondered if the developer had been in a meeting before this to go over just how much money he had lost this quarter from rejected development plans. Maybe that was why he was so angry.

Still, Christie didn't flinch at his verbal abuse. She was looking right at him, her gaze and voice steady, and her posture erect.

"Did you inherit Carrillo Contracting from your father, or your parents?"

Jed thought steam might come from the man's ears as his whole face turned red. Instinctively, Jed's muscles tensed. He was ready to drop everything and go into the room if the man needed some… calming down.

"No! Of course, I didn't. I built Carrillo from the ground up when I moved to New York!"

"Oh," Christie responded, feigning genuine surprise as if she didn't already know everything there was to know about him—and his business. "That must have been quite the difficult undertaking."

Carrillo's chest puffed out again as he gave a quick, sharp nod. "It was."

"That's very admirable," she mused. "But my question seemed to anger you a good deal. Is your relationship with your father strained?"

The pudgy man shook his head, beginning to sweat, likely from the heat under all those clothes.

"No, of course not. My father is a good man. He moved our family here from Mexico when I was very young. He did all he could for us."

Christie nodded along. "Well, your business has come under a lot of public scrutiny these past weeks."

"What?" Carrillo demanded.

"Oh," Christie gestured, making it look as if it was no big deal. "Word on the street is that you don't like homeless people very much, and with the murders of homeless people in the past weeks... you've fallen onto our radar."

Carrillo's gaze darkened.

"You insult me greatly, Ms. Whatever-Your-Name-Is... but–"

"Detective Jamison to you, Mr. Carrillo."

A shiver slid across Jed's shoulders at the way her tone sank from pleasant and neutral into tempered aggression as she corrected him. Jed saw the annoyance glint in Christie's eyes.

The man nodded and swallowed before he continued.

"Right. Well, *Detective*, I have done nothing but been a benefactor to the state and City of New York. My work has always been beneficial to all the citizens of the state, and I've done everything in my power to help this sorry city solve its homelessness problem."

"And how have you been doing that, Mr. Carrillo?"

The man was so puffed up now that Jed thought he would burst into pieces.

"By providing housing solutions, of course! That's what we do. We build apartment complexes and home solutions for the citizens of New York to live in! We're the best in the state. Even your department will agree with that! So, how could I hate the homeless?"

Christie looked down at the papers in front of her, not immediately answering, letting the question simmer in the air for a while.

"How did it feel to lose that twenty-five million in profit just because of twenty homeless people?"

Now Jed was sure he would explode. He jumped up from his seat, pointing a trembling finger at Christie, who never moved or flinched. When the door opened, and Jed walked in to stand behind Christie, towering over both of them with his arms folded over his black muscle tee for full effect, Carrillo sat down without hesitation.

He was boiling. A thousand emotions were racing through his features all at once, and Jed could see rage, embarrassment, fear, shock and contempt surge through his eyes.

"Listen, you—" He paused, trying to regain his composure. "Listen, Detective, that is classified information. I don't know how you've managed to inveigle it, but so help me God, I'll—"

Christie's head tilted when his words slowed, and Jed knew her gaze was razor sharp, even from where he stood behind her.

"How did it make you feel to know that your big, flashy project was rejected in favor of some lousy drug addicts, Mr. Carrillo?"

"I will *not* answer that question."

Christie nodded and pressed on. "Where were you on the night of September 16th at nine pm?"

"At home with my wife and children."

"If we called your wife, would she say the same thing?"

"She would. I get home at seven pm every day, and I never leave again until the next morning at seven am for work. That's our family time."

Christie made a note on the paper in front of her.

"So, you wouldn't have had a reason to be on 55th at that time on the 16th?"

"55th?" The man looked genuinely bewildered. "I don't even know what that is."

"55th Street, Mr. Carrillo."

He nodded like it suddenly made sense to him. "Then let me correct myself, Detective. I don't even know where that is."

Jed looked at the sweating man, whose suppressed rage poured out from his eyes and twitching lip. He had been angry since Christie first opened her mouth to speak. The profit loss had sent him over the edge.

Carrillo was glaring at Christie, and Jed was glaring at him, eyes on his every move, down to the rise and fall of his chest as he breathed. He would take him down if he even tried to make a move. He'd take anything down that tried to get close to her, frankly.

Carrillo's fists were tight as he rose from his seat, and he nodded stiffly to Christie, who nodded in return as he headed for the door. He didn't even look at Jed. He was angry alright. But angry enough to kill? That was still up for question.

When they were alone, Jed watched Christie stare down at the papers in front of her like she had done after the first interview.

"Thanks for coming to my rescue, Gray."

Jed grinned.

"Anything to save a damsel in distress, Detective."

Christie tried to glare at him but gave in to the smile that tugged at her lips.

"That interview was… interesting. We need to put in a request for his financials since we've talked about him potentially hiring the job out. I'm not sure whether we'll get those back right away. There's always lots of red tape when it comes to accessing people's financial records."

Her hands were deep in her pockets, and Jed watched her shoulders slump a little as she finished her sentence.

"Don't get discouraged," Jed said firmly as he squeezed her arm. "We'll get to the bottom of this."

CHAPTER 6

LATER THAT EVENING, THE team of policemen finally arrived at his apartment, and Jed was watching them do the installations. He had suggested they install a motion sensor and camera near his front door so they could see when he came in and left. That way, the body cam could be saved for whenever he left the house, instead of him having to wear it while he did everyday tasks, like cooking and lounging. That would just be awkward. This way, he could relax at home.

These were the sort of cameras that recorded everything—date and time stamps, temperature, weather, down to the moisture content of the air. In addition, these cameras were equipped for night recording, and the one in his apartment even had heat sensors for filming at night.

As for the body cam he would have to wear, he had already unboxed it. It was a miniscule, wireless thing, something he could attach to his tie or breast pocket like a clip.

The group chatted while they completed the installations. It was six in the evening on a Tuesday afternoon, and Jed hadn't been to the office since he had left at three yesterday. Yet, there was a group of policemen standing in a bundle at his door. His life had changed drastically in the last few days, and he was still reeling from it all.

While they had been negotiating the terms for the surveillance, Christie had also brought up the option of a search as an extra layer of precaution. *This is not mandatory, but doing a search of your apartment would give us an added layer of evidence as to your innocence. The killer uses a specific type of dagger, and he always leaves them at the scene of the crime. We haven't been able to trace any large purchases of knives or daggers made city-wide recently, so that means he has them at home. Searching your place and coming up short of those knives would make a strong case for your innocence.*

Jed agreed on the condition that she would be the one who did the search after the cameras were installed, so that the search would be on record, too. He didn't want some random police officer searching through his things. He didn't want anyone searching through his things, but if it was Christie, he could tolerate it. In any case, those daggers were something he needed to look into for his case research.

It was three hours later when the group of officers were through. He hadn't realized it took so long to set up a couple of cameras and motion sensors and connect them to his Wi-Fi. That was because it didn't. They'd spent more time laughing and talking about arbitrary things than they had spent working. It made him glad he had negotiated for Christie to be the one doing the search of his apartment. They would have taken another four hours to do that and probably would have left the apartment absolutely ransacked, the way they had left the boxes and papers from the cameras at his doorway.

Cursing under his breath, he gathered them and picked them up, tossing them down the garbage shoot. Christie was at the door, waiting for him, when he returned, and they entered the apartment together after he opened the door for her.

"Welcome to my humble abode," he said as they crossed the threshold.

Smiling up at him, she whispered a thank you.

"Well," he gestured, "it's all yours."

Christie looked around, feeling awkward and excited all at once.

"It's a pity you had to come over for the first time under these conditions, though," he, thought aloud. "I'm a great host."

She grinned cheekily. "Well, then, you can invite me over another time."

"It's a date."

Jed moved into the kitchen, grabbing two bottles of water from the fridge and handing one to her. Her heart was pounding.

Christie took a sip in a bid to calm herself down. Being in a man's space was always an opportunity to learn so much about him. Right now, she could confirm what she had already inferred about Jed. He was clean, organized, and by the looks of it, a good cook—and incredibly attractive, leaning on the counter across from her the way he was, eyes on her.

"Have you decided where you'll begin your search?"

She'd been staring, and he'd been letting her stare, sipping on his water slowly, as he watched her. She cleared her throat.

"I'll start right here in the kitchen. That's the most obvious place to hide knives, isn't it?" She teased.

"I wouldn't know," he responded, smiling.

They both laughed. The search began. In the lower cabinets, she found multiple cast iron skillets, which were seasoned and looked well-used, a blue Le Crueset stock pot, and crisp, white pottery casserole dishes nestled inside one another. Inside the cutlery drawer, everything was in its place—stainless steel utensils that looked to be commercial-grade.

Jed sat at the dining table while Christie worked her way through each drawer and cabinet on the lower level. He watched, a bemused smirk on his face, as she tried to reach the upper cabinets above the stove and sink. She huffed, frustration getting the better of her. Jed walked up to her right then, his hand settling next to her on the white marble, pressing against her waist slightly, while his other hand reached over her head to pull open the cabinet she'd been trying to reach.

"Thank you," she breathed, staying still as a mouse as he slowly moved away.

He hummed in response.

She made her way through the uppers. His cabinets were organized, with simple, clean cobalt blue plates & saucers arranged neatly inside. Beverage glasses were lined in rows according to their sizes, and to the left, stemmed glass ice cream dessert bowls sat, nestled perfectly against the cabinet wall.

When she was through, he came over again to close the cabinets while she opened the ovens and looked in the fridge. Even it was organized, cut into sections that reminded her of the TikToks she had seen online of people restocking their fridges. The rest of the dining and living room was straight-forward. The space was an open concept and felt comfortable and familiar, like a dear friend's home that you visited often.

It was a simple, yet homey design. Everything was in its place and had a purpose. There was a charcoal gray couch that looked inviting & cozy to curl up on for a movie night, a leather armchair with an industrial reading lamp next to it, and a side table with a couple of books on it that all had bookmarks in them, marking various pages—it was the perfect reading spot. Above the couch was a large piece of abstract artwork that displayed an array of black, white, red, and yellow that tickled her brain as though she had seen it before.

She knocked on surfaces, kneeled to look under furniture, and checked for loose floorboards. He watched her work, lending his assistance when she needed to shift a piece of furniture or lift something.

Next up was the bathroom. The slick white subway tiles in the large walk-in shower glistened, Christie noticed the shower was plenty big enough for two. She swallowed. A few select toiletries were on the shelf in the shower—Method Men and Native. No wonder he always smelled so good, she thought. The charcoal gray bathmat and towels were all in their place.

The bathroom, office, and hall closet searches went off without a hitch. In the bedroom, she found a queen-sized bed with industrial, black iron accents and large timber bedposts. There were large pillows on top of a charcoal gray & navy striped duvet. There was just one side table with alarm clock and small lamp. That made her smile. There wasn't enough room in any New York City apartment for two side tables. Across from the bed was the door to his closet and a window that overlooked the street below.

Inside the closet, his clothes were hanging neatly on one side, and on the other, there were shelves laden with folded clothes. Under the shelves lay a box on the floor and shoes placed neatly under the hanging clothes. She opened the box and rummaged around, pausing mid-search. He'd been sitting on the bed behind her as she rummaged through the bottom of his closet, and when she paused, before she could turn around or say anything, realization dawned on him. *Fuck.*

"Are these... handcuffs?" she asked, picking up a pair, "... and silk rope?"

Jed noticed she didn't bother to touch the rope. She examined the cuffs, turning to look at him with wide eyes.

"Professional grade handcuffs?"

"Can't have my prisoners escaping." He shrugged, seemingly unaffected by the fact that she'd stumbled across his playthings.

"Why do you need these?" Christie asked, naively.

"Why do you think?" he asked, cocking his head to the side.

Heat washed over her, both from sudden embarrassment and desire.

She replaced them in the box where she'd found them before closing the closet and turning around, cheeks red.

"Everything alright, Detective?" he queried, his voice quiet and soft in the large room. "You look a bit... flustered."

She blushed an even deeper shade of red, and he chuckled. "You are especially beautiful when you blush like that."

Her ears burned. When she finally mustered the courage to look over at him, she found his tender gaze on her, his expression still kind and calm. She'd expected to find him smiling, smug... something that would let her know he was just messing around.

She did not find what she was looking for—neither in his expression, nor in his apartment. There were no knives here. Only soft bedding, very firm bedposts, military grade handcuffs, rope, and a man she was suffocatingly attracted to.

"Thank you, and I'm fine. I think this concludes our search."

He nodded, rising, and led her back into the living room.

"Are you staying for dinner?" he asked, watching her head for the door.

She turned to look at him. He'd paused partway into the kitchen, likely on his way to start cooking. She did want to taste the food he made, but she couldn't think straight. That wasn't the only thing she wanted to taste. Christie wanted more than dinner. She wanted to know just how strong those cuffs were that she'd found. She needed to leave.

"Not this time," she answered. "Save it for the next visit? I feel like I've violated your space enough for one day."

He nodded, eyes watching her intently. She felt like he could see right through to the thoughts and images playing in her brain. But he couldn't.

"I will," was his reply, and he walked over to pull the door open for her.

She took a deep breath, crossed the threshold, and turned back to face him. Jed was leaning against the doorframe, an arm above his head. He towered over her in that position—more than he usually did—and her heart raced within her. She wasn't sure if it was because of the long day, the caffeine she drank earlier, or the way he was looking down at her in the dim hallway lighting.

"Call me when you get home so I know you're safe," he instructed.

Christie swallowed. Was it just her, or did he suddenly sound even more dominant than he usually did?

"Okay," slipped out of her lips.

A smile tugged at his.

"It was my pleasure having you. Come again soon, Detective."

CHAPTER 7

THE DAYS HAD flit by quickly, and the world around him had almost returned to normal. Almost. Jed kept his body cam on, only removing it when he walked into his office in the mornings and when he walked into his apartment in the evenings, and there were cameras in his apartment. So, things were as normal as they could be, given the circumstances.

It was another Friday, and he was in his office, looking out the windows as he waited for his line to ring—the usual. His routine—exercise, work, home—had resumed, with the occasional 'walk to the police station' added to it. Christie had called earlier, and their conversation had been brief, but tense.

Jed's sigh filled the room. The team was in knots, and Christie was head and shoulders in the middle of the ropes. She had thrown herself into her work with a vigor and interest Jed rarely saw, and she seemed to spend every waking moment consumed by thoughts of the case: potential angles, new evidence, and motives. Even though he found it unimaginably attractive how dedicated to her work and justice she was, Jed still worried about the pressure she was under. Then again, he was no different.

This week had been harder than usual for him, too, though for different reasons than the previous week. Last week, he'd begun an investigative therapy partnership and then had walked into the middle of two murder cases in the span of three days. It had been stressful.

Was it purely a coincidence that, right on the heels of him taking on a permanent investigative therapy partnership with the NYPD, two homeless men—the target of his role as an addiction therapist—were murdered? It was a thought that had been ruminating over and over in his mind. Jed had a slowly intensifying, sad premonition that the murderer, whoever he was, would not stop at just two.

For a moment, Jed allowed the beams of light drifting from his window onto his office rug to distract him. The sunlight was rippling across the floor, patterns forming from where it was shining through the trees. He looked up and through the window, watching pigeons crowd around a woman who was perched on the edge of a bench, eating a sandwich like she hadn't eaten anything in a week. She still tossed a piece to the eager birds. When she got up to walk away, Jed's reverie ended.

The lack of a concrete motive for the killings added to his uncertainty. It was a thought he'd meant to run by Christie on their call yesterday evening, but he'd gotten distracted by the details of the results of evidence analysis they'd received. There was finally information available about the weapons the suspect had used in his attacks. The good news was that they had traced the origin of the two daggers to a producer in the UK. The bad news was neither knife contained fingerprints or DNA of any kind. Apparently, the killer was more knowledgeable of crime scenes and evidence collection than they had realized.

Jed had had his doubts about that. With the seemingly sporadic murders and an unclear motive, Jed hadn't been able to figure out what kind of thought process ran through the mind of this killer. Now, knowing the origin and quality of the blades, at four hundred dollars apiece, and that the killer had gone to great lengths to protect his DNA by wearing gloves, Jed surmised that these killings weren't so sporadic after all and that the killer wasn't operating out of impulsivity. He knew the killer seemed to be following him, but were the victims just in the wrong place at the wrong time, or were they the intended victims?

These facts greatly decreased the potential of the killer being a substance abuser and ruled out many of Jed's potential hunches. Was he just a psychopath that enjoyed killing? Were homeless people just easy, dispensable targets?

Ring.

The clock rested on four-thirty. "Hello?"

"You already know who and how it is, Mr. G."

Relief washed over Jed like the cold, crisp water at the lake house he so badly wanted to visit. He hadn't realized just how anxious he'd been about whether Max was alright or not, though the recent murders had been outside of Max's zone.

"Maxwell. It's good to hear from you. How are you doing?"

"Alive and kicking, man. Alive and kicking."

There was a distinct tone of amusement in the boy's voice, and Jed's brows raised.

"What do you mean, Max?"

On the other end of the line, Max took a slurp of something.

"Yeah, man. Your side of town's been going crazy lately. Two murders in—what? Two days?"

Jed resisted the urge to correct him and focused on taking notes. He couldn't get his wires crossed. He worked with multiple clients, all dealing with substance addiction and abuse, most of them homeless or running away from the homes they did have. Jed knew word would spread. He'd been preparing to hear about it on his calls, particularly from Max, who never shied away from any topic.

"How have these incidents left you feeling?" Jed asked, deflecting the query neatly.

"I don't feel no type of way, man. But word on the street is crazy. All the guys are acting like… scared or something."

More notes. He scribbled on his paper, tossing his pen aside and reaching for another when the ink refused to come out of the tube.

"What are they afraid of?"

"Nobody knows who the killer is, man. Whoever it is, it's not nobody from the streets."

More scribbling. Max continued.

"Usually, if one of our guys gets dropped out, it's because of some kind of feud or some territory shit. Y'know how these mo'fuckas are when it comes to shit like that."

There was a pause as Max slurped from his drink again.

"The streets are going wild. Everybody's on edge. Everybody's expecting to be next."

Jed's heart dropped into his stomach. "Even those enemies of yours? Are they afraid, too?"

Max chuckled, but the sound was void of humor.

"They've been hit the worst. They're turning on themselves, arguing, fighting; the only thing left for 'em to do is start firing shots at each other at point-blank range. That's how I know it's not none of us, man. Everybody's proud to claim it when they turn another idiot into a corpse. They like using that kinda stuff to make people scared. Y'know. Show like they're tough or whateva."

If the top of the chain in the drug underbelly of New York were thrown into confusion by these killings, this was worse than Jed had estimated. He needed to call Christie.

"And you're not bothered by any of this?"

Max hesitated to respond, and Jed could hear him swallowing again.

"Man, listen," Max cleared his throat. "I could die at any given moment, anyway. So, whoever this punk is that's running 'round swinging daggers doesn't scare me."

Jed hummed, and Max continued. "In any case, he's only attacking old, helpless homeless people. There's plenty of young, strong homeless men around, and he don't seem to want smoke with any of them. He doesn't want smoke with any of *us*."

Jed sorted his belongings into his bag as he prepared to leave the office and found himself lost in multiple streams of thought. His conversation with Max had been a fruitful one. The boy had shared his recent thoughts about his relationship with his father, more about his hesitancy to meet with his mom, let Jed know he'd collected the cell phone Jed had gotten for him during the week, and had, ever so casually, dropped a prospective bomb about the case. His acceptance of the cell phone was a big milestone in their relationship—and a big indicator of Max's progress.

Jed had left the phone in front of his office's building, in his own locker. He'd told Max during a call earlier in the week, *I bought you a phone so you can keep in contact easier with the people you want to keep in contact with. And so you're not bound to that ten-minute call limit anymore. It's in my locker in the downstairs entrance of my building—you know where the building is. Locker number 1258, the code is 6299355. Come get it.*

Max had called because he thought he might not be able to call at his regular time on Friday, but in the end, he was able to make it.

Though all Max had done was laugh when Jed had finished giving him the details he would need to collect the phone, he had come to collect it sometime during the week and used it to call in today. If he'd come in for the phone, it meant that, eventually, he'd be okay coming in for sessions, too.

"Max should really consider getting into the police force," Jed mumbled under his breath as he swung his bag over his shoulder and turned to head out the door. "He is amazingly perceptive and incredibly street smart." Even though he knew that would not be a possibility with his police record and rehab history, Jed wished it could be.

Max was right, and the insinuation about the killer's age had left Jed floored. He wished he'd seen it sooner, himself. The killer was probably a younger man. Both the victims had been older men, and both had been attacked and overpowered, with the first victim being attacked while in a sitting position. That pointed to what could be strategic positioning that would give the killer a distinct advantage. Strength.

In the CCTV footage of both incidents, each victim had put up a brave fight but had been overpowered in the end. Could the killer have been relying on the advantage of youthful strength? Did the killer know better than to attack a younger homeless person like Max was suggesting?

As he closed the door to his office, the door next to it opened.

"Jed?"

He was pulled out of his thoughts, and Jed looked over. It was Hugh. Jed's neighbor stepped out of his own office, a grin on his face. Jed nodded to him, noticing that he was once again dressed like he belonged in a lawyer's office—a dark blue suit, complete with a jacket and the watch he always wore. Jed felt a little out of place in his simple, cream buttoned and tailored pants.

"I take it you're headed home?" Hugh asked. He looked down at the watch on his wrist.

"Yes. It's that time of the evening." Jed responded.

Hugh nodded, still smiling. "I realize that now. I still have a bit of work to do before I'm free for the evening."

He stepped into the hallway fully to face Jed, pulling his own door shut behind him. "I wanted to catch ya before you left," he went on.

"What's up? Can I help you with something?" Jed asked, caution in his voice.

Hugh's grin widened, and Jed wondered if he ever stopped smiling.

"Nah, nothing formal like. I actually wanted to invite you to grab dinner with me one evening next week."

Jed raised a brow. "Dinner?"

"Yeah, as buddies like."

Jed nodded, and Hugh laughed. That pulled a smile out of Jed.

"What? You thought I was inviting you to some kind of romantic, candle-lit affair?"

A snort of laughter echoed through the hall. "No. I just didn't understand what exactly you meant."

Hugh, who had been laughing just as much, nodded.

"Whatever, man." He grinned. "Wednesday? There's this new spot that just opened up on 68th that has been getting rave reviews. They've got a bar and dining section, too."

Jed nodded.

"We'll leave from here."

The sun was setting behind the buildings across the street when Jed finally made it through the front door of the office and out into the world. Crowds were milling about in the Monday evening glow, and as he struck out for home, he decided to stop by Jamie's stall. Since he was going to pass by it anyway, he might as well stop to pick up a hot dog for a savory dessert after he made himself dinner.

"What for you, my loyal customer?" Jamie teased as he walked up to the stand.

Jed laughed, bumping into the woman next to him and apologizing. She was much shorter than he was and had long, bleach-blonde hair that was tucked behind her ears. Three border collies wiggled their butts up at him from the end of the leash she was holding. He scratched their ears and heads and laughed when their wiggling intensified.

"That's okay," she responded, smiling as she watched an especially eager pup jump up onto Jed.

"I'm a regular by now, Jamie. C'mon! You know what my order is." Jed laughed.

"You're such a good girl," he cooed to the collie, whose pink ribbons gave everything away. The other two, who were also wiggling, wore blue ribbons on their ears. It was almost too precious a sight to see.

"Let me guess, this time you want three of 'em," Jamie teased again.

The trio laughed.

"Two will suffice, thanks."

Hotdogs in hand, he bid Jamie and his new friend Lana, the dog walker, goodbye, and turned down the street, still smiling. It had been windy all day, and he'd enjoyed watching the wind play in the trees during some of his longer calls. He always looked for a way to mentally stimulate himself so he could stay as alert as possible on his calls—without being too stimulated to end up distracted. Today, the wind had presented the perfect muse. Now, still, the wind whirred through the air and past the trees, sending loose leaves flying through the air all around. He smiled again as he passed a particularly heavily shedding tree and had to shield his food from the downpour of leaves.

Chapter 8

As his route led him closer and closer to home, his thoughts turned back to the case. He was walking the same way he had been that night after leaving the police station, past the Starbucks outlet, past the bookstore and small chain café, and then past the same trash can where Warren had been standing, warming his hands over the flames. Today, the can was dry, soot from its last burning still on the curb below it. Heaviness settled in Jed's stomach as he continued on.

Finally, inside his apartment, he dropped his bags next to the sofa, removed the body cam he'd gotten so used to wearing on his tie as a clip, and gazed out the floor to ceiling windows across from the kitchen, his eyes moving out and over the city. Being on the fifteenth floor definitely had its perks. As the pasta boiled on the stove, and as the cheese sauce simmered next to it, his mind raced. He wondered where his outing with Hugh would take their friendship.

Did they have a friendship? Hardly—they had only spoken twice, and today, the invitation to dinner, was one of those times. He wasn't sure how to feel about the man.

Over the years, he'd become more and more aware of just how much his relationship with his father, or rather the lack of it, affected the way he felt about and interacted with other men. It was something Jed was always aware of, and though he wanted to work on this area of his life, he rarely went out of his way to connect with other men. He was great at his job, but outside of work, he usually kept to himself and avoided new interactions. Since Hugh was new to his floor and so outgoing, it gave Jed an opportunity. Maybe this was his chance to have a close guy friend.

Jed's thoughts turned to Max—he'd made a great deal of progress today in his journey to rehab when he opened up about his relationship with his dad. He hadn't intended to, but it had answered Jed's question about why the boy was so hesitant to meet with his own mother. And Max's views on the case could benefit from a talk over with Christie. Two heads were always better than one when it came to analysis, especially since they were partners.

So why was he so hesitant to make the call? Jed looked at the time. It was eight-thirty. He should have called earlier. He didn't want to interrupt her evening, or whatever activity she was doing. Jed realized he didn't know whether she had a partner. The topic had never come up. What if she was at home with someone and his call interrupted their groove? His jaw tightened at the thought.

Time had flown by earlier as he'd done a quick clean-up of the apartment before starting dinner. The call could very well wait until morning, but Jed wanted to get the information off his chest now. He hesitated for only a moment longer before pressing the green call button.

"Hello? Is everything okay? Did something happen?"

She had answered on the first ring. He balked. He hadn't expected her to pick up at all.

"Um, yes. I'm okay. Are you... okay?" He returned the question.

"I'm fine. I just—I thought you had run into trouble. Your theory about this killer potentially being after you hasn't faded from my mind, and when I saw the phone ring, I thought—well, I thought you'd been attacked."

Remembering to stir his sauce, Jed turned to face the stove. He couldn't help the smile that spread on his face.

"I'm sorry to have worried you, Detective. Wouldn't want you to be analyzing my crime scene next," he joked.

"Please don't say that," she groaned. "Are you home?"

"Yes. I—" he started.

"You're safe." She ended for him.

He looked down at the screen almost incredulously. "I hadn't realized you were worried about me."

"You must be joking. Are you joking? You're my partner, Jed, and this is the first case we're working on together—a case that seems to be revolving around your life."

He continued to stir, tossing a handful of freshly-grated hard cheddar into the warm mixture.

"I know all that. I just…" he paused as he turned the stove off. "I just hadn't thought you'd be so concerned."

He tossed the pasta gently in the sauce, mixing in the tender baked chicken he'd finished making earlier in the evening. Christie hadn't responded.

"I'll call you more often in the evenings when I get in, so you know I haven't fallen victim to my theory."

Christie sighed. "Thank you."

"So…" Jed began as he plated his dinner and packaged the leftovers into his favorite glass Pyrex for storing. "I hope I'm not interrupting your evening too much?"

Christie chuckled.

"You aren't interrupting at all," she replied.

Jed nodded to himself. "Good. Because we'll be here for a while. I wanted to talk about the case, and some new ideas and realizations I… happened upon."

On the other end of the line, Christie swirled the wine in her glass before standing and heading for her desk by the window. It was where she worked when she was at home. The rug was soft beneath her feet as she padded across the living room. She pulled her chair out and sat down. Her apartment overlooked the city, too, and she watched cars drive by and people walk as Jed continued.

"In the office today, I had a sort of realization that opened up some other realms of possibility about our case. The first thing is that I learned that the homeless community is very shaken up by these two attacks. No one has the slightest clue who has been doing these killings. I'd even go as far as today that they're all turning on each other because of it. I happened upon a bit of info that made me realize that the only disturbances within the community are usually related to territory—you know how we were talking about the state's decision to leave derelict city spaces to them so they can have some kind of shelter?"

Christie listened, her pen gliding swiftly across her notebook in the dim light as she made notes about what Jed was saying. "Yes, I remember that discussion. We looked into that when we were discussing Carrillo's potential involvement in the case."

"Exactly. The homeless community is peaceful unless some kind of squabble is happening about who gets to sleep in this empty building or who gets to claim this sleeping spot as their own."

"Right," she chimed.

"So, since the community, itself, has no clue what's going on, that means it's definitely an outside attack."

"Okay," Christie bit her pen. "So, we can be sure that the motives for these killings aren't related to territory or internal squabbles."

Jed hummed, and Christie sighed.

"Day by day, the motive options we have lose their plausibility. And day by day, we struggle to come up with more." A hint of frustration bled into her voice.

"We just haven't come up with the right motive yet." Jed countered, echoing the hopeful sentiment she always had whenever he felt down in the dumps. "We just haven't figured it out *yet*."

In her dim apartment, she nodded. "If that was the first thing, what's the second thing?"

"Well, this is where it gets a bit interesting," Jed began. He had paused to eat some of his food, not wanting the warmth to fade before he had a chance to taste his dinner.

Christie heard the clink of glass and grinned. "What's for dinner Gray?"

He chuckled.

"What, am I chewing too loudly in your ear, Detective?"

Christie laughed along with him as he took another bite of his chicken.

"No, you aren't. You actually have very good eating hygiene, from what I've seen. So, I'm not worried about you chewing my ear off."

Jed laughed. "That's such a roundabout way to compliment me, Detective."

She smiled, watching as a couple holding hands crossed the street below her window.

"Well, take it or leave it," she teased.

He sighed, dramatically. "I'll take it. Dinner is chicken fajita pasta—and a hotdog for a savory dessert experience."

"Savory dessert?" Christie asked, trying to hold back her laughter.

"Yes." Jed admitted, amusement taking over his body. "Are you laughing at me, Detective?"

"Oh! No, of course not," she replied, still struggling to keep the laughter out of her voice. "Why would I be laughing at the fact that you're eating a hotdog for dessert?"

Jed chuckled. "Whatever you say, Detective."

The line was silent for a while as they both thought about their playful banter and Jed finished up his dinner. Rising from his sofa to set the dish in the sink, he stopped by the fridge to get a bottle of water on his way back to the living room.

"So," he began as he sat down. "I came to the realization that, in both instances of the murders he committed, the killer attacked two older males."

He paused, and Christie's brows pulled together as she tried to connect that information to what she already knew about the cases.

"I think I need a bit more information to connect the dots here Gray."

"Both victims were older, to the point of frailty, and one had been in a seated position when attacked from above."

Christie's mouth turned into a wide 'O'.

"So, you're saying that the killer might be younger, based on his target demographic so far and how he launched both attacks?"

"Exactly," Jed replied. "He initiated his attacks from overhead, both times, and that could be a strategic decision that gives him the advantage as a result of his strength. The CCTV footage of the incidents shows us that both victims fought back before he overpowered them."

"That's an incredible observation, Jed."

Christie's pen was racing across the pages of her notebook again as she tried to keep up with the pace of the conversation—and her own thoughts. Jed didn't respond. It wasn't entirely *his* observation, but it was, indeed, incredible.

"Do we think that this killer, somehow, knows better than to attack a younger homeless man? Because he'd have to work too hard to overpower them?"

Jed hummed his agreement. "I think that he knows he'll have to work too hard to even inflict injury on a younger homeless person because those younger men on the streets are often deep in the throes of addiction. Their involvement with substances makes them volatile—and very violent if provoked. They're also likely armed just as well—or even more so—than the killer, himself. Most of these homeless men either have weapons or have friends who have them. The killer might be the one who ends up dead if he were to attack a younger homeless man under those conditions."

Christie nodded to herself as she made notes.

"I also think," Jed continued, "that this may mean the killer has some knowledge about the homeless population and doesn't actually want to erase the homeless community, since he seems hesitant to face or attack the younger men. As far as 'troublesome' homeless persons, New Yorkers would tell you they're more concerned about the younger homeless men than the older ones—again, because of the volatility they have because of substance abuse."

After clearing his throat, he said, "That's a round-about way of saying that I don't think the killer's motives are as deep as we've been trying to make them."

"Oh?" Christie looked up from her notebook and stared into the air as her ear cradled the phone. "What motives do you think he has?"

"So far, I haven't narrowed it down enough or thought it through enough to propose anything that's fully plausible, but that, in itself, is a problem. What if this killer is just bored? Or they're trying to draw attention to either themselves or the community of homeless people? What if it's all of these things, encased in a larger, much more complex casing of other elements and contributors? What if it's none of these at all, and we're way off the mark?"

Neither of them spoke for a while until Christie broke the silence. "This case is quite the doozy."

"It is. And it's why one of the first things I do with my clients is establish their 'why'. Without it, all efforts toward rehabilitation, reintegration, or recovery will falter. If there's nothing to fight for, there's nothing to win."

"And I quite admire that about you."

As soon as the words left her lips, Christie tensed. She hadn't meant to say that out loud. It was just an inside thought—one she'd been having very often since they had begun to work together.

"Why, thank you," Jed replied with a smile in his voice.

She could feel that the energy in the conversation had shifted. He was basically across the borough, completely removed from her space, and from her person. But here in her small apartment, in her dark living room, wearing the silkiest nightgown she owned, she could feel the masculine intensity he was exuding and the way it made her toes curl as it filled the room around her.

At home was where her femininity was safest. In her line of work, she was constantly surrounded by men, and to fit in and be respected, she has always had to blend in. At home, she liked to re-connect with her feminine side and the strength she gained from it—which meant that her conversations with Jed were even more intimate when she was at home.

"But what is it you admire?"

There it was. Now she had no choice but to reveal her thoughts. She pushed through the tight lump in her throat and spoke.

"Your work ethic. How dedicated you are to your clients and your job, and just how well you've been managing the ethical nightmare it must be causing you. Your work is with addiction patients—and I've been told that a lot of those patients are homeless people. So, to see how you've handled our current case is, well… admirable. I've worked with partners in the past that, as soon as an incident happened that hit too close to home, they weren't able to go on. They cracked under the pressure. And it's understandable, of course. But you…" she trailed off.

"But I…?" He prompted, voice lower and firmer.

Christie's heartbeat quickened.

"You do a good job of separating the two," she answered. "I don't think I've ever worked with someone who was as competent, or as dedicated, or as insightful… or as young."

On the other end of the line, Jed grinned.

"This is very high praise coming from you, Detective," he answered. "Thank you."

She hummed in response.

"Is my age a concern for you?"

"What?" she asked quickly—maybe too quickly.

"You mentioned that element, almost reluctantly. So, I just wondered if it was a problem."

"Oh! No, it isn't. I'm just used to working with older—usually married—men."

"Ah, I see."

She could hear a smile creeping into Jed's voice. "And here comes a single, thirty-four-year-old wrench in your plans, aye? Sorry if I'm throwing things off for you, Detective."

Every time he called her 'detective', Christie shivered with delight. She was overcome by a tingling sensation that always ended and blossomed between her thighs. She needed to get a hold of herself.

"Oh, I don't mind. Working with fifty- and sixty-something's as a thirty-year-old wasn't always a great time."

"So, I guess that means you won't be requesting a partner change anytime soon?" he teased.

She laughed. "Nope. You're stuck with me."

After running through the details once more, in hopes that something they might have missed would dawn on them, they finished for the night.

It was ten o'clock, and Jed needed to get to bed right away if he was going to have any hope of resting well for the day ahead. As the hot water of the shower hit his skin, and he reflected on his conversation with Christie, he found himself wondering about her past partnerships.

She'd mentioned that she had worked mostly with older men who'd been married. That explained why they had given their roles up as soon as something happened that was too close for comfort. A man at that age had a family to protect, and when it came to involvement with criminals and criminal investigations, you never knew which convicted suspect would pin a vendetta on your head—or even attack your loved ones in your stead. Like Christie had said, it was understandable why her partners would have backed off in certain cases.

He, on the other hand, had no intention of dropping his role as an investigative therapist. This was his dream, the career he'd been longing for since he had committed to going to rehab. Jed owed his life to those that had helped him beat addiction. He knew his purpose was to do the same for others. Nothing would come between him and his goal of helping people restore their sense of normalcy and control over their lives, and he loved helping the city solve cases with the additional perspective of a mental health provider. No matter what happened, he wasn't going to ditch Christie. He hoped she knew that.

She had brought up his age, and though she had brushed it off as not being a bother when he asked, he sensed that wasn't the whole truth. He had noticed that she had the tendency to be a little shy around him, scratching her arm, avoiding eye contact, acting a little bit like she was nervous. It had been most evident when she'd come over to search his apartment, as well as after they'd spent long hours together in her office discussing the case. Jed wondered if he was somehow making her uncomfortable.

His hands stilled above his head, where they had been lathering the shampoo in his hair. The thought of causing her discomfort knocked the wind out of him. He could hardly bear it. It was so important to keep the air clear in male-female relationships, especially since they were partners in criminal investigations, and this was far more than just the average male-female friendship dynamic.

He needed to bring that up to her when he next saw her. It was no use asking her over the phone; he needed to see her body language when she answered. As Jed rinsed his hair and the water poured down his back, he pictured her standing in front of him, big brown eyes behind the rim of those glasses she wore, lips glossy and pouty, squirming under his gaze as he asked her, *'Do I make you uncomfortable, Detective?'* He switched the water to cold.

CHAPTER 9

"Gray," came Christie's voice through the receiver.

Groggy, but on high alert, Jed rolled himself into an upright position. The clock across the room read four-fifty-eight.

"Detective?"

She blinked, losing focus for a second on the other end of the line as Jed's gravelly, deep, sleepy voice caught her off guard. "I'm sorry to wake you at this ungodly hour, but there's been another incident."

"Another death?"

"Yes."

Her voice was soft, the sadness palpable in the single word she uttered in response.

"Are you okay, Christie?"

"No, I'm not." She answered. Then she sniffed and wiped away what sounded like tears.

"Where are you?" Jed was suddenly wide awake. He got to his feet and went into his closet, pulling sweatpants up his legs and a shirt over his head.

"I'm at the station. I just got back from the hospital and the crime scene."

"I'm coming."

He grabbed a bottle of water on his way past the fridge.

"That's okay, you don't have to—"

"I'm coming." There was no room for negotiation in his voice.

She sniffed again.

"I'll be right there," he said.

Jed all but burst through the doors of the police station, and in the elevator, he cursed under his breath. "Hurry up."

He pressed the number for the floor almost a hundred times, something he never did. Jed wasn't a naturally impatient person, but the urgency that had washed over him when he realized his partner was crying had turned a fifteen-minute walk into a five-minute run and had eliminated all the grogginess he would normally feel. He scowled as the doors to the elevators slowly closed and it began to move at a crawl. He should have just taken the two flights of stairs up.

After a minute that felt like an hour, the doors finally opened onto the second-floor landing, and he turned down the hallway, urgency still in his steps. When he reached the door, he knocked, and without waiting for a response, pushed it open.

Christie rose from where she was sitting behind her desk as he walked in, tears streaking down her cheeks. She tried to swipe them away as he entered. But Jed tossed the water bottle into the chair across from the desk and walked around to her. He took her by the hand, pulled her up from the seat and into his arms—a hug that left her heart racing and brought fresh tears.

She smelled like roses and dark spices, and for a moment, he breathed the scent in without speaking. Her arms slipped around him, and he hugged her even harder. He released her for a moment to look down at her. Her eyes were a little puffy, and her nose and cheeks were red from all the crying. He wanted to smile; she looked so beautiful, even with tears in her eyes and a pout on her lips.

Jed enclosed her in his arms again, and she sighed into his chest. Christie hadn't realized just how much she had needed that hug. She felt so safe in his arms. The pair separated after a long minute of holding each other, and he wiped the tears from her cheeks with his thumbs, watching her sigh as he did.

"Can you tell me what happened?"

She sniffed, swiping at her nose and nodding. She turned to make her way back to her desk, but stopped when his arm reached out to take hers.

"Stay here, so I can hug you again if you need it."

"The documents with the details of the new victim are on the table—"

"Let them stay there." Jed's voice was a soothing coo. "Talk to me here; just tell me what you remember."

She nodded, wiping at her eyes again. "It was awful. His name is Ethan Davidson, and he—"

Jed's heart dropped into his stomach. Noticing his expression change from concern to shock, the words died in her throat.

Stammering, Jed asked, "Ethan Davidson…? In his twenties? Five foot eleven, shaggy black hair, tattoos on his…"

Christie nodded along to each detail he mentioned, and eventually, his own words got stuck behind the lump in his throat. He squeezed his eyes shut. Christie's stomach turned, and she stepped forward to hold onto his arm.

"Jed," she began, her voice barely audible in the dark room, "did you know him?"

He didn't speak, but the short nod was enough to tinge the room even darker with sadness. Tears burned in Christie's eyes anew, and she covered her mouth in a bid to stop the sobs from pouring out. Jed, whose eyes had refocused on her, pulled her into his chest once again. She protested feebly, choking on her tears.

"No—I should be consoling you. You knew him."

"But you were there. You saw what happened."

She didn't have a response to that.

"You can tell me more when you're able to."

Christie nodded against his chest and, reluctantly, pulled away from him. She cleared her throat. "He was found in an alley, with needles and syringes all around him, and—"

"Fuck."

She watched Jed's hands come up to cover his face and listened to him groan.

He rocked forward. "No, it-it can't be."

Her eyes burned, and tears blurred her vision. "I'm sorry, Jed. He passed from an overdose of…"

"Fentanyl?" His voice shook as he muttered the word, hoping with everything in him that she would say no—that it would be something else. Anything else. Her small nod was a blow he could not bear. He sank to the floor on his knees. Christie was hugging him around the neck, her own tears dripping onto his shirt.

This isn't happening, thought Jed. *This can't be happening.*

Ethan was clean. He'd been clean for a year. He'd gone through the rehab system. They'd kept in touch after he had gotten back into a stable job. He couldn't be dead. He definitely couldn't be dead from fentanyl. Was that why he had called Jed's office a few days ago and left a message? Had he been trying to reach out because he needed help? He had an appointment this coming week.

Guilt was suffocating Jed. Nothing was making sense. He felt like the world was caving in on top of him all at once, and it was Christie's icy hand on his cheek that pulled him out of the grief that was wracking his body.

Jed looked into her eyes, glistening with tears, and watched more tears pool there, sliding down her lashes and falling to the floor. He closed his eyes. He couldn't bear the sight of her crying. He couldn't bear the weight of this news. Jed felt like he could barely bear the weight of his existence. They sat in silence for a while as he struggled to process the grief. In moments like these, he could hear his internal therapist telling him what to do—just like he would speak to his patients.

He focused on his breathing, intentionally slowing it, and taking deeper, longer breaths. He focused on the beating of his heart and let it remind him he was alive. Still sitting on the floor, he focused on what he could feel. Jed placed his hands on the cold floor and let the sensation climb up his arms. The sound of Christie's breathing, and her occasional sniffle, were the only things he could hear. Jed let his mind focus on those sounds until his own breathing fell in time with hers.

A few minutes later, when he'd done the emergency emotional processing ritual he so often preached to his clients, he sat in the chair across from Christie, watching her stare, bleakly, down at the table and the papers scattered over it. Guilt was written all over her face and in her body language. Judging from the way she was avoiding his eye contact, Jed knew she felt that this was her fault.

"I should have waited until morning to call."

There it was.

"What makes you say that?"

His voice sounded coarse, even to his own ears, and she looked up at him.

"I brought you into this mess. Maybe I should have waited until I processed the situation better to call you. I normally arrive after the person has already died, so I never encounter that kind of suffering. All I could do was stand there and watch—"

Jed cut in, sternly. "Call me as soon as something like this happens, every time it happens."

"But, Jed, I don't think that's a good idea."

"Why do you think it's a bad idea?"

"Well, I didn't say it's a bad idea either."

He cocked his head to the side and watched her for a long moment. Christie looked back at him. But then she looked down at her hands and squirmed a bit. There it was again. He got to his feet.

"There's something I've been meaning to ask you. Could you come over here for a second?"

She did, and when she was standing in front of him, leaning on the wall for support, he stared down into her eyes for another long moment, his hands deep in the pockets of his sweats.

She fidgeted almost immediately this time, rubbing her arm.

"Why do you do that?" he asked, careful to keep his tone gentle. She looked like a deer in headlights. With all the crying and emotional turmoil, he didn't want to add to her stress.

"Why do I do what?" she asked, her voice small in the large room.

Her eyes were so full of depth, like the clear waters surrounding the small islands in the Caribbean—a place he wanted to visit, and never return from. Except, Christie's eyes were brown and welcoming, like the bark of the towering trees in the forest near the lake after a long rain. The perfect combination of clear and homey.

"The minute all my attention is on you, you seem to be… uncomfortable."

Her eyes widened a bit, and her lips parted. No words came out of them. Jed could see that his statement had caught her off guard. He stepped closer.

"Answer me truthfully, please. Do I make you uncomfortable? In any way?"

She pushed her hair behind her ear, butterflies beating their wings aggressively in her belly. She swallowed. He was looking right at her, analyzing her every movement with those deep brown eyes that he wanted to drown in.

"I-I don't think uncomfortable is the right word to use…" she offered.

Something in his expression changed. He nodded.

"Do you know what the right word is?" he queried.

She swallowed again.

"Why did you bring this up?" she asked, looking all around the room, hoping to change the direction of the conversation. The slow smile that crept onto his face told her he could see through her ruse.

"I brought it up because, like I mentioned, you sometimes seem uncomfortable making eye contact with me. I'm concerned that it might be because I'm doing something to make you uncomfortable. I don't want this to harm our dynamic in the long-run. So, if I'm doing something, I want you to tell me what it is."

She nodded. "Okay. I understand. You aren't doing anything wrong."

No, indeed, Christie thought. He was doing everything right. She felt her heart quiver within her when he stepped even closer.

"What are you doing?" she asked.

He cocked his head to the side again. "Calling your bluff. You visibly tensed when I moved toward you."

She froze. Now he was sure to press the issue until he found out. The backs of her eyes burned. She didn't feel like confessing the feelings she was trying to hide when there was no chance of him being interested, and especially since it was exactly what would ruin their dynamic—as he put it—even if he did feel the same way.

Jed retreated to his original distance from her. "I'm not going to press the matter, but I want you to bring up what's bothering you—when you're ready."

Christie suppressed a sigh. His gaze was always so intense, so raptly intent on her that it made her want to whimper.

For Pete's sake, Christie, get it together! She chided herself. He finally looked away from her, out the windows to the sun that was barely peeking above the skyline. She took a deep breath.

"What happened at the scene?" he asked.

They sat down again, and he took a sip of his water, preparing himself to hear the story. Except, it wasn't a story. It was real. Ethan was gone.

"We arrived at the scene at around one-thirty, and we found him on 59th, in an alley like I mentioned earlier, with needles and empty syringes all around him. He still had one syringe in his left arm. He was alive when we got there."

Jed's heart sank. He knew Christie had watched Ethan die.

"He was gasping for air and clutching at his chest with his right hand—he must have had three heart attacks in the time we were waiting for the EMTs to arrive. They gave him several doses Narcan at the scene, but it didn't help. We were just too late."

He took a deep breath, and she continued with the story.

"By the time we got to the hospital, he was non-responsive—just his eyes wide open, quick shallow breaths, no visual or auditory responses. A few minutes later, I watched him fade away."

Jed caught her swiping at her face again. He wanted to comfort her, but what could comfort someone who had witnessed two gruesome crime scenes and watched a man die from an overdose? She continued, flipping through her folder to a page that only had a few lines of ink on its surface.

"There are some things about this that I haven't been able to reconcile, though."

Jed braced himself for more impact.

"Of course, we checked your body cam and surveillance footage right when we got notified about the incident, and the data showed you had arrived home much earlier and hadn't left again, so that took care of that. This incident was definitely different than the ones before it, but we're keeping it on our radar. It happened in the vicinity of the first two murders, affected the same demographic, and there appeared to be a struggle at the scene. We're working under the assumption that the murderer was interrupted and fled the scene before he could stab the victim the way he stabbed the others."

Christie stared up at the light on the ceiling for a moment before she went on. "What puzzled me, though, was that Ethan's left arm was visibly broken, which likely caused him to clutch at his chest with just his right hand. He couldn't move the other arm."

Jed's brows pulled together.

"I don't have the post-mortem results yet, but I noticed a few bruises on his body as we were pulling him into the hospital that made me wonder—he looked as though he'd been in a fight. His lip was split in three places, he had a black eye, his shirt was torn all over, there was a bloodstain on the back of his shirt…"

Her voice trailed off, and she looked over at Jed, eyes filled with sadness.

"There were so many signs of foul play."

Jed swallowed the last of his water, his mind racing.

"They are still processing the crime scene and looking for the murder weapon now. I didn't see it, but it was very chaotic when we were trying to save Ethan."

CHAPTER 10

SUN WAS STREAMING IN through the windows as usual, and Jed was knee-deep in work. Catching up on his tasks after the initial aftermath of a new case was the hardest part of managing both jobs.

He'd gotten his workout in, eaten a light breakfast, packed his lunch for work, and arrived with time to spare before the workday officially began. Wading through case files, updating rehabilitation reports, and speaking with clients on a normal day was workload enough. Today, learning that one of his previous clients—and a success story at that—had fallen prey to death by overdose took all the enthusiasm out of him.

Jed could still hardly believe it. He'd spoken to Ethan just a few weeks ago, on their monthly check-in as mandated by the rehabilitation program for the first six months after successful completion of rehab. He'd reported that he was doing well, settling into his job well, building his savings and investment portfolios, and even hoping to get back into dating. Then his life was snuffed out, right in the middle of his recovery.

Christie's mention of foul play still rang through Jed's mind. Why was his arm broken? And why was it broken on the same side the syringe had been used on? Why had the killer attacked someone so much younger than the other two victims? Why did he have a black eye and split lips and trauma wounds from a stab? Had Ethan already been found on the streets, inebriated, and the killer decided to deliver a fatal stab since he was an easy target? To top it all off, what added to the confusion was the matter of this incident occurring on 59th Street.

There were no CCTV systems on that leg of the street, and conveniently, that was where Ethan had been found. The witness had reported that they'd seen a man in an alleyway gasping horribly, and they were unsure whether or not to try and approach and assist him. By the time the police arrived, he'd been convulsing over and over, dying a slow, agonizing death. And Christie had watched it unfold.

Ring.

The sound pulled Jed away from the case and back into the present. He picked up the phone to dive into another one of his weekly client calls with an older homeless man that had turned to addiction therapy in a bid to save his relationship with his family and get back on his feet.

"Hello?"

He'd almost forgotten what day it was; they were flying by so fast. It was Wednesday. That meant one thing. Jed was going to have to face the reality of the commitment he'd made to Hugh the previous week. They were going to dinner that evening. He knew it would most likely work out well—the most that could happen was that he'd say something silly, and even then, Hugh would probably just laugh it off without thinking too much of it.

As he wrapped up work, saving his progress on his clients' progress charts and data sheets, a knock sounded on his door. Jed's shoulders tensed, immediately knowing who it was and what it was about.

"Come in," he called, still focused on closing out work for the evening.

Hugh entered the room, and after closing the door behind him, sauntered across the space to sit before Jed's desk on the small sofa as though he'd done it a hundred times already. Jed looked up from his computer and glanced across the room at Hugh, who was flipping through the magazines on the side table next to him.

Why is he so comfortable being in here? Why am I never this comfortable anywhere? Jed asked himself. He saved the final document and started the powering off sequence on his computer. *Then again, why am I so uncomfortable with him being comfortable here? He's my guest.* He puffed out a heavy breath, and Hugh looked over.

"You're wrapping up, right? I hope I didn't just waltz in here while you're still working."

Jed managed to smile. "No, you're good. I'm closing out."

"Great," Hugh exclaimed, the usual grin appearing on his face. "I managed to finish all my work before you today! What an achievement!"

Jed raised a brow, his own smile widening. "I didn't realize we were competing."

Hugh laughed.

"That's because we aren't. But you're Mr. Efficient—you get things done during your workday. Meanwhile, I'm here late all the time, working."

Jed laughed outright, and Hugh watched him, grinning. He put his laptop into his bag and checked the desk to see if he was leaving anything behind that he would need, or that needed to be stowed away in the locked cabinets in the corner of the room. Leaving patient data around carelessly that could fall into the wrong hands was not something he'd ever do—not even accidentally.

"You're ready?" Hugh asked as Jed got to his feet.

"Yup. Ready and starving."

Hugh tossed the magazine back onto the side table and stood up. "Well, let's go, then."

They left the building together, walking up the block, away from the heart of Manhattan and into a part of town Jed was less familiar with.

"I should tell you," Jed began as he fastened the camera to his tie, "that I'm wearing a body cam that's been mandated by the NYPD because of my involvement with the recent homeless murder case."

"Oh, that should be fine. You know round these parts?" Hugh asked as he looked over at him.

Jed shook his head.

"I live around these parts. You live a couple blocks down from work, right?"

"Yeah," Jed looked closely at the man walking next to him.

Hugh was still smiling, and he nodded.

"Cool. I see you walking in that direction after you leave work, so I figured you lived near there."

That made sense, and Jed nodded.

"Our destination is just across the way at the end of this block," Hugh said, pointing. "I didn't know if it would be crazy packed or not, so I asked the hostess to save me a table."

He winked over at Jed. "The hostess is my best friend."

When the pair entered the restaurant, they were greeted by a flower wall with a neon sign that was lit up in a deep green color. Chive.

So that's what this place is called, Jed thought as he followed Hugh in. The hostess greeted him with a hug before waving to Jed and leading them into the bar and dining area. It was dim, with colored LED lights all around and music playing from a booth in the back. They sat, and Hugh took up his menu right away, scanning through it.

"Between me and you," he started, eyes scanning the menu, "I'm starving."

Jed grinned, picking up his own menu and looking down at it with great interest.

"I recommend the barbecue pork double decker burger, the shrimp jalapeño pasta, and the sirloin steak and potatoes. I've tried those, and I'd bet my paycheck that you'll love 'em." Hugh grinned.

"In that case, I'll go for the pasta and the burger."

"Ah! And you've got good taste, too." Hugh added.

Jed laughed, flipping the menu over to check out the drink menu, and his smile slowly faded as he read over the options.

"They don't serve non-alcoholic beverages here?" he asked Hugh.

"They do, but not very many options. This is an alcohol lover's paradise. They've got everything from wines, to tequilas, to brandy, to chardonnay... everything."

Jed nodded, shrugging. "I realized that when I looked at the menu. They don't have anything I like. Well, that's a pity. I was actually starting to like the place."

Hugh's smile fell. "You don't drink?"

Jed shook his head. "I'm not a drinker."

Hugh gaped at him. "By choice?"

Jed laughed at the incredulous expression on his face. "Yes, by choice. I chose sobriety a long time ago."

Hugh stared at him for a while. "Wow. You don't mind if I drink, do ya?"

"Nope, you can have whatever you like."

Hugh nodded, signaling the waiter nearby. "We're ready to order."

Later that evening, after dinner and a long chat with Hugh, Jed had made his way home feeling like he'd gained a new friend. The euphoria had faded quickly, though, and as he walked into his apartment, he felt the weight of the past two weeks come falling down on him. He sat on the couch and tossed his bag next to him, removed his shoes and socks, and sighed aloud into the empty apartment, wishing for the five-hundredth time that he could visit the lake to clear his mind.

In theory, it would be easy. Get in the Jeep, drive down to the lake, and go MIA. But that was why it was hard. He would have to schedule all his interviews, filing, and reports around the visit in order to be truly free when he went. He had done that often enough before, but he'd never had to factor in an active investigation, or a partner. For the time being, he was stuck here, and there was no way to avoid his reality when he lived in the heart of the city.

Every morning on his way to work, he passed by people who reminded him of those who had been cut down in the past two weeks—elderly men walking by with their canes, some with women leading the way, others struggling on through the crowded streets alone. He passed by homeless men sitting on their corners, on the curbs, on the benches outside restaurants, hands outstretched and begging for money, begging for food, begging for help. Some even had cigarettes in hand, and around some, the stench of weed was strong. Coming home, he would stop by Jamie's stall, buy a hot dog—often two, sometimes three—and hand one to each homeless person he saw.

Even though he had been working so closely with them over the years, Jed had never quite been so ultra-aware of what they were going through on the streets as he was now. It pulled his mind back to his past, made him remember how he'd been forced to spend nights on the streets, away from his warm home, laid up in an alley somewhere with the rain pouring down onto him. It had been his own fault; he'd been high on the hill of addiction, and his loving, sweet mother had been far too terrified to allow him into the house on those days when he was at his worst.

Jed owed her everything—everything and then some—for the way she had stuck beside him through that period of his life.

He needed to call her. He hadn't done his weekly call in a while. It wasn't that he meant to avoid her, but when his mind was like this, it was hard for him to reach out to the people that mattered—the people that could help him. He didn't want her worrying about him, and he didn't want her scared for his life the way he knew she would be when she found out how close he had come to being one of those attacked.

But it had been far too long. He longed to hear her voice and wanted to tell her about Christie, about the cases, about work, about making a new friend. There were so many things on his mind—he had no idea where to start.

He looked at the time. It was just before ten pm. He dug through his backpack for his phone, typed in his password, opened his contacts, and clicked the green button before his anxiety could change his mind.

Ring.

Ring.

Ring.

"Hello? Jed?"

When his mom's voice came through the line, he felt the back of his eyes begin to burn.

"Jed, are you there? Is everything alright?"

He swallowed, trying to get the lump in his throat to move long enough for him to respond.

"I'm here. And I'm alright, Mom. How are you?"

"You know better than to lie to me, honey," she responded. "Where do you think you got your ability to see through people's facades? You've forgotten so soon, city boy?"

He smiled at her teasing.

"Everything is going wrong" he managed to say. "Everything is going horribly."

"Well, don't just sit there. Tell me what's going on."

"It's a long story."

"Then, it's a good thing I have all night."

Jed nodded. He should have known she'd say that. She was always there for him, no matter what silly thing he was ranting about, or how seriously he had messed up. His eyes burned again.

"Since the last time we spoke, I started a new job, of sorts. It's an investigative therapy position, and I'm working alongside the NYPD. Chief Lucas is the one who reached out to me, after he saw my track record as an addiction therapist. According to the chief, I'm the 'best in the city', and they wanted to pair me with someone who was the best at investigating crime scenes. So, I got paired with this woman—her name is Christie—and she is a joy to work with."

"She sounds delightful. What's she like?"

He considered his answer for a while, thinking about her eyes, her smile, her drive.

"She's beautiful. She's so dedicated to her work, she feels things deeply, and she empathizes with the victims and their families so much. She moved here to take on this role, and she let it slip that in her previous state, there hadn't been much action. Well, since she's moved here, there has been too much action. I'm afraid New York might be wearing her down already."

"Action? What kind of action are we talking about?"

This was the part he had been running from, the reason he hadn't called sooner. Jed didn't want to tell his mom just how close he had come to being a part of two murders. He sighed heavily.

"Well… I don't even know how to say this. The night after I met up with my partner for the first time, and we toasted to our partnership, the first murder happened. A homeless man was killed right after I walked by him. It happened so close to the time I walked by that I was the number one suspect on the case. Fortunately, the CCTV footage cleared me. The killer entered, walked onto the scene from the left, and attacked the homeless man after had already gone down the street and was heading home."

"Oh my God! That's so scary!"

Jed flinched but pushed himself to continue. "A couple days later, while I was walking home from the police station, another murder happened after I walked by—another homeless man. By the time I got home and got into bed, my partner called me to tell me that there had been another murder. CCTV footage is what cleared me again. After that, I took it upon myself to have surveillance cameras installed in my apartment that monitor when I leave and enter, and I've also been wearing a body cam when I'm on the road."

"Is that why you haven't called all this time?"

"Yes?"

"Jed! What if you hadn't called at all and something ended up happening to you? I wouldn't have known that any of this was going on."

"I know. I'm sorry, Mom. I didn't want you to start worrying about me."

"I'm your mom… I'm going to worry about you, regardless. But this is a big deal. You could have gotten hurt. Or even worse."

"I know. I'm sorry."

"Am I going to have to start calling you every single day to get you to tell me what's going on? Because I will."

Jed stifled a chuckle. "No, you won't. I should call more often."

He heard his mom sigh and mumble something under her breath. "Why does it seem like everywhere you are, a murder takes place? I'm not sure I'm even comfortable saying that because I don't want something to happen to you."

"That's something I mentioned to my partner as well—that it just seems like I'm the revolving target."

"I would hate for that to be true."

"Well, I guess the third murder disproves that theory, in a sick kind of way."

"Third??" His mother's surprise reverberated through the phone.

"Yes… a third murder took place a couple of days ago. It was one of my past clients. He had been homeless and used to be addicted to drugs. They ended up finding him overdosed on fentanyl, with broken bones and all sorts of crazy stuff."

"Oh my God! Does that mean he went back to drugs after you helped him?"

Jed looked down at his toes. His head felt heavy. "I'm not even sure what happened, to be honest. I spoke to him a couple of weeks ago, and he was doing well. He was telling me about his job, his goals—everything seemed to be going just fine after he finished rehab."

"So, this has come out of nowhere? Not really, this is always the risk and reality of addiction. It is never really over. It is a lifetime battle."

"So true."

They were both quiet for a while.

"Jed?"

"Yes, Mom?"

"I love you, and I'm proud of you for getting the position in the first place."

He nodded, expecting her to go on and say she was worried about how dangerous the job has turned out to be or why she thought he should reconsider the position.

"How have you been holding up with all of this happening? Especially the last one—the one you helped?"

That had not been what he was anticipating hearing.

"I'm not sure. I have been trying to process my feelings, trying to stay present, doing all the practices that teach my clients for high-stress emotional situations. But it just seems like too much for me to take in all at once. I've also been trying to be the strong one since my partner has been going through it the past few days. She was on site at the overdose case and watched him go through the heart attacks. She saw him die at the hospital."

"Oh my God! She must be devastated. I can't imagine witnessing something like that. And especially witnessing it so many times in a row, all in the same situation."

"Yeah, she hasn't been handling the last one so well. So, I've been trying to be there for her."

"But Jed, this person was your client. You helped through their addiction, rehab, and reintegration into society. You must be devastated, too! I can't even imagine how that feels."

He pinched the bridge of his nose. He had learned his own emotional availability and empathy from his mom during his teenage years. When he was younger, it used to annoy him just how soft she had been. And after his dad had walked out, she had remained soft, except for the times when she needed to discipline him—those were the times she had been firm.

Now, he appreciated that empathy to no end. She seemed to know exactly what he needed to hear. At the same time, what he needed to hear was about to make him cry.

"I am. I don't think it's quite sunk in yet. I still can't believe he's gone. It just doesn't make sense."

"And he never showed any signs of falling back into addiction?"

"He didn't. He swore he was done with drugs. And I had no reason to believe that he wouldn't be truthful. But lying plays a huge role in addiction—someone stuck in the throes of a high will say anything to remain undiscovered and continue using. After what he had been through on the streets, I hoped he would stay off for good. Now I wonder if I'm the one that's to blame—if I'm the one who missed the cues. I don't know. Maybe I overlooked a cryptic message he might have laced into a story—something that would make this plausible… something that would make him go back."

"Oh, Jed. My poor baby. I wish I could give you a hug."

He smiled through his tears, and his mother continued. "If it had been there, I know you would have caught it. You're very attentive to your clients, and you give your work your all. Maybe there was no sign. Or maybe he was just too good at concealing that he was still struggling. Or maybe it was a moment of weakness where he didn't have access to you, and he thought he would just be able to get a quick shot in or something…"

Jed's smile widened, listening to his mom trying to make him feel better.

"I know that. But I still wonder about it. It just doesn't make sense."

"Well, I'm sure there will be something that shows up that helps you figure out what's going on. I know you're more than capable of solving this case. And with your partner by your side, you two will have this wrapped up in no time. But

I know you're caught up about it. Have you been working out?"

"Yes. I work out most days. I've only missed a couple since this whole situation started."

"And have you been eating well?"

He laughed. It was just like his mom, worrying about his routines.

"I have been eating well. I actually went to dinner this evening with a friend."

"A friend? Tell me about them?"

"Well, he's a guy I met at work. He's a strange character, at times, but I think he means well. He's very outgoing and seems comfortable in every situation. So, he's pretty different than me."

"Well, it's good that you've made a friend."

Jed smiled to himself.

The line was quiet for a moment before a lilt came into his mother's voice. "Do you consider Christie a friend?"

His smile faded. "Yes, I do."

"Hmm. Are you sure you don't consider her maybe a little bit more than a friend?"

"What are you trying to say, Mom?"

His mom giggled on the end of the line. "Don't use that tone with me, mister! I'm just asking because of the way you spoke about her. She seems to tickle your fancy—just a little bit?"

"Just a little bit," Jed relented.

"Aha! I knew it! The way you said her name, and the way you said she was beautiful! I just knew there were stars in your eyes!"

Jed spoke with a wide grin. "Mom, you make me sound like a lovesick puppy. That's not the case at all."

"Maybe not yet, but I have a feeling it's going to get there."

He shook his head. "Of course, you do."

"Well, Jed, I just want you to know that I'm very proud of you. All things considered, you're holding up really well under the pressure of it all. You're managing two difficult jobs, and you're doing so well!"

He swiped at his eyes.

"But, please be careful. I know you can throw yourself into your work to the point where you start forgetting to prioritize your routines."

"I will mom. I will."

CHAPTER 11

"WHAT DAY EVEN IS it?"

Jed couldn't tell. He looked at the bottom of his screen and saw that the date read Wednesday. He groaned, wiping his hand across his face. Jed paused his work and got up from his desk to walk around. He stopped on the rug in the center of the room and reached his arms up into the air, stretching to work out the kinks in his back. Jed had gone to the gym extra early this morning to get in a longer workout. He had even managed to achieve a new personal record in his squat and deadlift. Both were 250lbs. By the time he had noticed that it was almost time for work, it was too late for a complete cooldown routine. But Jed knew he would be fine until he got home.

Jed made his way back to his desk and looked at the file on his screen. He was filling out a rehab intake form for one of his clients, who was a regular caller on Tuesdays. He had spoken to him yesterday and had finally gotten him to agree to go to rehab. Jed smiled at the thought.

He loved his job. It was always a celebration when a new client, or an old client, finally decided to take control of their lives back. Sometimes it took a few weeks, sometimes it took a few months, and sometimes it took a year. No matter how long it took, though, Jed was content to keep working with a client as long as they would keep working with him. No matter who his caller was, he always listened to as much as they were willing to share. He never rushed them off the line or tried to get them to share more than they were ready to, but he always encouraged them to keep fighting for the life they wanted. It was the why that was so important.

For this client, he wanted to give his dream of becoming a chef a second chance. It was after the man had been rejected from culinary school that he had gotten sucked into the drug world. Sometimes, in the face of rejection, people forget to look around for new opportunities, or another way to reach their goals. This is what had happened with this client. He was so distraught about the rejection that he never even thought to look for another way to pursue his dream. When Jed had learned about the rejection, he had asked the man whether he had tried to learn from a chef or apprentice at a restaurant.

When the man had said no, he had chuckled. He hadn't even thought about doing that.

Jed had seized that opportunity to drive his point home. *Well*, he said, *now's your chance. It's never too late to try.* The man had been a bit hesitant at first, still a bit insecure that he had lost his skill or that cooking wasn't what he wanted to do anymore. A couple more questions about what he could see

himself doing for the rest of his life, and he was convinced.
He would give it a second chance.

Now, Jed was doing the man's paperwork for his intake into
rehab. He couldn't be happier. He reread the file to make sure
that he had not missed any important details and had filled out
all the necessary sections. As he clicked the submit button, his
phone rang.

"Gray."

"Detective?"

"Some new information just became available for the case.
Are you available anytime soon?"

He looked down at his watch. "I can be over in ten minutes."

"Okay. I'll be in my office."

They hung up, and Jed stared down at the phone for a
second. What was that all about? As he closed out his tabs,
signed out of his systems, and packed his computer away into
his bag, he wondered what the update could be. The way
things had been going lately, Jed thought this case could go
in any direction.

He stopped at Jamie's stand on his way past and picked
up his usual order, one for him and one for Christie. His
walk to the station was slower today than it usually was since
her tone hadn't conveyed any immediate need for urgency.
He watched the light breeze spin the leaves on the curb and
couples crossing the street together. There was even a couple
walking their dog—the cutest little Pug.

In the office, as they sat across from each other, neither of them spoke. He watched her sort through the papers in front of her, not really looking at him as they ate.

"Good afternoon to you, too, Detective."

"Good afternoon," she responded, looking up at him then.

"Have I done something to anger you?"

Her brows furrowed, and she cocked her head to the side. "Not that I can remember."

He watched her take a bite from the hot dog, her hair spilling around her cheeks. She was wearing white cargo pants, and a white oversized tee. *Special occasion?* He wondered.

"Have you been at work all day?" Jed asked as casually as he could.

"No. I just came in around an hour ago. I was out."

He nodded and considered asking further questions, but Christie spoke. "So, about the case update, we have a bit of an update to our suspect list."

"Oh?"

"Her name is Lauren Finch, and she's an ex-partner of one of our victims—Warren."

Jed nodded along. "Right. What would her motive be?"

Christie flipped the page.

"Based on the information we have, she and Warren were the perfect couple with all the prospects of having a happy married life together and settling down permanently—until he gave it all up for drugs. We're only now discovering her relationship with him because we struggled to connect him to any family or friends, and she was out of state visiting her sister. For a while, it seemed like he had no past at all."

"How did you manage to make the connection in the end?"

"There were some faded pictures in his pocket of him with a woman, but they were too water damaged to decipher their faces. On the back, was written 'Lauren, my love.' That, too, was so damaged I couldn't make it out."

She raised her head right then to look at him. Jed waited for Christie to go on. "Well?"

"Called in a friend of a friend who's a graphologist. He cracked it in five minutes."

"Ah."

"Indeed. So, maybe she might have wanted to get back at him for hurting her, given the context of their breakup?"

"In theory, it seems plausible," Jed said, brushing his hair out of his face with his free hand. "But in practice, it's unlikely."

"Why's that?"

He crossed his arms over his chest, and her eyes dropped to his biceps. The corner of his lip twitched as he noticed.

"If I'm in love with someone and they fall into addiction, murdering them in cold blood would be the last thing on my mind. What I would be doing is frantically searching for a way to help them. It's the default reaction of most people. They try for years to save the person, and if they can't, they give up. Much less likely to turn to murder planning right away."

Christie nodded.

"Besides," he added, watching her tuck her hair behind her ear. "Does she match the killer's profile that we have from the CCTV footage?"

Christie flipped to the previous page.

"She is 5'6", slim build, green eyes, long brown hair…"

Jed huffed. "I think we can mark her off the list as a plausible suspect."

Christie's brow raised. "Women can't kill men?"

"If she's 5'6" and has a slim build, we can guess she weighs around 130lbs–140lbs."

"So?" Christie asked.

"Warren was tall with a medium build. We can guess he weighs around 175lbs. I don't see her overpowering him very easily. The postmortem results returned no evidence to support that he had drugs in his system at the time of the attack. That means that he would not have been disorientated or floundering around the way someone caught in the high would be."

She nodded, her eyes resting in the distance as she thought. "That means she would have had to take him down with just her raw strength. We know that Warren was eventually overpowered, which means that the killer had to be stronger than he was."

He nodded. "So, you see, it's not that women can't kill men, but given the circumstances of the attack, and the body mass and relative strength stats, she wouldn't have been able to overpower him. When it comes to brawn, the odds are in favor of men. She could, however, have had help from a jealous new partner."

Jed watched a thought alter Christie's features, then she nodded.

"Something on your mind, Detective?"

"Just… thinking about the brawn stats you so casually dropped. Her weight is 134lbs, and Warren weighed 174lbs."

He nodded. "I was close enough. Those margins would have still yielded the same result."

She just looked at him. His lips pulled into a smile.

"What is it now?"

Christie grinned and shook her head, looking down at her paper. "Working with you, I never know what to expect. One minute, you offload about mental illness. The next, you're analyzing weight and height ratios and debunking our suspects. Either way, she'll be in tomorrow for interviewing."

"Does not knowing what to expect make you uneasy, Detective?"

"No."

Not in that way, at least, Christie thought to herself. The way his eyes sparkled right then, she wondered again if he could hear her thoughts. Had she accidentally spoken out loud. But she would have heard herself say it, right? Instead of embarrassing herself by asking, she pressed on.

"Well, since you've debunked the suspect, we had…"

His laugh interrupted Christie and echoed through the room as he threw his head back. His shoulders shook for a while, and as Jed righted himself in the chair again, he went off into another peal of laughter at the sheepish look on her face.

"Your sarcasm is immensely amusing, Detective."

"Why do you call me that?" she asked.

He smiled. There it was. "That's what you are, isn't it?"

"It is. But you could use my name – you choose not to. You only use my name in certain situations. Like yesterday, when you asked me if I was okay."

"I was worried about you. It wasn't the time to be playful."

"So, you're being playful when you use it?"

"Yes."

Christie paused, and Jed grew concerned.

"Do you mind?" he asked.

She shook her head. "I don't mind."

Jed eyed her for a moment and decided she was being truthful. "Now, what were you saying about me 'debunking' the suspect?"

An exasperated sigh rocked through Christie's body. She rested her head in her hands. "We're back to square one."

He shook his head. "No, we aren't. We're back to the square we were at before we added her to the picture. Or… she could have had help."

They looked at each other in silence for a heartbeat.

Jed was the one to break it. "You look beautiful today. White really brings out your eyes… and your hair."

"Thank you," she said with a giddy smile. "I went out with friends earlier, so I wanted to wear something other than boring navy pants."

"Your navy pants are anything but boring, Detective. Because that color suits you, too."

"Are you trying to get something from me?" Christie teased. "Come on! Spit it out! What favor do you want?"

They both laughed, and as he shook his head, she swore she saw what looked like desire gleam in his eyes.

"Oh, nothing…" he toyed, playing along.

Their laughter dulled to a chuckle as Jed bit down on his lower lip, and she choked on the words she had been about to say. Christie was mortified as she fell into a coughing fit.

He rose to his feet, his pants stretching tightly around his hips as he stepped toward her, which made her cough all the more. Jed's hand circled around her arm, and he pulled her upright, swiveling her around to face the wall away from him. Then he started hitting the middle of her back, far too gently to be effective.

Her coughing turned into peals of laughter, and his hand stilled where it was poised to strike her again. She turned to look at him, still laughing, her hand over her mouth. His lip twitched into a smile.

"Are you… laughing at my effort to help you, Detective?"

"You were hitting me like you were trying to burp a baby."

She still hadn't stopped laughing, and he sighed.

"I didn't want to hurt your back. You know—brawn and all." He raised his free hand to flex his biceps.

"Whatever, Gray. You can keep your brawn."

He grinned. "Is that all you called me for? Or did you just want my company?"

She rolled her eyes and sat down again. "I called you to talk about the case."

He watched her intently for a moment as she closed the folder and set it aside. Christie took a swig from her water bottle.

"You've been struggling, haven't you?" Jed crossed his arms.

She swallowed, and his eyes caught the movement of her throat. Christie said nothing.

"Why didn't you tell me?"

Her eyes searched the room, and Jed could see she was looking for an excuse. She didn't find one. "I didn't want to distract from the case and end up taking up your whole day."

Christie wondered how he managed to see right through her the way he did. She hadn't dreamed that working with a therapist would leave her feeling so vulnerable and, yet, so comforted. His expression was suddenly very serious, and his attention was fully on her, with that intensity she loved so much but was so very afraid of.

"Take up my whole day."

"What?"

"We're *partners,* Christie. On this emotional rollercoaster together. We laugh together, we celebrate together, we cry together, we struggle together, we survive together, we overcome together. We solve cases together. How do you expect to continue working on this case if you've got all those heavy feelings in your heart that you refuse to talk about?"

"I didn't think it was that... serious?"

His eyes narrowed. "Why are you afraid to come to me when you're struggling?"

She blanked. The silence stretched.

The resolve on Jed's face was clear. "We're not leaving here until we sort this out. Talk to me."

"Jed, please don't make this complicated."

He waited, his eyes unmoving.

Christie relented. "I'm just not good with processing death sometimes, even though I'm literally a criminal investigator, okay? There. I said it."

He watched her lean back in the chair and cross her arms. He nodded.

"Okay. For now, I'll work with that."

"What do you mean, for now?" she asked, her tone immediately defensive.

His voice remained level and calm. "It means that I understand that you don't want to talk about it right now. Eventually, we will have to talk about this because it will continue to affect you unless we address it, head-on. I will wait until you are ready. But you will have to be ready, eventually."

"What if I don't want to be ready?" she demanded. "Are you going to force me?"

His brows pulled together, and his head cocked to the side, his eyes boring into hers.

"There will be no use of force in our relationship. Not now, not ever. When you are ready, we will face this together."

CHAPTER 12

"GOOD MORNING, LAUREN. How are you doing?"

"I'm doing alright."

The woman's tone was snappy, Christie noticed. It was likely a defense mechanism. Her long brown hair was pulled back into a sleek ponytail that highlighted her features, and she scratched at her left hand with her right one, revealing a large tattoo of a snake and rose extending up her forearm to her elbow. Her green eyes moved back and forth all around the room, as though she was expecting some hidden person to jump out at her from the shadows.

"I'm glad to hear that you're doing alright. That's a very nice tattoo, by the way."

The woman smiled a little.

"Thank you. I had it done a few weeks ago."

"Do you have many tattoos?"

Lauren's shoulders softened. "I do. I have a few bigger pieces—and a lot of smaller ones. I've been getting tattoos since I was fifteen."

Christie nodded as Lauren raised her left arm, revealing a small script tattoo that went across the back of her hand. "So, you've got quite the collection of them then."

Lauren nodded. Christie smiled, more to herself than anything else.

"Body art can be an amazing way of self-expression." Christie continued, sure that she had put her interviewee at some level of ease. "Do you know why we had you come in today?"

The woman nodded and, suddenly, looked as though she might throw up. Her face paled, her eyes adopted a glazed look, and she held her hands tightly together.

"I heard that—that Warren was murdered," she stuttered.

Christie gave the woman time to compose herself. Tears had begun streaking down Lauren's face, and her previous, put-together appearance was shattering under the weight of just one question from Christie.

"I was so shocked to hear the news," she went on. "I still can't believe it."

"Why was the news so shocking for you?"

Lauren had given up swiping the tears away. They were running freely down her face now, dripping onto her jeans.

"I don't know who would have done such a thing. He was so harmless. He just needed help..."

She broke down, head in her hands and sobbing, Lauren cried, what seemed like, her heart out in front of Christie. The room silent save, for the sound of her sobbing, Christie sighed and waited for Lauren to compose herself a bit before saying anything else. After a minute or two, the woman raised her head again and apologized.

"I'm sorry. But I still can't believe that he's gone. I thought we had hope of getting back together and…" She swiped her hand across her cheek in another feeble attempt to keep the tears at bay. "… and now he's gone forever. I didn't even get to say goodbye."

Christie's heart cracked for the frail, crying woman, but she pressed on, as gently as she could.

"You mentioned that Warren just needed help. What do you mean?"

Lauren sniffled. "He needed help to overcome his addiction. It wasn't what he wanted—the drugs, I mean. I knew he was just hooked on the feeling. He wanted to be different. He'd told me over and over that he wanted to quit for good. He was in recovery when we met. And then he got injured a couple months ago at work in construction and hurt his back. His doctor gave him Percocet for the pain, but he refused to refill his prescription, even though Warren was still hurting. He couldn't stand the pain, so he went back to street drugs to manage it all, and that's when we broke up. But just last week I received a letter from him telling me that he had started seeing a counselor."

Her sobs started again, breaking free into the room from around the hand she pressed to her mouth to try to keep them in. When she had composed herself enough to sit up again, Christie resumed.

"You think he turned back to illegal drugs and took to the streets because of the struggle and not because he wanted to?"

Lauren nodded in response. "He lost his job. Money became a strain on our relationship."

"How did it feel for you to know that he chose the drugs over you?"

That question seemed to unleash an even more intense torrential downpour of tears. Christie's heart sank as she watched the woman, but her expression never betrayed her feelings.

"It was awful…" she said, her voice breaking as she tried to speak. "I've never felt so betrayed and abandoned in my life."

Behind the glass partition, Jed looked down at the floor. These interviews had been hard enough in that they weren't yielding the kinds of results and further leads they had been hoping for. On top of all that, they were huge emotional rollercoasters.

"I couldn't function for weeks," she continued. "I lost my job because I missed so many days. I didn't eat—I couldn't even get out of bed."

Christie nodded. Jed admired how she was holding it together in front of Lauren. There was no sign of pain in her own expression, except in her eyes when she looked over at him. The eyes. They could never hide what they truly felt—unless you were trained in how to mask.

"I had to start therapy. I wish he had tried therapy sooner. Maybe we would have stood a chance. Now I know it was the addiction that chose the streets over me. He wasn't in control anymore."

Jed's jaws tightened, and he closed his eyes. *Deep breath in, deep breath out,* he told himself as he let the agony of her statement flow through him. He would have stood a chance if he had tried therapy sooner. He could have made it. Jed knew all too well the resistance addicts had to work through before they would allow therapy into their lives. If only he had tried to reach out. If only he had received the support he'd needed if he had reached out.

Christie was looking at the floor right then, and he knew she was thinking the same thing.

"So, Ms. Finch, where were you on the night of September 16th at nine pm?"

"At the movies with my friends."

"What film did you see?"

"We were watching *Scream* at the Film Forum. It's a three-screen Soho cinema, and it's one of the only spots left in New York City where unusual film selections take precedence over big Hollywood bonanzas. My friends and I go there to watch silent films, classic films, underground films—they're all showcased."

"What time did the film end?"

"It ended at around eleven. Then we all walked home."

"So, you weren't on or near 55th at nine pm on that evening?"

Lauren shook her head. "If I had been, maybe I'd be dead, too. Because I'd have tried to save him."

"Do you know of anyone who would want to hurt Arthur? Did he owe anyone money?"

Lauren thought for a moment. "I'm not sure. He never liked borrowing money from anyone. He was too proud, too sure he could make it on his own."

And then, it was over. Jed watched Lauren leave the interrogation room. She was still swiping her eyes, trying in vain to stop the tears that were pouring out of her. She had asked Christie to keep her updated on the case and had expressed, in between sobs, that she hoped they would catch the killer.

"It wouldn't bring Warren back, but it would be the least we could do so he can rest in peace. I want that killer to rot in jail." She'd said it as she was making her way out. Jed was glad she was in therapy to deal with the grief. She was grieving two things at once—the loss of their relationship when he slipped into addiction again and it took control of him, and losing his life, which made the loss of their relationship permanent. It must have been a hard blow for her.

Jed hadn't sensed any significant levels of anger, spite, or narcissism that he could identify as a link to the possibility of her being the killer. All he had read from her was a sadness so deep that it was taking her into a nosedive. He hoped her therapist was working overtime to get her back into safe waters.

Jed joined Christie, who was looking down at her papers, deep in thought. He watched her in silence for a while until she sighed. "We need an alibi check. I'll get on that."

CHAPTER 13

AT HOME THAT NIGHT, Jed found himself in a slump. He'd already satisfied the demands of his routine, working out, dinner, and a shower. Now he was staring out into the city through the windows from the safety of his couch.

From the bedroom, he heard his phone ring. He launched to his feet, but his face fell when the ringing stopped right before he picked up the phone.

"That's odd," he murmured to himself. "It only rang once."

His call log showed *No Caller ID,* and as he went to call Christie to see if it was her that had called with a case update, a new notification banner popped up on the screen. *One new voicemail.*

He headed back to his spot on the couch and clicked the voicemail. The message was playing, but it was silent for a while until the sound of static and a man's voice reached Jed's ears. The speech was horribly distorted. He could only just make sense of it. He frowned. Who was this?

You must be pretty cut up about Ethan, huh? The voice droned.

Jed's heart dropped, and his stomach lurched. What did he just say?

Tsk. 'Tis a fucking shame. Maybe you should teach your clients how to fight so I can't overpower them so easily next time? The voice laughed. *He'd already started using fentanyl again, anyways, so your little therapy shit failed. You're a fucking loser, Gray. Always were, always will be.*

Jed couldn't believe his ears, and he stared down at the phone in shock for what felt like an eternity. A searing hot pain pierced his heart, and he clutched at his chest and leaned over.

Ethan had gotten back into drugs before he was killed. Had his therapy really failed? Jed could hardly breathe as he sat clutching his phone tightly in one hand and his chest in the other. Was he dreaming? Had he suddenly taken ill with a high fever and become delirious? He looked down at his phone, and with a shaking hand, replayed the voicemail.

It was still there. He had heard correctly. He'd tried to keep these thoughts at bay since Ethan's body had been discovered, but now they were roaring through his mind. This was his fault.

Thirty minutes later, when his phone rang again, he picked it up immediately. It was Christie.

"Gray."

"Detective?"

Christie sighed. She sounded exhausted.

"Lauren's alibi didn't check out. She got to the movies late—very late. We have no account for where she was at ten-thirty, when Warren was murdered. What's most interesting is that she showed up to the movies with a man. It was a date. I guess she's not so heartbroken after all."

CHAPTER 14

"So, WHAT YOU'RE SAYING is, there is absolutely no DNA on the syringe that was in Ethan's arm?"

Christie nodded, then shook her head. "That is what this report says. Though I can hardly believe it."

Jed leaned back in his chair, arms once again crossed in front of him.

"If Ethan's prints weren't on the syringe, but the syringe was in his arm, how did it get there? And how does that factor in the bruises and broken bones we confirmed in the post-mortem reports?"

Christie shrugged, unsure what to say.

Jed sat back up and reached out a hand. "Let me take a look at the report. I have to see this for myself."

He skimmed over the pages until he found the section he was looking for.

Findings: No exact copies of the DNA of Ethan Davidson were found on the syringe that was removed from Ethan Davidson's arm. Samples of DNA and fingerprints were removed from the body of Ethan Davidson. In addition to no exact copies of Ethan's DNA being found on the syringe, our tests did not report the presence of any kind of DNA material on the syringe. Our tests use methodology that has a 99% detection and identification accuracy rate that would have identified any copies of the DNA on the syringe if they had been present.

He handed the paper back across the table to Christie.

"I don't know what to make of this either," offered Christie.

Jed was deep in thought. The crime scene photos were spread across the table, and the pair was analyzing the report they had just gotten back from the forensics department. It seemed, apparently, that ghosts were real. Except that Jed knew they weren't. Not after that voicemail he had received the previous evening.

"Reading that must have been difficult for you," she remarked.

A sad smile claimed his features. He couldn't let Christie in on what he'd discovered just yet. He needed to play the part just a little bit longer until he could figure out what to do.

"It was. Very difficult." Jed straightened in his chair. "Though I suppose this is some sort of consolation for me. If Ethan's prints aren't on the syringe, that means he didn't intentionally overdose, and that comforts me—tells me that he hadn't secretly been struggling and had given up. But because they aren't there, that also means that the foul play you were sensing is now glaringly obvious. This is a case of first-degree murder."

Christie's cheeks puffed up as she took a long, deep breath.

"So, someone beat him, broke his arm so he couldn't resist, and injected him with a lethal dose of fentanyl?"

"That's how it appears," Jed said.

Maybe you should teach your clients how to fight so I can't overpower them so easily next time? The voicemail kept playing in his head, over and over. His temple was pounding. Christie was focused on taking notes, pen already gliding across the page in front of her.

"And it's perfectly plausible—the killer we're already profiling always wears gloves. And again, no DNA detected. There was no weapon found at the scene, though. Maybe someone interrupted the killer and he had to flee with the weapon this time."

Jed's response was only a thoughtful 'hmm', and Christie continued taking notes. She was right. They were running into walls with the other two cases when it came down to DNA evidence, and this case was turning out to be the same. Something was missing. There was something he couldn't see. And last night's turn of events with that distorted voicemail was Jed's confirmation that he needed to do some digging.

Before he could open the door to his apartment, his phone rang. Jed didn't even turn the key in the lock before he answered and waited for Christie to speak.

"Gray."

"Detective?"

"We've got another murder. Another elderly homeless man, this time on 65th. Identifying the victim is going to take some time on this one; there's not much left to identify. Fits the profile: older homeless male, stabbed to death and the same kind of dagger found on site. The medical examiner will call us when they know more."

He sighed, his hand falling from the key as it sat in the lock. "Do you need me at the scene?"

"No. You must have just gotten home. Just rest your pretty little head, and I'll update you later. We're still processing the scene."

"Tell me you checked my body cam location without telling me you checked my body cam location."

She laughed, and he grinned.

"Call me if you need me, okay?"

Jed heard a little smile in her voice as she said, "I will, Gray."

He entered the apartment and pulled his leftovers from the fridge, thinking through his day. His walk home had been uneventful as usual, except that he had run into Lana, who was walking two different dogs this time. They had stopped to chat for a while, and she'd talked about being a dog walker. He smiled at the memory. Imagine spending time with dogs for a living. The pups had been so sweet; this time a golden retriever and a husky who were brother and sister. Then Jed tried to envision all the homeless people he passed on his way home and wondered who this last victim was.

As his potatoes warmed, he dumped his backpack at the foot of his bed and stripped down to his boxers. As he tucked into his meal, Jed realized he'd taken the potatoes off the fire too quickly. They were only just warm. He continued chewing anyway, eager to shower and drop into bed.

These days, it felt like he was living the same day over and over again. Wake up, work out, get to the office, talk to Hugh for a bit, start working, do filing and admin work, work on rehab reports, finalize intake and outtake documents, take calls and see clients for their appointments, head to the police station for more casework with Christie, arrive home late, eat, shower, and head to bed.

Routine was his bread and butter. But this was a new routine—one he was unused to, and it was taking a toll on him.

He sent a message to his mom before getting into the shower. Jed had promised to keep her updated on his daily life, and well, he wanted to stick to it—add it into the routine, if you will. He knew she was at home worrying, mulling over their conversation and trying to piece the fragments of his life together to see how she could give him good advice.

That's what moms are for, Jed mused, but he knew better than to think that was the norm for everyone. His clients often had horrifying stories about their mothers—either things they had watched her go through, or things they had suffered at her hand. Max, in particular, was a troublesome case.

He walked into the bathroom, not bothering to turn the overhead lights on, lest he give himself a headache right before bed. Max had shared with him recently the real reason he did not want to meet with his mom. She wasn't a 'bad person' according to Maxwell, but she had done a lot of damage to him, emotionally, as a young child. His parents had split up, and instead of encouraging her son and supporting him through the disintegration of their family unit, she had spent every chance she got tearing down Max's dad in her son's presence, poisoning his mind against his father.

It was so bad that Max had told Jed that he'd hated his father so much, he told everyone who asked that he was dead—because that's what he wanted him to be. Even though his dad kept trying to reach out to him and mend their relationship, it wasn't until he had left home that Max realized the truth. According to him, distancing himself from his mother was the best decision he ever made. He'd run into his dad, they had got to talking, and two seconds into the conversation, he'd realized his mother was a liar.

Everything she'd lamented about his dad's character proved untrue in those few moments. His father was kind, jovial, and very supportive. His mom was the angry, abusive, narcissistic manipulator. Since that day, he'd refused to see her.

Jed lathered his hair with shampoo, letting the water and steam soothe his muscles. Every morning, and every night when he took a shower, he gave himself a pat on the back. A large, standing shower had been on his list of non-negotiables for an apartment. Boy, had his grit in the search for the right place paid off.

As the fog swirled around him, Jed couldn't help but feel blessed for his amazing mom. Even though his and Max's story were so similar, his mom had been the anchor that had kept him from spinning completely out of control. He watched the soapy water run down the drain and sighed, feeling the weight of the day wash off his shoulders.

In true form, Christie had called him with an update on the investigation of the fourth murder in their case. The news had left his stomach turning.

"We're still working on identifying the victim, but we do know that he passed from shock and hemorrhage, and we're at a count of fifty-three stab wounds. And, Jed, this took place on your route, nine pm on the 28th, ten minutes after you had already walked by him."

There it was again. Ten minutes after he'd walked by. The killer was still on his trail. He had managed to think up an idea for how to catch the person that was doing it, and this new murder confirmed that it would work. For now, though, he thought as he looked at his bed, it'd been a long day. He needed some sleep.

Hugh had convinced him to get lunch together, and since he'd finished his leftovers for dinner and had woken up to the realization that his fridge was empty, Jed allowed himself to be dragged to the café a block down from their office. It was Friday, the end of the week, which was why his fridge was empty. He wasn't too bummed about it. That just meant he had done a good job of eating well this week.

Hugh was reminiscing about his glory days in high school and college, and his stories were cracking both of them up.

"No, really!" He exclaimed as they crossed the street. "My mom showed up to school in curlers and a face mask, demanding to speak to the principal. I was so embarrassed. Absolutely inconsolable. I didn't go back to school until the week after—by that time, I figured everyone had forgotten."

Jed smiled as he asked the next question, already figuring that he knew the answer.

"Well, did they forget?"

Hugh turned to him and narrowed his eyes.

"Forget? The second I walked into the hallway at the front of the school, I was getting whistled at, and people were making all sorts of comments about how hot my mom was."

Hugh visibly cringed and shuddered as though repulsed by that thought, and Jed roared with laughter.

"It isn't funny!" Hugh muttered miserably.

"Oh, but it is. It's absolutely hilarious!"

Hugh huffed, and the two fell into an easy silence as they neared the shop. From the corner of his eye, Jed caught sight of something that glinted on the highest wall of the Starbucks they were passing. His steps slowed.

"So, that's where it is!"

Hugh, who had walked on ahead of him, turned to see what he was talking about. He walked back to Jed and stared up at the building.

"What are we looking at?"

"Hm? Oh! The CCTV camera that's on this leg of the street."

Hugh stiffened, but Jed's attention was on the camera. He recovered quickly. "What?"

Jed looked over at him. "CCTV? For city surveillance?"

Hugh looked up at the black camera. "Right. Let's go on."

He turned without another word and marched forward. Jed blinked. When he caught up to him, he prodded. "What? You're camera shy?"

Hugh snorted. "Hardly. I just wasn't aware that there were CCTV systems so arbitrarily placed."

"They're not at all random from what I've gathered. Most streets in the borough have at least two or three of them."

Hugh slowed, looking over at Jed.

"What? Really?"

Jed nodded, amused by Hugh's wonderment over something so simple.

"Yup. It's city policy to keep them up and running for security purposes. It deters a lot of criminals. Though, of course, most criminals aren't bright enough to notice them."

Hugh burst into another smile right then. "Right. Then it's a good thing we're always on our best behavior! Never know who's watching people mill about on the city streets."

He winked at Jed, then looked down at his watch, as though in a hurry.

"Let's go. We don't have much time left to get food and eat without needing to run back to the office."

Jed nodded.

On their way back to the office, Hugh was uncharacteristically quiet and solemn, but Jed put it down to the café they'd visited. It was packed, and they had either had to wait half an hour to be seated or go somewhere else and face, potentially, even longer wait times. It was the lunch rush hour, and they both knew nowhere would be less crowded. Their best bet would be to wait, and wait they did.

Eventually, they'd been able to order. Jed had opted for their signature shrimp burger and had picked up a few of their sweet treats for later. He needed to get groceries as soon as possible—in fact, as soon as he got back to the office, he was going to order groceries on Amazon Fresh. He wasn't feeling like walking through grocery aisles tonight.

Once their orders were ready, they had taken them to go, since they wouldn't have enough time to eat and get back to the office before their hour was up. It was amazingly busy in the café.

When Jed was back in the office, eating his burger, his phone chimed. It was Christie. His heart skipped a beat when he read the message.

Hey, Jed. Do you maybe wanna go get some ice cream tonight? Just to take our minds off work?

Yes. He would love to go get some ice cream tonight. He let the message sit for a minute, both so he wouldn't seem desperate and so that he could calm his thundering heart. He'd been meaning to ask her out—to, like she had said, get both their minds off work. The case had become so intense so quickly that it was consuming all their energies, individually and combined. A break was in order. Just Jed, Christie, and ice cream cones.

He took another big bite of the shrimp burger in his hands, understanding right away why it was their most popular menu item. The shrimp was tender, seasoned to perfection, and the sauce and cheese combination they had paired it with were impeccable. The buns were melt-in-your-mouth soft, and the lettuce gave it the perfect amount of crunch. He would have to go back to that café to try out their other options and, most definitely, get this burger another time.

Washing his last bite down with some water, he opened his brown paper bag and pulled out one of his sweet treats. A cinnamon roll. It had been glistening so beautifully in the glass case inside the café that his self-control had all but evaporated like a puddle in the heat of summer.

He groaned as he took a bite, transported by the flavors back to the lakeside with his aunt and uncle, where his aunt spent long evenings in the kitchen, teaching him how to cook. Her cinnamon rolls were his favorite, and though this one came close, it couldn't compare to the homemade, small batch taste of his aunt's. After Jed's dad had left, his aunt and uncle had really stepped up to help his mom, and they'd become an even bigger part of his life. His aunt, in particular, had taken to him even more. She'd visited mom more often, and she and his mother had grown closer as sisters.

He picked up the phone as he tucked the last piece of sweet bliss into his mouth and typed out a response.

Tonight at six. My treat? I'll come for you at the station.

He took a deep breath and set the phone down, dusting away any stray crumbs and folding away the wrappers. It was time to get back to getting some work done.

CHAPTER 15

"Hey, Jed!" Christie's voice greeted him as he waltzed into her office. "How are you?"

To him, she seemed a little nervous, though her cheery voice gave nothing away. Her hair was down around her face, just the way he loved to see it, in bold curls that looked like she had taken a little extra time on her hair today. She was wearing a long-sleeved white blouse and jeans. He'd never seen her wear denim before, and as she turned to take her purse from the side of the chair, he realized he wanted to see her wearing denim much more often. He was still looking straight at her when she turned back to face him.

"Good afternoon, Detective. Just thinking about what flavor ice cream I'm going to get," he teased.

She smiled. "We will have a ton of options at the ice cream cafe I'm thinking about going to."

"Have you been there before?"

"No. I haven't been inside, but I have passed their cute little cafe multiple times on my way home from work. They tend to be full during the days, but in the afternoons they're always much quieter."

Jed nodded. "Let's hope no one else has the same bright idea as us."

His eyes twinkled as he watched her close her files and put them away neatly in the drawer. Then she locked the drawer with a key that she tucked into her bag—always so organized. She looked over at Jed one more time, tucking her hair behind her ear as she walked over.

"Well," she said. "Let's go."

"After you," he bowed, ushering her on before him.

Outside, she led him down a street that took them east, away from the heart of the bustle in the middle of Manhattan. There were songbirds chirping from the trees that lined the street as they wound their way through small groups of people, stalls, and the occasional dog walker.

"Jed!"

Christie watched a young, blonde-haired girl came running up to Jed, and she tensed ever so slightly when the girl flung her arms around him. Jed leaned into the hug, laughing down at something she must have said that Christie couldn't hear. It was always awkward when her friends saw people she didn't know, Christie mused to herself, emphasizing the word *friends* to herself over and over. *We are work friends, and Jed is allowed and supposed to have non-work friends.* She shifted her weight from one converse to the other. *Of course, some of them would be women.* She watched one of Jed's arms tighten around the girl before the two separated. *Finally.*

Is time moving more slowly than usual? Christie wondered to herself, ripping her eyes away from the two friends who were laughing and chatting to look down the long street.

"This is Christie," Jed said, reaching out an arm to wrap around her and pull her into their conversation circle.

Tingles spread through her at the warmth of his palm where it still rested on her waist, and his eyes twinkled down at her before his gaze turned back to the blonde-haired girl, who was smiling at Christie.

"It's so nice to meet you, Christie! I'm Lana. I walk dogs for a living."

Try as she might, Christie could not detect even an ounce of sarcasm or ingenuity in the girl's bright eyes and enthusiastic grin. She smiled back.

"It's so nice to meet you," Lana continued. "I've heard Jed mention you when he's too busy to chat in the evenings. Something about work or other."

The jealous bubble inside her suddenly melted away.

"Yes, we often have quite the flood of work to take care of."

Lana nodded, and Jed interjected then, his hand tightening almost reassuringly around Christie as he spoke. Warmth flooded through her again.

"Yeah well, this is one of those afternoons where I'm busy again. We've actually gotta run now."

Lana nodded with understanding. "Of course! I need to go pick up my dogs for the afternoon and rush home afterward to study. It's exam season!"

Jed pulled the girl in for another quick hug before she bustled off down the street.

"All the best with your exams, kid!"

"Thanks, Jed!"

He watched her walk away for a minute before turning back to Christie, something like amusement in his eyes as he looked down at her.

"Ready?"

She nodded, not trusting herself to speak without embarrassing herself by asking more about who Lana was to Jed. She didn't need to know, and she was almost sure that asking would make her feel even more awkward than she already did. They started off down the street again, and she pressed her lips together. Jed had called the girl *kid*. That was a good enough indicator of their dynamic. Christie could at least accept that as a consolation prize.

Inside the café, the amusement in Jed's expression almost doubled. This was the most cutesy décor he had ever seen, and it was making his cheeks hurt from wanting to smile. The décor was a mixture of Japandi and the classic pastel, colorful amine café styles. There were plushies on some of the seats, tall olive trees in the corners, and a faint lo-fi-esque song played in the background.

Christie was looking at him. "What are you thinking?"

Jed finally gave into the smile that had been trying to form on his cheeks for the past minute or so since they had entered.

Placing a hand on the small of her back, he led her forward to the counter as the line dissipated.

"This café reminds me perfectly of you. Soft, feminine, but with flavors as robust as they come."

As he looked up at the menu, Christie blinked, trying to process the layers within the compliment he'd so casually issued. She wondered if he complimented all the women in his life the way he did her. She hoped he did because it was such a sweet, kind gesture. But she also secretly hoped he didn't because that would mean there'd be more compliments reserved for her.

She waited patiently for him to browse the many options. She had already decided what she would try. Word on the street was that the best flavor at Cream's Café was the Banana Cheesecake Ice Cream. The server walked up to them and greeted them with a friendly smile before all but going googly eyed on Jed.

"Hi! Welcome to Cream's Café. What can we get you today?"

"We'll both have the banana cheesecake ice cream," Jed answered.

Christie's face contorted in surprise as he turned to look down at her, a smile spreading across his cheeks at her adorable expression of confusion.

"How many scoops do you want?"

"Two," she managed to say.

"Two for the lady—three for me."

The cashier nodded, ringing up the order while Jed paid, and then led her over to the section of the café that looked out onto the street.

As they sat, the question came blurting out of her. "How did you know what flavor I wanted?"

Jed did that thing where he tilted his head to the side to look at her.

"You mentioned it when we met for dinner. You said, verbatim: *There's a café I've been meaning to try out, and all my friends keep raving about the banana cheesecake ice cream. I have to try it out.*"

The memory suddenly came back to her. They talked so much and so often that, sometimes, she could hardly figure out what parts of her she had shared and what parts she hadn't. It felt like he already knew everything hidden within her.

"And you remembered me saying that?"

His eyes narrowed just a fraction. "I remember everything you say to me."

Christie's eyes fluttered to the floor.

Jed cleared his throat. "I should tell you, by the way, that you should wear more denim more often. It brings out your eyes."

Christie laughed outright, and Jed grinned too, taking a sip of the water the waiter had poured for them while they waited for their ice cream.

"My eyes, huh? Of course."

Jed's own eyes sparkled across the table at her, amusement and contentment filling him—a feeling he so often got whenever he spent time with her.

Christie looked at him, and her gaze softened. "I'll keep that in mind."

"I hope I'm not intruding too much on your private time on this fine Friday evening, Detective," he said with another slow smile that made her stomach coil.

"I'm the one that invited you out," she said. "But not to worry. I won't keep you out too late."

Jed hummed, watching her over the rim of his glass, the look in his eyes making her remember her own feelings of possessiveness just a few minutes ago.

Their orders arrived just then, and Christie grinned.

"It's so cute!" she cooed down at the bowl of ice cream.

Jed watched her reach for her phone and take a picture of the arrangement: a small clear glass bowl, two pretty scoops of a pale-yellow banana cheesecake ice cream, tiny banana slices around the rim of the glass, and the lightest drizzle of chocolate on top.

His bowl was arranged the same, albeit a bit larger because of his third scoop. He watched her smile grow as she picked up her spoon.

"Ready?" He watched surprise fill her eyes.

She smiled over at him. "You were waiting for me to start?"

"Of course."

She nodded, still smiling. "Okay, Gray. Let's tuck in."

They both closed their eyes as they savored the first mouthful, and Christie had to stop herself from groaning out loud. Her friends were right. She would have to come here more often.

After they had separated and Jed was on his way home, he decided that now was as good a time as any to put his theory to the test. His plan was simple: take the long, deserted route home in hopes of drawing out whoever it was that was killing these people right after he walked by them.

On all the occasions when this had happened, Jed had walked by the homeless person, made his way straight home, and then gotten a call from Christie to say that there had been a murder minutes after he had passed the person. Tonight, he would walk by a couple of homeless men, heading in the direction of home, and instead of going home, would double back on the same path where the killer entered the scene, hoping to catch him in real time.

He hadn't thought through what he would do if he came face to face with the killer. Would he hide? Try to intervene? He wasn't sure. He hadn't gotten that far in the planning, but he was willing to take the risk. At this stage of the case, there was already an established pattern he could rely on.

Jed spent the next three hours walking past homeless people he thought might be prime targets for the sadistic killer they were dealing with. He kept his hands in his pockets and looked as unassuming as he could as he strolled. He passed closed cafes, antique stores, vintage bookshops, restaurants, grocery stores, and empty parking garages. Jed hadn't been on the streets of New York this late since he'd been an addict himself—sixteen years old, roaming wherever he pleased, whenever he pleased, until the wee hours of the morning.

At the four-hour mark, when he'd retraced six of his regular routes, he had the bright idea of walking through the darkest alleys he could find. He looked at his watch. It was twenty minutes till midnight. He was sure that this meant the killer likely wouldn't be bothering to act tonight. All the murders had taken place between eight pm and two am, so he'd still keep walking. There was still time for the killer to show himself.

His phone rang out in the silence as he was making his way through an alley, and he grabbed it and put it to his ear.

"Where?" Jed answered, eager to see if his theory had worked.

"Exactly, Gray. Where are you? Why did I get three pings that you've been walking around the city at midnight on all the streets where we've had murders?"

Shit. He'd forgotten that he was wearing the body cam and that his locations were being recorded. And he sure as heck didn't know they'd programmed it to ping in the crime scene locations. He froze.

But Christie wouldn't relent. "Jed. What are you doing? Do you have any idea how dangerous what you're doing is?"

Christie's voice was almost hysterical, and Jed sighed.

"Yes, Detective, I do. That's kind of the point."

"Listen, I don't know what you think you're doing, but you need to get home *now*—and that's an order."

"I'll get home soon enough. I need to—"

"Now, Jed. Go. Home. Now."

Under different circumstances, Jed would have been amused at her tone. Now, however, he simply sighed in response.

"I will be watching your live location until you get home, and if you're not home in the next ten minutes, I'll send state troopers after you with their horns and sirens blaring. Do you understand?"

"Yes ma'am."

"Good. And don't pull this stunt again. Ever."

Jed heard Christie hang up and sighed into the silence where he stood. She was right. This was incredibly dangerous. But he knew that if he had told her his plan, she would have refused to let him go through with it. He headed home, feeling defeated.

CHAPTER 16

JED WOKE UP TO the sound of knocking at his door. Confused and half-asleep, he looked at the time on the clock on his nightstand. It was six thirty in the morning on a Saturday.

He dragged himself to the door and opened it to find Christie, livid.

She let herself in, brushing past him to stand in his living room, arms on her hips and fire in her eyes. Jed took a deep breath in and closed the door before turning to face her.

"What the hell was that, Gray?"

Jed crossed his arms, and Christie tried not to be distracted by the fact that he'd obviously just woken up.

"I was testing a theory."

"Testing a theory? Alone, like a target in the middle of New York City at midnight?"

"Yes."

That seemed to make Christie even more angry. "What do you mean 'yes'? Why didn't you say something so I could come with you?"

Jed shook his head. "Because I'm never going to put you in harm's way. That's why."

"So you acknowledge that was a stupid thing to do?"

Jed didn't answer.

"What's with you? This isn't like you. What's going on?"

Christie watched Jed's lip twitch, her ire growing as his silence stretched on. "Oh, so *Mr. We're-A-Team* suddenly doesn't have anything to say?"

Jed looked out the window for a minute. He was wearing sweats, and this was the most inconvenient time possible to be aroused by her anger. It was also just plain rude. "I knew you wouldn't let me do it, so I didn't bother to mention it."

"I wouldn't have let you do it because whatever 'it' is was irrational and extremely dangerous. But we could have at least organized a stakeout if you had let me in on whatever it is you're hiding!"

Irrational. The word burned through his skull. She was right. It *was* irrational. And they could very well have organized a stakeout if he had brought it to their attention. He sighed.

"I didn't know how to bring it up. It's my fault so I felt like I had to redeem myself."

"What is your fault, Jed?"

"Ethan's murder."

Christie's brows furrowed. "What do you mean it was your fault?"

"That's what the killer said," Jed began. He stopped when a look of utter confusion and shock crossed Christie's features.

"I got a voicemail," he added quickly. "And that's what he said. That my therapy had failed and Ethan had already started to do drugs again. Which was why he could overpower him so easily."

Christie's eyes were wide, and Jed sighed, pushing his messy hair out of his face.

"I wanted to see if I could lure him out by walking by a homeless person—to give him a target—and then doubling back on the route and catch him in the act."

A look of horror overtook Christie's face. "What?! You wanted to catch a serial killer in the act, all by yourself, with no backup, and not even a vest?"

She was yelling, and when she said it all out loud the severity of his actions settled into Jed's mind. He hadn't thought it all the way through.

"Catch him in the act, and then what?" She demanded. "Become one of the victims and leave me to clean up your body off the sidewalk, too?"

Jed flinched. "No. I didn't-

"Yes, it's clear you didn't think it through, Jed."

Her voice cracked when she said his name, and regret flashed through him.

"Fuck. I'm sorry. I didn't mean for it to go this far. I just sort of got lost trying to figure it out on my own and decided to try it out last night to see what happened."

He reached for her arm cautiously, and when she let him take it into his hand, he pulled her in for a hug.

"I'm sorry."

"You scared the crap out of me," she replied, tears streaking down her face.

"I'm sorry."

"You could have gotten hurt. Or worse."

"I know. I'm sorry," he murmured into her hair.

She sniffled, and Jed sighed.

"Will you forgive me?" he asked.

"Only if you promise never to pull a stunt like that again."

Jed nodded. "You have my word."

She hesitated for a moment before nodding against his chest.

"Okay."

They separated, and Christie swiped at her eyes briefly before pulling a pen and notepad out of her back pocket.

"Now then, what did you discover?"

Jed roared with laughter, and Christie smiled sheepishly.

"Oh, come on. You must have noticed something. And what was that voicemail all about?"

CHAPTER 17

THE WEEKEND HAD COME and gone. Jed had spent most of his time catching up on small parts of his routine that had dropped off the radar in the past weeks. He bought groceries and planned his meals. He did all his laundry, deep cleaned his apartment, and caught up with his mom.

What little free time was left after that, he spent talking over the case with Christie and preparing for the week ahead. The newest murder, number four, was taking some time to be processed because of the unusually gruesome way it had happened. His stomach had turned over when Christie called to let him know processing was delayed, and he'd honestly not known what to say at the time.

He sighed where he was, sitting behind his desk, reflecting on the past week the way he always did on a Monday. How could he move forward? How could he improve on the results of the last seven days?

Right now, he was thinking about his conversation with Max last Friday before he had gone to get ice cream with Christie. Even though they had made so much progress the previous week, Max had all but refused to talk about his mom. Jed knew better than to force a conversation about an unhealed aspect of his client's life, so instead, they had talked about Max's dad.

Max loved to talk about his dad, and in doing so, he inadvertently spoke about his mom. In every other sentence, he would say, *'and that's why he left'*. He would say something about his dad's restaurant business and then say, *'and that's why he left'*. He would say something about his dad's new girlfriend and say, *'and that's why he left'*. The teenager was currently rewriting the narrative his mom had told him about his dad's estrangement from their family.

Jed was happy to listen. Actually, he was very excited to listen. Rewriting trauma narratives was a very important part of the process toward healing. If he could get to the bottom of what he truly believed about his reality, the stories he had been told by those around him and in power over him, and begin to see the story for what it is, or at least take control of the way he tells and lives the story, he would be well on his path back into society.

Of course, the teenager did not know that. In his mind, he was only emphasizing how much of a liar his mom was. Jed couldn't imagine just how painful it would be to realize that your mom, the one person who was supposed to be on your side forever, no matter what, lied to you and tried to manipulate you into hating your father, the other person who was supposed to be with you for the rest of your life. That single action robbed Max of both of his parents. Now, he was estranged and angry with his mom, and before, he had been estranged and angry with his father.

Jed was content to move at Max's pace as long as they were still moving. He would keep encouraging him, working alongside him, and helping him process the things that were keeping him away from rehab.

Rehab. Max needed to go to rehab. Jed knew the boy wanted to go, and he would not let him give up on that desire just because of his subconscious processes and fear-based programming. Maxwell needed to get out of the environment he was in, and to do that meant entering into rehab. After rehab, it would be easier to get him housing. There were sober housing options that he could transition into, and then there were programs to help with subsidized housing to get him and his girlfriend on their feet.

The boy had his wits about him. He needed to, or he would have long been dead by now. Jed had successfully worked with him on harm reduction, and Max hadn't used cocaine in over six months. His drug of choice now was cannabis, and he had admitted his increased awareness of when he allowed himself to use the drug because he knew he needed to stay on high alert to stay safe.

Jed lazed in his office chair and watched the sun come streaming in through the windows.

Hugh had come knocking earlier, but he had decided not to entertain his friend today. There was too much to be caught up on. Jed looked back down at his papers. He had a client coming in today who had been through the rehab system and was a name on his list of success stories. For the last week, every time he saw a check-in client for post rehab rehabilitation, he had thought of Ethan. Ethan, that sweet soul. Jed wondered who would have so great a vendetta against him that they would use the same drug he had been addicted to, and haunted by, to end his life.

He didn't know. But he was sure as hell going to find out.

Just then, a knock came on the door.

"Come in," he called.

"Hi, Mr. Gray! How are you?"

Jed grinned, watching the man enter the room before they shook hands, and his visitor sank into the sofa across the room the way he usually did when he came in.

"Well, Greg, I should be asking you that. How are you? How have you been? Don't hold out on me!" Jed teased.

The two men laughed, and Jed watched joy split Greg's cheeks. He hoped that meant good news.

"Truth is, I've never been better."

That's what Jed liked to hear.

"I've been out for two weeks. Time has flown by."

"Two good weeks, I hope?" Jed queried with a grin.

Greg laughed a little. "It's been almost like a dream. A fever dream, but in a good way. I moved back in with my wife. She got a new dog for company while I was away, so I finally met the little critter. We even have plans to start the home-buying process. She wants to move a little further out of the city so we can get a condo or something of the sort at a better price. And speaking of price, I got my job back!" He announced each achievement with pride.

"Yeah?" Jed felt like his face would burst open from his grin.

"Yeah! When I was signing up for rehab, I told my supervisor, and he told me that I could always come back when I was through with rehab. He told me that he was proud of me for taking the step while the addiction was in its young stages and that he wanted me to reach out to him when I was back so he could see what he could do to get me back into the company."

Jed nodded along, his pen gliding across the papers in front of him, making him think of the way Christie always took fervent notes when he was speaking. He smiled a little at the thought of her. Then his smile grew for Greg, the man beaming in front of him. He loved listening to his clients' testimonies. It always refreshed his spirit for the week ahead and reminded him what he was fighting for.

"How does that make you feel?" he asked.

"Why, I feel incredible! He told me he had a promotion for me whenever I returned and guess what? When I walked into the office—two weeks ago, today—the promotion papers were waiting for me right on my desk. He told me he was proud of me. And he said that he admired just how hard I fought not to let my addiction mess with my work ethic."

The man's eyes moistened a bit, and Jed gave him some time to recompose himself.

"He told me that he had a cousin who has been through the addiction cycle and tried her hardest to recover, but never did. She ended up passing away from an overdose. Because of that, he always tries to give extra support to those who are struggling with addiction. His speech almost made me cry!"

Jed nodded. "I'm happy he was able to share that experience with you—and that he commended you for how hard you worked. You deserve the commendation. As a matter of fact, it's my turn to commend you. You did a tremendous job reaching out when you did, as soon as you identified that you were in trouble. A lot of people get to that point of consciousness where they recognize that this is a struggle and that they're not able to overcome it on their own. But they're too afraid to reach out for help, so they keep going. Once you pass that point of consciousness, it's so much harder to come back. You did good."

Greg nodded along, swiping at his eye when he thought Jed wasn't looking.

"And, based on the reports I got back from your performance in rehab, you did really well there, too. Everyone spoke and wrote highly of you."

The two men sat in silence for a while, Greg absorbing the praises he was receiving, and Jed making notes on his post rehab forms, occasionally glancing at Greg to see if he needed any support. In true form, Greg asked for the support himself.

"So… is this where you and I end?"

Jed grinned. "Is this where you want it to end?"

"No! Of course, I don't... that's not what I'm saying at all. I just—"

"Yes?"

"I don't really know what happens after the rehab ends, with you and me."

Jed nodded. This was usually one of the hardest parts of the process for his clients, and for him. He had gotten them to the point where they no longer needed him. As far as addiction therapy, his job was done. All that was left was light maintenance.

"Well, Greg, here's how it works moving forward. You and I will have a check-in session every two weeks for the first three months, just like today is our first session two weeks after you left rehab. After the three-month anniversary when you left rehab, our sessions will go to every other month, and they will continue like that until you decide that you no longer need me or that you want to see a more generalized therapist."

Greg nodded, a smile breaking out onto his features. "What if I decide to never get tired of you? Can I keep you forever?"

"Well," Jed grinned and tapped his pen against his desk, "that's up to you. It's your call to make—but you should keep in mind that I *am* an addiction therapist, so sooner or later, we might run out of things to talk about."

Greg huffed out a small laugh. "I understand. I guess there's no reason to fret about it now, is there? When we get to that bridge, we'll figure something out."

"We will."

They both nodded, contentment settling into their hearts as Jed continued to make notes and Greg looked out the window for a moment.

"Now, about that condo you guys wanted to buy…"

CHAPTER 18

"AFTER WE'RE THROUGH HERE, we'll get dinner—on me."

Excuses began to form in Christie's throat as her lips parted. They were doing what felt like their hundredth run-through of the interviews, the results of their checks on alibis and financial statements, and what had been said in the interviews themselves. Jed cut in before she could think of a good excuse not to.

"That wasn't a question, Detective. After we're through here, we'll get dinner on me."

She shut her mouth again, choosing to nod along. When they were through, they headed out of the station and down the darkening street in silence.

While the interviews for all three suspects had varied in their levels of emotional demand, Lauren Finch's had been the most emotionally demanding. In their first interview with Whitman, then with Carrillo, both men had been stubborn and uncooperative. All three interviews had revealed plausible motives and poor alibis for the suspects, based on the information they were able to pull.

John's alibi had been disproven, and so had Lauren's. Their request for Carrillo's financial statements was still processing.

As Jed and Christie left the station, heading into the evening to a Korean BBQ to have dinner, Christie sighed. The street they were walking down was deserted, and Jed was on high alert.

"Can you believe this investigation?"

Jed snorted.

"Tell me about it," he remarked sarcastically.

"It sucks. It really sucks. I thought I had it all together. All planned out. And I had it all under control—until I started doing the interviews and then it all came crashing down on top of me."

"What came crashing down?" Jed asked.

"My expectations."

He snorted again, trying to keep his laughter inside his body. Christie turned to gaze at him, her eyes narrowing as she tried to look straight at him through the glare of the halo that the streetlight behind his head created. She was being serious, he could tell, but some amusement still danced in her eyes.

"Are you... laughing at me, Gray?"

"That I am, Detective, but not in a bad way. What were your expectations going into the interviews?"

"Answers. Something concrete that I could say, 'Alright, he said this, and this was inconsistent, so now we are on the killer's trail for real.' Instead, I got a whole bunch of attitude—and a bunch of being yelled at."

Jed's footsteps paused, and he reached out for her arm and pulled her around to face him. The streetlight next to them was beaming down onto her delicate features in a way that made him want to commit the moment to memory.

"I wanted to bring that up, but I didn't know how to," Jed remarked.

"Bring what up?

"The way you've handled the interviews is very commendable. I wanted to ask about how you've been feeling after them all… if the verbal lashings took a toll on how you were feeling."

"Are you always this perceptive?"

"Yes. By trade, and by experience."

Christie hummed in response, breaking contact with his gaze to look down at his chest for a moment. She had felt his attention consistently on her while she had interviewed all three of the suspects, especially when she had been interviewing Carrillo. He had been quite the doozy, with the way he had responded to her at the end of the interview, when she had asked about the twenty-five million dollars in losses. That had really set him off.

"I feel a bit beat up," she admitted. "But it's all part of the job. And with emotional responses, it can mean we are getting closer to the truth."

A smile pulled up at the corners of Jed's lips. "Protecting the lives of civilians is part of the job description of a police officer. But getting shot on the line of duty still hurts."

Christie's eyes grew wide. She hadn't thought of it that way.

Jed hunched down and whispered to her, "We need to address all the wounds we sustain in the name of the fight for justice. Otherwise, we won't be able to fight."

She swallowed and nodded. As usual, he was right. The two continued on to the restaurant, tucking into their meals, not talking much as they devoured the food before them. They had pork ramen with extra pork, kimchi fried rice, dumplings, and udon noodles. It was divine. Jed watched Christie eat across from him, letting his mind run over their day as she chewed and stared out the windows into the dark street.

She had pulled a lot of heavy weight in the last few weeks. Jed realized that, despite having worked with her for the past weeks, those intense interviews were the first time he had really seen Christie in *action*. The way she had held her own, the way she had kept her tone level and professional, the way she hadn't even flinched when Carrillo got up and threatened her—it impressed Jed.

It was all incredibly admirable… and incredibly attractive. Christie popped another dumpling into her mouth and closed her eyes as she chewed. She was clearly enjoying herself. He was glad because, whenever he was with her, Jed was enjoying himself, too.

"I have a week off from work next week," he mentioned as casually as he could.

She stopped chewing. Her eyes wide, she put her chopsticks down and wiped her hands on her napkin. "What? You're leaving me?"

Jed chuckled. "No… you'll always be able to reach me via call and text. You just won't be seeing me."

Christie pouted, and his eyes zeroed in on her lips.

"Where are you going off to?" she asked. "To visit your girlfriend or your wife and kids that you've been hiding from me?"

"Something like that," he mused.

"Ha. Ha. Ha. Very funny, Jed."

"You started it."

"Yeah, whatever, Gray."

His brow raised as he chewed on a piece of juicy pork. "What's the matter? Jealous?"

She stuffed another dumpling into her mouth without answering his question. That made him laugh.

"I see how it is," he said, smiling.

Jed looked around for a moment, taking notice of the people inside the restaurant. It was late evening, and there were quite a few patrons milling around—and more coming through the doors. They were also making deliveries, so the staff were taking orders for both carryout and dine-in service. He even saw one woman walk in wearing what looked to be her pajamas. In her defense, she was visibly pregnant and only just barely able to waddle to the register. Maybe she was having a really intense craving. He couldn't blame the baby. The food was that good.

"So, is it a secret?" Christy pressed.

"Is what a secret?" Jed asked as he turned back to look at her.

"Where are you going off to? I asked, and you didn't answer."

"Oh! I'm sorry about that. I got lost in thought for a mom ent.'" He drank a bit of the soup.

God. This is so good, he thought to himself. His list of restaurants to revisit was growing steadily longer.

"I'm taking the week to visit my aunt and uncle's property in the woods, far away from civilization. I need to do some recalibrating. I feel I haven't been as much help to you as I should be on this case. Also, I think there's some things about it we're not seeing. After the emotional hit of losing Ethan, and having his murderer tell me it was my fault that he was able to kill him, I think some time in nature will help me reset."

Christie watched Jed take a long drink of water before he continued. Finally, she nodded and pushed her fork around her plate, and they ate in silence for another short while.

"When will you be leaving?" she asked.

"Tomorrow morning, bright and early, I'll be off."

She nodded again. "I'm supposed to get an update on the most recent incident tomorrow morning. I'll try to update you on the details before you ditch."

His eyes narrowed just as a fraction. "Interesting choice of word there, Detective."

She forced a smile. "Can't take a joke, Gray?"

"Oh, I can take a joke. But you aren't joking, are you, Detective?"

When Christie failed to respond, instead opting to shovel yet another dumpling into her mouth, Jed nodded.

"That's what I thought."

CHAPTER 19

THE NEXT MORNING, JED woke up so early that, at first, he thought he had barely slept. A quick check of the time showed that it was five in the morning, and it was just pitch black outside his floor-to-ceiling windows.

Since his bags were already packed, he padded to the shower and blasted himself with the water as cold as he could stand it.

There was just something magical about how quickly the human body could jolt awake when it was submerged in icy cold water, and Jed was planning to do a lot of submerging at the lake. He could almost smell the crisp air.

After drying and dressing, and securing his body cam to the neckline of his muscle tee, he dragged his bags out the door before pausing to look back into his apartment for a minute. Then he closed the door and headed for the elevator. He needed to get out of the city early to avoid the traffic. And to do that, he needed to go downstairs to the parking lot, resurrect his Jeep, and settle in for the three-hour drive to Highland Lakes.

Christie had called when he'd gotten out of the shower and caught him up to speed on the details of the fourth murder. She would email him all the documents, crime scene photos, and CCTV footage for him to review.

"Death of one Larry Wilcrow by shock and hemorrhage as a result of repeated sharp force trauma. Suspect sustained a total of fifty-three stab wounds—fifteen to the neck and shoulders, thirteen to the face, and twenty-five in the abdominal area."

His head still reeled from the gruesome recount of the condition of the body, and he hadn't missed Christie's careful guarding of her tone as she recounted the details. He knew it was eating away at her. It was eating away at him, too, and he hadn't even been at the scene of the crime—he couldn't imagine what it must feel like for Christie.

As the elevator descended sixteen floors to the underground parking garage, Jed sighed and ran his hand over his face before bringing it back up to pinch his cheeks. That concern was exactly why he needed to take the week off and use this time to process.

He sighed for what felt like the ninetieth time as the doors of the elevator opened and walked out and into the maze of cars to find his own. When he'd been working for the first few months, he'd saved most of his income to buy a car. Lots of people might find that a silly fixation to have—why buy a car when you walk, bus, or take the train everywhere in New York? But New York City wasn't the only place he frequented.

Because his family's lake house was such a safe haven for him, his only true place of refuge when he needed time and space away from it all, his car had been one of those investments that was geared at making long-term sense, no matter how silly it seemed in the present moment.

Driving himself was almost one hundred dollars cheaper in gas than taking the bus, then flagging a taxi down to take him the second leg of the journey. Who could be bothered to embark and disembark a bus, then embark and disembark a taxi, all while lugging suitcases around? And who wanted to have to deal with the odd personalities that often traveled the public routes? Jed definitely didn't. He was content to either walk to his destination or drive.

As he climbed into the matte black Wrangler Unlimited and nestled into the seats as the air conditioning came on, he felt contentment settle in. Money well spent.

The drive down would be long, but he was looking forward to the change of pace and scenery. It was barely six-thirty am, and the streets were starting to wake up. Usually, he'd be just now beginning to prepare for work after a good, long session in the gym. Now, he was enjoying the view of the Hudson as he rolled out of the city and away from his problems.

Jed couldn't help that Christie crossed his mind. Leaving the hustle and bustle was harder this time than it had ever been before. He hoped she would be safe and that she would take care of herself emotionally the way he'd been trying to get her to.

Of the three reasons he was taking this break in the first place, Christie was entwined with them all.

First, he needed time away to process how he was feeling—and how he'd been coping over the last weeks. Second, he needed to reconnect to his 'why' and his 'how'. Investigative therapy had been a blur, what felt like a fast-paced montage he had to keep up with. Third on the list was that he really needed to sit down and break the case. He hadn't truly had the dedicated time or mental resources lately to sit down and face it all. With the details of all four murders in hand, suspect interviews taken care of and transcribed, and a killer's profile, he had all he needed to make this madness make sense.

Or so he desperately hoped. At the end of this week off, Jed would return to his routines, equipped with the tools, answers, and energy he needed to continue to support his partner through the case wrap up. He needed the break—no doubt about it. But watching Christie struggle was more incentive to go.

Last night before bed, he'd done a deep dive into two of his favorite research resources for investigating people—Reddit and Discord. It was truly amazing what one could find on those platforms, and if you needed dirt on a popular person, something that could really take them down if it ever got into the hands of the public, those were the places to look.

His first task had been finding anything he could about Carrillo. He hadn't gone into the search expecting much, but he'd happened upon an entire Discord server and two subreddits dedicated to slandering the businessman and his company. There were thousands of reports of his aggressive, abusive behavior on the job, recordings of him yelling at workers, and even a video recording of him berating a secretary at his company. Turns out, most of the people who worked with him, particularly the contractors and day workers who were usually immigrants like himself, despised his guts.

The redeeming quality about him from what Jed had seen as he scrolled through the servers was that the compensation Carrillo offered was unmatched statewide. He paid them well, they had good health benefits, and because his business was respected, the workers managed to inveigle other preferences and benefits here and there by using their work identification cards around the city.

All that information spoke to his character, but it hadn't raised enough of a case to fortify his presence on the suspect list. But at the very top of the Discord server was a message dated August 11th, mere weeks before the murders started. It was a video recording. Since Jed had scrolled from the bottom upward through what felt like millions of messages of workers complaining, listened to hundreds of audio recordings, and clicked through thousands of pictures, he had contemplated letting the video remain until later. But he had scrolled through it all, so he would finish the job now. There was no need to leave it until later. He could sit through a couple minutes more of footage.

It had left his jaw on the floor. The video was taken in what looked like a conference room, where a group of nine people were sitting around a long desk. That was all well and fine. But Carrillo was in the center of the frame, going absolutely nuts.

"What do you mean the city council rejected the plans I sent them? That's not possible. There must be some kind of mistake. Come open the email on my computer so I can see it for myself, and I swear if I find out that you've been trying to sabotage me all this time, you'll have to move out of this city to find someone to hire you."

The frail, frightened blonde-haired secretary had opened the email on his computer and backed away from him immediately, almost tripping over her own heels as she did. Carrillo read the email on his screen and turned a shade of red only a hair lighter than a tomato. Everyone around him flinched when he banged his fist on the table and jumped to his feet.

"Who do those people think they are!

How dare they reject my development proposal AGAIN! And for what? Homeless scum that are a stain on the beautiful City of New York?"

Carrillo had looked up and spun to face a profusely sweating bald-headed man that was sitting on his left.

"Luthor, what are our profits and losses for this quarter so far? I swear they'll regret this."

Luthor spent a few tense seconds clicking buttons on his wireless mouse before stammering a response.

"*P-profits are at ten million dollars, Mr. C-Carrillo.*"

Carrillo was so enraged that he hardly seemed to hear the man.

"*Losses. What are the losses?*"

"*L-losses are—*" Luthor had cleared his throat, "*—twenty-five million.*"

Jed had thought the man might die on the spot. Shock, disbelief, rage, sadness, and fear were in his expression all at once, and he sank into his seat, his hands coming up to cover his face.

The room was deathly silent for a few moments until Carrillo managed to compose himself and speak again.

"*We will recover those losses before the year ends. The city council will regret this.*"

That was where the recording stopped. Jed had stared at the black screen of his computer for almost five minutes after the video ended. His mind raced. If he had ever doubted the presence of a motive that could drive Carrillo to the point of murder, those doubts had been expelled. The video was mostly blurry and shot from a strange angle that made Jed think this person had secretly been recording from behind what looked like a water bottle and a computer.

In the Discord server, the video had been sent with the caption: "*All this man cares about is money. It's disgusting to watch.*" Jed had saved the video to a new folder on his computer, along with a few other recordings and pictures he thought might help the case. He had also printed out a few pages of the Discord server and taken a web snapshot that would serve as proof that the webpage had existed, just in case it ended up being deleted later on.

As if that discovery hadn't been enough, he'd found what he was sure were John Whitman's and Lauren's secret Reddit accounts. John's username was 'whitmanchangedNYC'. If that weren't confirmation enough, Jed didn't know what was. Whitman wasn't a formalized mental health worker or anything of the sort, but he worked with the homeless a great deal. He organized private funding drives to prepare care packages for them that included food, over-the-counter medicines, toiletries, and clothes. Because of this, he thought of himself as some kind of New York City hero. And he was, in a way, but he was basically classifying himself as New York's savior. Talk about a grandiose sense of self-importance.

In any case, Jed had spent a few minutes scrolling through the man's latest posts, which were all very spaced out according to the date and time stamps attached to them.

There were a great deal of questions about various things—how to begin private fundraising, the best way to package food so that it wouldn't spoil, how to buy clothes for people when you didn't know what size they wore. Finally, Jed stumbled across something that had left his mouth open yet again, something he hadn't seen coming. It was a post from earlier in the year, in May.

"None of you know who I truly am, so this will not harm me in any way. I have decided that today is the day where I finally

confront a part of my life that I have left behind [hopefully]. They say confession is good for the soul.

As a young adult, when I first moved to New York City, I was obsessed with bullying people. I know what this sounds like, just hear me out. I just loved to see the look on people's faces when I was a prick to them. It almost gave me some kind of sick joy to watch women be offended whenever you stormed past them like they didn't exist, or to watch other men try to size you up and figure out why you were so confident when you brashly told them to get the hell out of your way. It was just fun.

Anyways, I got pretty sick a couple months after I first moved to the city and spent some time in hospital. I guess that's when I decided that being mean to people was bad for my health? Well, that's what I gathered from what the doctor pointed out—I was under too much stress, and it was messing with my nervous system. I needed to basically just chill out.

Anyway, I'm a changed man. I used to have fits of anger that would cause me to lash out, get into fights—I even stabbed a man one time. Well, it wasn't one time. It was a couple of times. More than a couple of times.

That's besides the point. The point is I'm a changed man. Now I'm changing New York for the better. Even murderers can be redeemed. No, I won't be elaborating. In any case, it was an accident. Nobody asked about it.

Anyways, bye.

After reading that post, Jed's routine had been the same. He printed out a copy of the web page with the post that had held his attention, took a web snapshot of the profile and post, and made notes about what he had read. It was a bit of the same for Lauren's secret Reddit page, except she didn't have much to look at, and it wasn't a secret page. Her username was 'finchleagleswings', and her profile showed Manhattan, NY as her location.

'Finch' and 'L' checked out, and Jed remembered seeing the tattoo of an eagle's wings on her upper forearm during the interview. She had a couple of posts from about a year ago and then nothing else. He wondered if the account was still active. In any case, what he did find was enough to raise suspicion. It was a question that had been answered, in detail, by the rest of the Reddit community.

How much money do you usually get from an insurance policy after somebody dies?

Why did she want to know how much she would get if someone died? Who was she enquiring about? Again, Jed had repeated the process. Printer copy, take web snapshots, make notes about what he read. He had sent all this info over to Christie, as a departure gift. Notes, URLs, snapshots, recordings, videos, everything. She had, of course, been very excited to hear that there was an update, since their face-to-face investigations hadn't gotten them very far with each suspect. She promised to look through them and get back to Jed with feedback about what she thought could be done based on the new evidence. Jed promised the same.

CHAPTER 20

HE HAD PULLED INTO the drive almost five minutes ago but hadn't made a move to get out of the Jeep. The engine had long been turned off, along with the radio and the cool air seeping through the vents. In their places was the sounds of the birds all around him in the trees on their morning breakfast runs, the soft trickling of water as the nearby stream emptied into the lake on its far side, and the crunch of grass and dead limbs as wildlife rummaged around the forest floor. The wind curled through Jed's hair as it came blustering through the Jeep's windows, and he leaned back against his headrest, taking it all in. Perfection. It was just perfect. The water sparkled a deep blue-green, and the waves lapped against the sandy shore gently. Butterflies went flitting back and forth across the windshield, one even getting far enough off course to find itself inside the truck, coming to a rest on Jed's outstretched index finger.

Memories of his childhood flooded back to him. He would spend his summers and long weekends out here—Christmas breaks, too. It was his favorite place in the world, and his uncle and aunt had given him his own room that was always ready for him to visit. Sometimes, he'd come to visit with the two of them, and sometimes with his mom, too. It was when he was older that he'd realized just how much his uncle and aunt helped out, giving his mom a mini vacation by allowing her to stay home alone.

Every Christmas, right through to New Year's, they went sledding, ice fishing, played tons of board games, and cozied up by the fire to watch holiday movies. Every holiday was spent between the four of them.

He smiled, watching the delicate white and gold wings of the small creature open and close. Perhaps it was tired, like he was, and had come here to rest. Perhaps they understood each other far more than was apparent on the surface.

He'd arrived at around nine in the morning, and when he finally pulled himself out of the Jeep, it was half past ten. Jed had spent over a full hour just watching the world around him move and thrive and pulse with life. He was home.

He entered the cabin, his first stop in the kitchen to light the pilot flame on the hot water heater. Afterward he set his body cam down on the windowsill next to the door to keep a track of his entries and exits. Then Jed went to lug his bags in and plop them into the corner of his bedroom. He stretched out on the bed, and a wave of relaxation and tiredness washed over him like it always did when he first arrived to the lake. Every time he visited, he took a nap, first thing—almost like his body needed time to recalibrate and acclimate to the slower pace of the countryside.

A few hours later, awake and refreshed, Jed sat on the balcony looking out over the water and into the trees beyond. He listened to the sounds of nature all around and let them anchor him in the present. The rippling of the waves, the chirps of birds in the trees, the crickets complaining about the heat of the noon sun enthralled him until the tone of his iPhone ringing interrupted his peace. He put the phone to his ear without looking to see who it was.

"Jed Gray speaking."

"Hi, Jed."

"Christie? Is everything alright?"

The sigh on the other end of the line told him the answer before she even went on.

"I'm alright. Just tired."

"Physically? Emotionally?"

He slipped into his therapist role so easily with her. It was something he still didn't understand, himself. None of his other relationships or friendships were that way. He didn't even get that mushy with his mom. Jed could hardly believe his own ears half the time when he was working on processing emotions and being present in the moment with Christie. It was almost… automatic.

"A bit physical. Mostly emotional."

He nodded to himself.

"I just saw your message, so I thought I'd call so you didn't think I was ignoring you," she added.

"Thank you for calling. It's good that you aren't ignoring me. Though I hadn't realized you would have a reason to."

On the other end of the line, Christie's mouth opened and closed.

"How do you always manage to have the upper hand in these conversations?" she asked, annoyance bubbling to the surface.

She hadn't called him to be psychoanalyzed. She just wanted to talk. Jed hummed thoughtfully. "Is that what it feels like when I call you out on your incorrect thought processes and patterns? Like we're in a competition, and I'm winning? Like I'm picking at your faults when I'm perfect?"

Her mouth opened and closed again, over, and over like a fish out of water. Eventually, she pulled the phone away from her ear and looked down at the screen, shock radiating out from her. She thought about hanging up.

Finally, she managed to say, "Yes."

"I'm sorry it feels that way. That's not what I'm trying to achieve."

"What are you trying to achieve then?" she asked, her tone snappy.

Jed, ever patient, smiled. "I want you to face the cycle of emotion you're stuck in, Christie. You feel something, you run away from it until you don't feel it anymore, you inch back into the situation and act like nothing happened, then the cycle repeats."

"Is the NYPD paying you a bonus or something to psycho-analyze me?"

Jed smiled again, his level, gentle tone never changing no matter how hers wavered between anger, denial, and surprise.

"For you, I'd do it for free."

Christie's eyes began to tear up. As though he could sense her shutting down, Jed prompted one more time, "Remember, Christie, I'll be here when you're ready to stand and face what you're feeling. I'll stand with you, and we can start small."

She huffed, and that pulled a grin onto his cheeks.

"I'm going now," she said.

Jed smiled.

"One more thing, Detective."

"What might that be?"

"I miss you, too," he said gently, "since that might be what you called to say, and you might have chickened out. Have a good evening. Call me if you need anything."

CHAPTER 21

"HEY, MOM."

Laurie was cooking, her potatoes boiling and her broccoli steaming away on the stovetop. She pushed her hair back out of her face, a little annoyed with herself that she'd forgotten to tie it up before coming into the kitchen.

"Hi, Jed! How are you?"

"Guess where I am?" he prompted.

Laurie was wrapping the hair tie she always kept on her wrist around her ash brown hair, careful not to tug on the ends of the fragile gray strands she was also trying to wrap up in her ponytail.

"Is guessing where you are going to tell me how you're doing?" she asked as she laughed a little.

"Yes, it will."

She tapped her finger against her cheek.

"Well, I guess this is a good puzzle for me to exercise my brain then, huh?"

On the other end of the line, Jed chuckled. "That's one way to look at it, yeah."

"My lucky guess is that you're at Highland."

Jed balked. "I don't know whether to be offended or happy. Have you secretly been tracking my location?"

Laurie laughed outright, tickled by the idea. "No, of course not, silly! It's the easiest answer."

"So, you're saying I'm predictable?"

"Well," she teased, "a version of that. You're a creature of habit. It's the only viable option. If you were at your apartment, I doubt you'd have brought it up."

She was right, Jed realized as he drank his water.

"And I doubt you'd be brave enough or crass enough to call me and boast about your manly achievement if you'd been… visiting your partner's house."

Jed choked furiously. He wiped water out of his eyes, and out of his ears, and had to blow his nose three times to get everything out. Jed coughed and hacked so hard at that insinuation that he could barely stand, and the water in his glass had spilled all over him. He was hunched over at the waist, trying to catch some air.

"Too far?"

He could hear his mom's sheepish comment coming through the line from his position on the floor.

"Yes."

Laurie laughed again, and he flushed as she continued. "I suppose it's not glamorous for a son and his mom to talk about the intricacies of sex."

"We haven't had sex. We haven't even kissed. Not that I—well I do, but I—" he huffed. "You know what I mean."

"Yes. I know what you mean, Jed."

He coughed again, trying to clear his windpipe.

Changing the subject, Laurie prompted, "What's the occasion?"

"What?"

"Well, you're at the lake. Usually, that means you're stressed out of your mind and you need a last-resort break, so you drove down."

"Last… resort?" he asked, feeling sheepish, like a child whose secrets were being exposed.

"Yes, last resort. Usually, you're already dead on your feet when you remember you've got the lake house to escape to."

"Well, Mom, that's not *entirely* true."

"Oh?"

He sighed before taking a deep breath. "Yes. I think about the lake all the time. I want to visit all the time. It's just that it's when I'm under pressure that I need the safe space the most."

In her kitchen, Laurie nodded along as she checked her potatoes. "I think I understand that."

"Well, yeah. That's where I'm at right now."

Sensing that he felt a little slighted by her remark about the lake being his last resort, she hurried to respond. "Of course, darling. I'm proud of you for taking the step you need to recover some of your strength. Especially after dealing with three murders in such a brief space of time."

Jed winced, realizing he'd so casually forgotten to mention the new murder to his mom.

"How is the case coming along?" she asked.

"Mom… there has been another murder since we last spoke."

Laurie placed her spoon on its wooden spoon rest and held onto the edge of the countertop behind her.

"F-four?"

"Yes. There's now four. That's the reason I came down to the lake."

"Has it been overwhelming you?"

"Yes, but more than that, I needed some time away to think. To look at all the elements and decipher them."

"I think deciding to do that at the lake was a good call. It's so calm and peaceful there that I'm confident it'll clear your mind and settle you enough to focus on the case the way you need to."

Jed nodded, standing up from his bed and pushing his feet into his house slippers.

"I sure hope it will. I've only got a week until I have to go back to my regularly-scheduled programming. I have no choice but to discover some answers this week."

After some chatting, they said their goodbyes, and Jed shook his head as though to shake off the grogginess that remained in him. He headed through the living room and out to the garage through the door at the back of the kitchen.

Jed had unpacked most of the things he'd brought with him—clothing, toiletries, snacks he couldn't do without—but the real treasure was in the back of his Jeep. He popped it open and caught the brown parcel as it slid out, almost crashing to the floor on top of his feet. That would have hurt.

After lugging it inside, he set it down on the floor in the open space between the kitchen and living room. He grabbed a knife from the cutlery drawer and ran the sharp metal down the side of the package carefully, peeling away the layer of protective paper and the bubble wrap beneath to reveal a whiteboard and a corkboard.

Just the tools he needed to really get into the meat of the case.

He padded back to the garage and into his trunk again to gather all his other supplies. There were thumbtacks, pens, card stock, and a mini printer so he could print pictures of all the suspects, victims, and locations of the murders. There were three balls of colored yarn, each color corresponding to a suspect, and lots of dry erase markers so he could draw lines, make notes, and process things out loud.

He left all the stationery in the same spot on the floor where he'd unboxed the boards and packed the food away into the fridge in the kitchen. Then, he went out onto the balcony to stare out across the open water. The sun was setting. His best bet, for now, was to have some dinner, take a dip in the lake, and organize his supplies afterward.

As his rice cooked and his chicken baked, Jed tried to keep a clear mind. Thoughts of Christie kept popping up uninvited. His concern for Max flitted across his mind, Hugh's invitation to lunch that he hadn't been able to accept this past week, somehow, came up as well. He made a mental note that he would have to try to make up for that by inviting Hugh to grab lunch when he got back into town.

Jed didn't like it, but Max seemed a little too sharp when it came to the 'word on the street'. Each time he called, the teenager would say something a little more outlandish—a little more random—and Jed had quickly realized that this was some sort of code he was meant to unravel. He'd written down all the cryptic pieces of information, but so far, he had not managed to break through to any of their meanings. It was quite the experience, really, being schooled on street code by a seventeen-year-old.

Fortunately, Jed wasn't one of those therapists that got super anal and up-in-arms about younger people teaching them things. Some older folks genuinely didn't believe young people had anything of value to share. Except Jed knew that wasn't true. It was a learned behavior, built from trauma they had suffered at the hands of their parents, that they were now turning over and reworking as a weapon against younger people.

The cycle of generational trauma was not easily recognizable. Where it was, it was easily breakable, but that didn't mean it wasn't hard. It took a great deal of conscious effort and a lot of dedication. Most people gave up before they even started.

He piled his dinner into a bowl, sitting down to eat at the kitchen island while admiring the golden sunlight as it came streaming in through the windows across from him. Jed remembered sitting in this kitchen as a kid, watching his aunt make cinnamon rolls, bake cupcakes, and make ice cream. He missed those carefree moments, missed how they would all run out to the lake for a swim after dinner, right before they settled in for the night.

There was no better night cap than a sticky cinnamon roll with a gleaming scoop of ice cream on top, and a tiny fork with which to eat it. He always struggled a bit before his aunt gave in and cut his cinnamon roll into small pieces for him. His uncle would chime in then, *"Make sure you let him start to do it on his own. We can't spoil him forever, you know."* Then his uncle would look over at him and smile. *"Ready for a swim now, Jed?"*

Jed's answer had always been always yes.

He peeled the shirt from his body and tossed it into a half-folded mess on the accent chair across from him. Then he stretched, raising his arms above his head and backward for a long moment.

Discarding his sweats in the same fashion, he ran toward the railing of the balcony, like he so often had as a child, and jumped over it into the water below. When the freezing mountain water touched his skin, his heart lurched, and he grimaced as he swam back to the top, bursting up from below as he gasped.

"Fuck," he muttered to himself, teeth chattering a bit. "I always f-forget just h-how cold it i-is."

Embarrassed by his stuttering even though he was entirely alone, Jed stopped speaking and focused on his breathing as he floated to the surface. He gazed out across the lake, where it spread as far as the eye could see to the horizon, and sighed. The pressure of the water against his chest fluctuated as he breathed out long and hard.

It's so beautiful here.

He turned to look at the cabin, its rafters rising high into the trees. Once you were in front of it, it was hard not to see the stark wood against the foliage all around it. But when you were driving up the winding road, the house was invisible in the trees. All you could see was water—blue. If you weren't paying attention as you pulled up to the water's edge, you'd drive right into it; it was that inviting.

He closed his eyes and let the overwhelming feeling of peace wash over him and settle into his bones.

Jed scoffed as he remembered his mom's statement that he only thought of the cabin as a last resort. It was so much more than that. It was his home. If he could have packed his things and left it all behind, this is where he would spend the rest of his days, tramping through the forest, listening to the birds sing and watching them flit through the air, and diving into the icy cold waters that came down from the Adirondack. If there were a perfect place on Earth, it was here.

After a few blissful minutes swimming and splashing about in the lake, Jed climbed out and checked the time, only to find that the clock read nine-thirty. That meant that he'd jumped into the lake exactly an hour after he'd finished eating.

Besides the time that had passed, Jed noticed he had a missed call from Christie. He stripped down to bare skin and toweled off on the porch, then strode into the house and to the bathroom in his room to turn the water on. He'd already acclimated to the ice of the lake, so he might as well get his daily scrubs in under the hot water from the pipes. Sure enough, when he opened the tap, the water that kept flooding down into the shower enclosure was even hotter than it was in his city abode. He showered quickly, then dialed Christie.

"Hi Christie," he said as soon as the line connected. "Is everything alright?"

As he dried his hair, he listened to the silence on the line.

"Theoretically speaking…" she began.

He grinned at that. That was his favorite game to play with his clients who were a little more resistant to the process—expressing the narrative retelling of what you are feeling, thinking, doing, or whatever else, through the use of an alibi or saying 'in theory'. It amused him to no end that Christie, of all people, was using it.

"What if I have done something wrong, and I need to confess, but don't know how to?"

"Why wouldn't you know how to confess? All confessing is, is owning up to your actions. Are you afraid of punishment?"

"Theoretically, there are no punishments. I suppose there are just the repercussions that come with expressing your feelings."

"That's an interesting way to put that. What do you see the repercussions of expressing your feelings being?" Jed leaned back in his seat.

Christie paused for a moment. "Theoretically speaking, I think there would be a lot of shame."

"Just shame? Or is that just the primary emotion that would be associated with self-expression... in theory?"

"It would be the primary emotion. But I also think that there would be quite a lot of anger and disappointment."

Jed's attention was fully hooked now. "Why would there be disappointment? Why that feeling, specifically?"

"Well, I guess because this person has always kept their feelings to themselves and sort them out alone."

"Right. But now this person is struggling to process their feelings on their own?"

"Yes. What does a person do at that point in time?"

Jed smiled. "That person must name and face the emotion that is bringing up the feelings of disappointment and shame. Shame and disappointment are not the primary emotions in this scenario. The primary emotion is fear—fear that this person might lose control over their situation or fear that their vulnerability might come back to haunt them."

He looked out the window for a moment, listening to how quiet the line was. It stayed that way.

"There are a couple of ways to handle the situation," Jed continued, realizing that Christie didn't know how to respond. "All in theory, of course. The way to solve this is through communicating, either with the self or with others. This person could choose to write their feelings out instead of speaking their feelings aloud to someone else. This is the more favorable option of the two because it introduces exposure therapy. Since you have the right and space at all times to really feel what you're feeling and note it down, it also spares your pride. It gives you privacy and keeps the threat of embarrassment at bay."

On the other end of the line, Christie was making notes about what Jed was saying.

"Are you still here with us, Christie?"

"Who's us?" she asked when she finally remembered to speak.

Jed chuckled, letting her attempt to deflect slide this time. "We three. You, me, and our good friend who's, sadly, stuck in a hypothetical situation."

"Yeah. I hope her freedom of expression helps her to stop feeling like she's going off her rockers.

"I'm confident it will. A combination of both those methods are necessary. However, since it offers the best of both worlds.

Your friend can benefit from an external listening ear when she needs answers and advice urgently, or your friend can benefit from an internal listening ear as they write and spend time thinking about and being present with what they are feeling."

Christie nodded along. She could see how that would make sense. "Well, Jed, I'd prefer to face this feeling face to face with you, and it's eating me alive. So... here goes."

Jed's hands stilled where they were running the towel across his body to get fully dry. Was this a confession of feelings? As soon as the thought entered his mind, he pushed it away. It simply wasn't. That wasn't even a viable option.

"I'm listening," he offered as encouragement.

"I miss you. A lot. It's really boring here without you—even though we spent literally most of our time talking over the most bizarre cases of murder and mutilation I have ever seen in my career."

"Can I give you an additional tool to make expressing how you feel more deliberate?"

She nodded, before realizing she had to use her words, since he couldn't see her.

"Why not? Go ahead."

"Well, when you're saying how you feel, it's very easy to stuff the confession into a longer, more complex sentence that works in favor of your confession being overlooked. It's self-sabotage. Say what you feel, alone. Don't add flowers, gifts, diamonds, nothing. Just what you feel. Allow it to be heard fully, received fully, and responded to fully."

He heard her take a deep breath before she spoke again. "I miss you, Jed. I miss you a lot."

She bit down on her lip, sure he'd merely congratulate her for completing the exercise.

"I miss you too, Christie."

She balked, staring at the phone.

Jed sat on the edge of his bed, closed his eyes, and leaned back. He pressed the phone closer to his ear. "So, how's your first day been without me?"

CHAPTER 22

JED'S MORNING PLANS WERE simple. Wake up, take a swim, make breakfast, work out, take a shower, then sit down to finally face this case, and that was exactly what he did when the new morning came. He rolled out of bed at six am, took a long swim to wake himself up, made his favorite breakfast to eat when he was at the lake—eggs, bacon, and fluffy pancakes—and went on a morning run to clear his mind for the day.

The morning air was chilly and crisp, and as he pushed himself into a steady running pace, the trees and just waking creatures of the forest whipping past him, he let his body fall into a rhythm that felt so natural that his mind could wander. This was one of the changes he had really needed. He loved his workout time at home, but running on a forest trail was an experience like no other. No cars honking, no pedestrians to dodge, no opening and closing shop doors to navigate around, no people walking dogs—just singing birds, sunlight streaming through the trees, and the natural sense of stillness that really helped him work through all that was on his mind.

Max. He needed to figure out what the boy had been trying to tell him with all the sporadic clues he seemed to drop during their conversations. Was it related to the case? Was Max trying to communicate something about his own life and relationships? Or was he just taking Jed for a ride?

Jed's feet struck the ground in time with his heartbeat, and he breathed in deeply as he passed by a smaller trail that led off the main one, deeper into the forest on the left side of the cabin.

Jed didn't think Max was trying to mess with him. The teenager had gotten better and better each week at communicating how he felt and correcting Jed when he said something that he hadn't liked. If anything, Max would be more likely to try to help Jed understand more about himself, even if he did it under the cover of prompting Jed to ask a leading question.

So, was Max trying to get Jed to understand something about himself? Max's usual pattern of prompting Jed to ask or discover things about him that were not on the surface was usually an unconscious process. Jed had noticed it in their recent session, where Max had inadvertently gone on and on about his dad, his dad's innocence, and his dad's business, which had allowed Jed to recognize Max's unconscious rewriting of the narrative his mother had taught him over the years. Max didn't usually come right out with confessions about himself or questions and wasn't direct in any of his requests for help.

Jed was almost at the end of the trail. There, he would turn around and head back to the cabin, keeping his pace as steady as he could. He looked down at his watch. It was almost seven, and he had done everything in his morning routine. Back home in the city, at this time of day, he would already be feeling the weight of the day ahead on top of him. But there was just something about the country that made him want to wake up early and get to work.

As he made a U-turn at the end of the trail, Jed decided these realizations about Max left him with only one option: Max was, somehow, trying to sneak him some insight into the case.

How would Max know this information, if that was what he was trying to do? Then again, Max seemed to know everything about everything that was happening on the streets of New York. Potentially, he might have been a bystander to one of the murders, or he knew someone that was a bystander, or he just liked to play detective. He was naturally very perceptive. Maybe he thought he had the case figured out and was trying to help Jed? And of course, Max was well aware of the difficulties with being explicit about confessions, murders, suspects, and victims on therapy lines. Even if he was talking to Jed, who had managed to gain his trust, Max wasn't stupid.

Jed was almost back to the cabin. He would have to revisit Max's input later on. For his first order of the day, he would be getting into the details of the case and trying to eliminate some of the suspects based on the information they had.

After his shower, he sat down in the living room in front of his whiteboard markers and all of his case files.

He marked off a small section in the left corner of the whiteboard, and with his red marker, wrote two words: 'why' and 'how'. Those were the first two things he needed to be clear on. They weren't case-related, but they were part of the reason he hadn't been able to make solid progress in deciphering this case.

His strategy for working with clients that struggled to overcome addiction was the same as it was for working on cases with the NYPD. The difference was that the 'why' and 'how' he emphasized and solidified with his addiction clients at the start of their therapy journey didn't cross over into investigative therapy in the same way.

As an addiction therapist, his job was to help his clients understand their why and their how. In investigative therapy, he needed to identify those two elements on his own. When he operated out of alignment with those two concepts, he realized his tendency to struggle with maintaining cohesive lines of thought as he tried to work through pretty much anything.

He stared at the whiteboard, tapping the marker against the wood table he was sitting at. The morning sun was just starting to come streaming through the kitchen window, and as the sun rose further into the sky, the line where the sunlight stopped on the wooden floor came closer and closer to where he was sitting.

The 'why' was easy. He was an investigative therapist because it gave him the opportunity to serve—to both solve crime and use his skills to bring about rehabilitation in hardened criminals. He did it because he wanted to repair the breach in society, where victims had been snuffed out by violent crimes. It was about solving their cases and bringing justice to the perpetrators. Defending the fallen.

He wrote it out on the board and sat back to look at the other word. *How?* The 'how' was hard. It was the complement to the 'why' because knowing what to fight for without knowing how to fight was no good to anyone. If anything, that would just drive a person to the point of insanity. Radical self-awareness without the tools to help oneself was self-destruction.

In the initial stages of his career as an investigative therapist, his 'how' had been straightforward, no nonsense, and to the point. *You're a therapist, so do what a therapist does. Analyze criminals based on their mental health, or any mental illnesses they appear to present with.*

It added a human element to case-solving, since rationales, motives, and the like, were controlled by, housed in, and showed outwardly by the mind. And it had worked. That was how he had gradually built his relationship with the NYPD and with the chief.

Now, though, that circumstances were so different. He would need a fresh approach. This time around, he wasn't just working on any case. He was working on a case that blurred the lines between his life as both an investigative therapist and as an addiction therapist. He was facing a nightmare—his clients were under attack.

Now, his 'how' required more than just cut-and-dry analysis.

His stomach started to turn over, the tasty food that he had just eaten beginning to turn sour. What this case needed was something he didn't want to give it. The case needed him. His story. His experiences. His memories. Memories he had no interest in dredging up from where he had buried them in his mind. But it was getting to the point where he had no choice. He was going to have to face himself to figure out who this murderer was and why they were targeting the homeless and the addicted.

Rising to his feet, Jed moved over to the whiteboard and wrote down his 'how'. *Face yourself to face the case.* At the bottom of the whiteboard, he wrote, *Why is the killer trying to frame me? What do I have to do with this?* That question had also been evading him. No matter what angle he looked at it from, he had trouble making it make sense in a way that would fit into the case.

Back in his position at his makeshift desk, he stared down at the to-do list he had haphazardly jotted down before bed. To make genuine sense of any of this, he would need to analyze things in a myriad of different ways. First, he needed to analyze chronologically—what happened when, what happened next, and what happened after that. Then, he needed to analyze the chain of events by victim, then by suspect. He checked the first thing off his list. He gathered his case materials and started a read-through of the details.

After jotting down the dates, times, and locations of each of the four murders that had taken place in the last few weeks, he sat down again and looked at his files. On the corner of his whiteboard, he had made a list of all the commonalities across the four murders.

All the victims were men, three of the four victims were homeless, three of the four victims were over the age of fifty, and all four of the victims had a history of substance abuse or were actively in addiction. All the victims died from a combination of trauma wounds, and a drug overdose in Ethan's case. Three of the four victims had been attacked in areas with CCTV surveillance, which had confirmed that those three older men had been murdered by a suspect with a consistent profile across three of the four murders.

There were three suspects. Thiago Carrillo, a business-man that had repeatedly demonstrated and expressed rage at watching his business crash because the city continued to reject his development plans. Next was John Whitman, a self-proclaimed New York philanthropist with a sneaky, violent past... and an alibi that didn't check out. Finally, was Lauren Finch, the second victim's ex-lover that appeared to be interested in the remuneration schemes of life insurance policies, who was already seeing someone else and also had an unreliable alibi. There was also one voicemail from a man who had professed to be Ethan's murderer that could either be from one of these two men or a very arrogant contract killer.

He took a break to get a drink of cold water from the cooler and stood in the doorway, gazing out across the water toward the woods beyond. It was a beautiful day, and Jed was tempted to take another quick swim before getting back to work, but hesitated. He should keep pressing on and try to crack into the heart of things for a couple of hours before just giving in to the call of the cold water. Jed would save the swim for sunset, as a little treat. He turned back to his work.

Jed shuffled his papers around, rearranging them according to the next stage of the analysis—victims on one side, suspects on the other. Crime scene details, clues, and location and time details were grouped together in one corner, while he kept the suspect's profile in the corner closest to him.

This piece of information had been consistent throughout the case, and it had often confused Jed. Whoever he was, the killer was around six feet in tall and was of slim build. Physically, that's about all they knew because he always wore a ski mask, hoodie, and gloves at the scene of the crime.

There was the time that the killer had looked right at the camera after finishing his attack on the most recent victim, though. Jed pulled up the replay of the CCTV footage from September 28th at nine pm. That was the most recent attack on record, and it seemed that the killer had been particularly blood-hungry that night. The sixty something year old Larry hadn't stood a chance. He'd been stabbed *fifty-three times.*

Thirteen of those stab wounds had been to the old man's face and head. It had taken them hours to identify the victim; he'd been a bleeding mass of flesh that was unrecognizable.

Jed remembered Christie's words as she recounted the formal details of the case.

"Death of one Larry Wilcrow by shock and hemorrhage as a result of repeated sharp-force trauma. Suspect sustained a total of fifty-three stab wounds, fifteen to the neck and shoulders, thirteen to the abdominal areas, and twenty-five to the face and head."

This attack had been different, though. The killer had revealed his eyes to the camera. At least, that's what it seemed like he was doing. Jed let the video play over and over, staring at it, eyes fixed on the man's actions. He'd gotten to his feet, taken a step back, and turned to walk back down the road in the direction he'd come from.

It was when the killer turned that the interesting thing happened. The man raised his head, and his eyes moved to the streetlight where the CCTV camera sat. His eyes were only in the position for a split second before the rest of his head turned, and he looked over to his right, as though checking his surroundings. Then he was gone.

Jed let the video replay for the fourth time. Such an insignificant gesture, there one moment, gone the next, but a niggling feeling began in the back of his mind. It could be a total coincidence. Was he was just turning his head and noticed something, or just turning his head and hadn't looked at the light at all?

Whatever it was, Jed knew without a doubt that for a split second, he could see the killer's eyes.

He sat back in his seat and let his thoughts run for a while. He could see the image clearly alright—clearly enough to see the man's irises, but not quite clear enough to see their color. Still, Jed could tell that the killer was Caucasian from the ring of pale flesh around his eyes where they showed through the opening in the ski mask.

After replaying the video seven more times, he was sure that the suspect's eyes were not brown, not gray, and not hazel. That left two options: green or blue. Jed's own eyes burned from watching the video on the highest brightness his computer would allow, and his stomach was turning over from watching the murder unfold repeatedly. He could see that there were large, dark patches of blood-stained fabric on the front of the killer's sweater as he turned and the streetlight illuminated him. He could also see a kind of wild, vengeful look in his eyes for the fraction of a moment he appeared to look at the camera.

Jed added 'blue/green eyes' and 'Caucasian' to the list of traits before him before shooting a voice message to Christie, explaining what he had discovered and how. Then, he took another quick break, again looking out over the water as it came to shore, glistening in the soft sunlight that was streaming down through small breaks in the clouds. It was beautiful out, but the bright landscape couldn't seem to break through the somber mood that had settled into his bones.

It was going to be a long day.

CHAPTER 23

AFTER MAKING AND HAVING a hearty lunch and clearing up the kitchen, his phone rang. It was Christie, and his heart leapt.

Jed picked up the phone to hear her voice on the other end say, "Hey."

"Good afternoon, Detective."

He was sitting on the patio now, taking in the afternoon breeze that was blowing in off the water.

"How are you? Are you having fun?"

Jed chuckled, then sighed. "Yes, but no. It's nice to be surrounded by nature and to just… absorb the peace here. But it's hard to have peace when the case is taking up absolutely all the brain power I currently have."

"I get that," she agreed as she tossed her pen onto the table in front of her and pressed her hand against the bridge of her nose. "Believe me, I get that."

"How have you been holding up?" he asked cautiously.

"I've been okay. Just… you know. Journaling."

"Journaling. That's always a good way to get our thoughts onto paper so they don't drive us insane."

"Yeah. That's what a therapist friend of mine told me."

Jed nodded, playing along, though he couldn't hide the amusement in his voice. "Your friend knows what they're on about. I reckon you should keep them around."

Christie laughed a little. "Yeah. He'd love to hear you say that."

"I bet he would. But has the journaling been helping? I know, sometimes, it takes a while before it helps us feel lighter."

"Well, it's helped with some things. With other things..." She trailed off.

Jed spoke into the phone, almost cooing, "Some things just need more care and time. So, we must keep treating them gently until they give way."

She sighed. "Right."

"And of course, you know I'm here for you if you want to work through something together."

Christie grinned to herself. "Thank you. I might take you up on that offer some day. Have you been finding peace in some of your moments, at least?"

He took a long drink from his glass of lemonade and thought about her question.

"I have, yes. Usually, when I'm on the phone with my mom, I feel at peace. She's such a sweetheart. She tries so much to help me, bless her sweet soul."

"I'm happy you have her support," Christie said.

Jed looked down at the phone where it was resting on the small wooden side table next to him. For the first time since he'd met her, he hesitated to speak. "I sense you might be trying to tell me something, except you haven't actually said anything."

"Maybe," was her only reply.

"I'm happy to have her support as well. If it weren't for her, things would be... different. She's my rock."

Christie nodded. "I can tell you two are very close."

"We are. Are you close with your parents?"

Jed's tone hadn't changed from the normal, conversational one he'd been using, but she could feel the soft concern in the question as tangibly as she could feel the soft sheets in the death grip she had them in.

"I was. But they aren't around anymore."

Jed stared at the phone for a second before looking out across the water again. "And is their absence temporary, or is it the permanent kind?"

Christie swallowed, willing herself to not just face the truth, but also to say it out loud.

"They passed away a few years ago. Both at the same time—in a house fire."

Jed's mouth wanted to fall open, but he kept his composure, even though he could feel his heart breaking for Christie. "I'm sorry."

"Yeah. Me, too."

"It must have been especially hard to lose them both at the same time."

"It was. Still is," she said. Her voice was close to a whisper. "But in a strange way, I'm glad it happened that way. My mom was ill—she couldn't move very much on her own. When the fire started, both of them wouldn't have made it out in time, and my dad just... refused to leave her behind."

"Wow. In a bittersweet way, that's sort of touching."

Christie smiled. "I know. My dad loved my mom very much. He wouldn't have left her behind, no matter what. The ultimate price to pay for love. It was still a terrible loss."

"How has the grieving process been?"

She scratched her arm, looking at the family portrait of her smiling parents and a much younger version of herself on the wall opposite her bed.

"I'm not sure. Some days, I'm fine. Some days, I think I'm fine and break into a million pieces."

Jed closed his eyes. He didn't like the image that was coming to mind—of Christie hunched over, sobbing silently, alone. Jed wished he could wrap his arms around her right then. He wished he could hold her until she was healed of all that pain.

Instead, he cleared his throat. "Up and down. Like a sine wave. That's usually how the healing process plays out."

Christie smiled at the reference. "What if I didn't know what a sine wave was, Gray?"

Jed grinned. "Then you'd say so and I'd explain. But you do, so you get the reference."

They both laughed.

Christie shook her whole body. She felt better. "Yeah, I got the reference. But speaking of references—"

"Before you segway into the case, I want you to know something."

Christie's heart pounded painfully within her for a few fear-stricken moments. Rationality won out against her thoughts of '*Is he about to confess something romantic?*' She rolled her eyes. That could only happen if he had feelings for her. She was sure he didn't.

"What's on your mind?" she asked, as casually as she could.

"You are."

She waited.

"I want you to know that I'm sorry for your loss, and even more than that, I wish I was there right now to give you the biggest hug. I hate I found this out while I'm away."

"It's okay," she managed to say, though tears welled in her eyes.

"Is it?"

"Well, it's already happened that way, hasn't it?"

Her voice was low, and her words were measured. Jed could hear the coming tears in her voice even though she tried to hide them. He stared at the railing in front of him.

"Yes, it has," he answered, raising his head to look at the tree next to the cabin, "but that doesn't mean we're not allowed to wish it were different. When I get back, a big hug is waiting for you."

She laughed a little, then sighed. "I'll be looking forward to that."

"So am I. Now, what were you saying about references?"

"I've been going through the info and resources you've been sending over the past few days. I think we're finally getting somewhere. In fact, I think I need to get a lake house of my own if this is how sharp it makes you on the job."

Jed threw his head back and laughed. On the other end of the line, Christie couldn't help the grin that spread across her cheeks as he laughed.

"It's a worthy investment—high long-term return."

Teasingly, Christie admonished him, "Spoken like a true businessman. Does the property belong to you?"

"No, it's my aunt & uncle's. But they love me, so they let me visit whenever I want to."

"Oh! I get that. It must be nice to have free access to it in that way."

"It is. Hopefully, though, I'll have my own piece of lake-front soon."

"We could buy it together after this lousy case is over. But only if you promise not to hog it all the time."

Jed laughed again, and Christie smiled. She loved hearing him laugh that way – it always made her heart expand with joy.

"No promises."

"Whatever, Gray."

CHAPTER 24

AFTER DINNER, JED SAT at the table in front of his whiteboard, yet again. He had set up the corkboard next to it and created his logic map. Pictures of the suspects, the crime scenes, victims, and the case details were pinned to the board, and red cord ran from connected detail to connected detail to help him visualize what was happening.

Except, it was only managing to confuse him. Jed hadn't figured out why that was yet. Earlier, he had given up in favor of making food—a yummy homemade pizza and his favorite drink, Lyre's. The bittersweet orange and rich peach flavors of the drink were a refreshing accompaniment to the pizza's summery palate, and he'd sighed a deep sigh of satisfaction after he'd finished the meal.

The overhead lights were on since the sun had begun to set, and he looked away from the boards and out the door. He'd promised himself he'd take a sunset swim today, and though he hadn't made as much progress as he'd like to have made, he still planned to honor his word.

He stood up. Pulling the shirt over his head, he tossed it to the chair. He pulled his feet free from his sweatpants and dropped them in a neat pile on the chair. He walked to the balcony that overlooked the water and stared down at the deep blue for a minute or two. This was his favorite feature of the house, how it jutted out over the water and turned the balcony into more than just a relaxing space to watch the sun rise and set. It was also a diving platform.

He jumped. Splashing around in the cold water, he dove, spending some time below the surface before breaching again. Thoughts of Christie wouldn't leave him be. He wondered if she was serious about wanting to buy land on the lakefront. He wondered what that would mean for their relationship—and for his relationship with the lake.

It was his private escape. If she was serious, would her presence in the future interfere with his feeling of rest when he visited? Yet Jed had to be truthful with himself. What he was really trying to figure out was if he would fall even deeper in love with the lake, because Christie would become associated with it. If that ended up being the case, would that mean that he was falling in love with her?

He pushed the thought to the back of his mind as he swam to shore. That would have to be tackled another day. Right here, right now, as the sun disappeared behind the trees on the far side of the lake, he needed to remain focused on the case. He needed to make some kind of significant progress before he went to bed.

Jed only had two more full days at the lake. The first three had flown by in blur-like fashion, and he would need to get back to the city for the weekend so he could reintegrate himself into his normal routines ahead of the new workweek. It was now or never.

As he sat at the table and stared at the evidence once again, he picked up his notebook and pen. It was time to work things out. He would begin with the least likely suspect—Lauren.

Lauren was a thirty-three-year-old waitress who looked older than her years. Life had taken its toll on her. She was 5'6" in tall, had green eyes, long brunette hair, and was the reason he had spent so much time trying to figure out if the killer's eyes had been green or blue. Even though the height profiles were different for Lauren and for the killer, who was six feet tall, Jed knew she could not have been the one to execute the murder herself.

If the killer's eyes had been green, he could have ruled that maybe, just maybe, Lauren had some relative who had been willing to kill Warren for her. Even then, why would she have gone to as much trouble as she did? Warren hadn't been the only victim. He had been the second of four. That meant that if Lauren wanted to kill Warren, she would have just killed *him*, right? Jed scratched his chin.

Maybe she had killed more than one person to cover up her motive. That could be plausible. But then, what would her motive be? Had she turned on the homeless because she blamed the homeless population for causing her to lose the love of her life? Jed tapped his pen on the table. Her Reddit profile had a few questions about insurance policies, and some about drugs. Both could be linked to the case since Warren had been in active addiction when he had been murdered.

Was it that Lauren wanted to kill him to get back at him for leaving her? For abandoning their relationship? It was possible. But something about it didn't sit right with Jed. If their relationship had been as bright and as promising as Lauren had made it seem during the interview, why would she have turned to vindication and revenge when the relationship ended? Jed found this especially doubtful because it had ended because of addiction rather than infidelity or anything else that would usually cause a partner to react negatively. For Jed, that part was not adding up.

He replayed the interview, scrolling to fifteen minutes into Lauren's section and letting the rest of the tape play out.

"We were perfect together. We were so happy. I knew he had a history of using drugs, but I never thought he would go back to using them. He promised me that he was working on it. That he was getting help. But he wasn't. He was using all our money that we had planned to save up to buy a home, to buy drugs. I had no idea.

On the day he got up and left, I thought it was a prank. I couldn't believe it. But he was leaving. He left. He chose the streets, and he chose his addiction. Nothing I said could change his mind, not even the future we had been working so hard on to build together. It all meant nothing compared to the high of drugs. He betrayed me. I still haven't been able to date anyone else. All I wanted was him. All I wanted was us."

That did not sound like the mindset of a woman who had been ready to kill. Emotions showed up at every chance they got—they were cocky things, always bursting to be at the surface, always showing up in the eyes, always showing up on the features or in the body language. He had watched Christie interview all three suspects, and Lauren had been the most non-threatening of them all. The only thing he had read in her body language, tone, and facial features was devastation and disbelief. Not only had she lost the man she loved in terms of their relationship, but he was also now far beyond ever being able to come back, ever being able to reconcile, or ever being able to work things out. He was dead.

On the flip side of things, though, she had lied about where she had been at the time of the murder—and with whom. She had not only arrived to the movies late, but she had arrived with a man. Jed and Christie had later learned was her date. Had they just been coming back from killing Warren?

Jed wrote his thoughts down on the paper beneath her name, then transferred the most important points to the whiteboard with his marker. He took a long drink of water before sitting back down to face the paper again. Next on the list was John Whitman.

Whitman was 5'11", sixty-five years old, and had dark brown eyes and black hair that was balding around the perimeter of his head. He was slim and limber—save for his limp. John was Caucasian and had a lot of large, brown freckled spots across his face and down his neck. Jed figured they continued across his entire body.

John's aptitude at moving between opposite emotional states was frightening. In the blink of an eye, he had gone from sweet and charming to an anger that felt like an explicit threat. His alibi had failed, too. He'd conveniently gone on a forty-five-minute walk right when Allan's murder had taken place. Had he left work to go murder a homeless person, then head casually back to work? Allan wasn't one of the men he'd previously had altercations with, so he wondered whether Whitman was trying to get back at the community because he perceived them as ungrateful or dismissive of his contributions and attempts to help them?

Whitman had a limp on his left side and walked in a way that looked very unsteady to the casual observer. He frequently looked like he was on the verge of toppling over, and Jed had noticed this in his observations of the man's daily activities on the streets of New York whenever he walked by the side of town Whitman frequented.

A limp like that could not be hidden. Jed opened his computer, clicked the replay of the first murder, and watched it through to the end. Then, he watched the second and fourth in like manner. This time, he was focusing on the gait of the killer. Whoever this man was, he walked calmly, unhurriedly, and with confident strides. There was no sign of a limp, whatsoever. That meant that John Whitman, with a limp that could be seen a mile away, was not the killer. At least, he hadn't done it himself. Jed looked over his findings from John's Reddit page once again.

Was this enough to conclude that John had a strong enough motive to hire someone to attack and murder homeless people? The same people he was raising private funding to help? The same people he had spent countless hours on Reddit asking questions about how to properly buy clothes and prepare food for?

John seemed to have a history of aggression in his younger years. His body language showed that much, and so had his confession on Reddit. Jed took a sip of his water. He refilled his glass from the cooler and stopped by the boards on his way back to his desk to write his findings under John's name.

He didn't like to think it, but it was feeling like the case was going to end up at a stalemate. A long sigh escaped him, and he looked out through the window into the growing darkness of the forest beyond the cabin. If none of these three suspects checked out as being the killer themselves, the probability of the killer being contracted grew. But if that were true, why had the contract killer sought out his number and called to gloat?

Thiago Carrillo was the last suspect. The evidence made the strongest case for him to be behind the murders. Despite Jed's feelings of doubt concerning the previous two suspects, he knew well enough that it would not be wise to write off the two just because he didn't think they were violent enough. The inner workings of the human mind were not always visible on the outside. He knew he could put nothing past anyone.

There was always a possibility that people had connections that weren't apparent, motives that were hidden, and ways of doing things that couldn't be understood right away. He planned to keep an eye on them, as well as their activity, and continue to do research to see if he could build a stronger case for their involvement in the situation. For now, it was looking like they weren't the ones he and Christie should be focused on.

Looking at all the evidence in front of him—the notes he had taken in the interview stage, the evidence he had found online, and the official documents the NYPD had acquired—Jed realized Carrillo had made quite a case for himself. He was an aggressive and unfair enough boss, so much so that his employees and colleagues felt the need to have an entire Discord server with over one thousand members lamenting about his unacceptable behavior on a daily basis.

He was cunning enough to threaten his employees without thinking twice about it but keep them paid well enough that they wouldn't leave, and he was determined enough to swear that the New York City Council would regret their decision to reject his building proposals. Not to mention that he was confident enough to openly declare that he would regain the money he had lost in the last quarter before the year ended.

How did he plan to regain twenty-five million dollars in four months? How did he plan to make the city regret their rejection of the proposal? In the interview, Christie had asked Carrillo how he felt about losing his business proposal because of twenty homeless men. Looking at things now, from the new perspective he had after watching the recorded video that was found in the discord server, Jed began to connect the dots that he'd been struggling with before.

Did Carrillo intend to win back his profits by eliminating the people who were standing in the way of his development? Was his plan to get rid of the homeless people so that the New York City Council would have no choice but to approve his proposals? Was he desperate enough to sacrifice the lives of twenty men just so he could build another two apartment buildings? The department still hadn't secured his financial statements, so the argument that he may have hired out his dirty work was still up in the air.

Jed could see that he was, in fact, desperate enough. In that two-minute span of video recording, Carrillo had declared himself an enemy of the state by threatening to make sure that the city council regretted their decision. Jed was no businessman, but how did Carrillo plan to regain all the losses of the previous quarter, plus the rest of the losses from the first two quarters of the year, in the remaining four months of the year? Jed paused his writing to count on his fingers.

September... October... November... December... Yes, that was four months.

Jed was sure the city council hadn't just decided to reject his plans for this past quarter, but rather that they had been rejecting his plans from the start of the year. It wasn't like those twenty homeless men had just appeared out of nowhere. They had always lived in those spaces, derelict buildings, that no one seemed to have use for anymore.

Did he have the motive? Yes, he did. Did he have the resources to execute it? Yes, he did. Did he have the time to execute it? Yes, he did. What Jed wasn't sure about were the logistics of how he would have done it, if he had done it. And where was the proof they needed to verify his involvement?

The forty-five-year-old was 5'11", had a potbelly, and was completely bald. Since he was Mexican by nationality, he had darker, more tanned skin than the killer did. His gait was different, too, Jed remembered. Carrillo walked swiftly and a bit unsteadily, like he was always in a rush to get to where he was going, and a bit like he was going to topple over from walking so swiftly. He did not have the lazily confident stride that the killer had in all three crime scene videos.

Jed watched the videos again to be sure. Besides his physical profile not aligning with that of the killer, Jed had already figured that if Carrillo was behind the murders, he would not have been the one to do them himself. He was a man with much to lose. He had a family—a wife and two little kids—a big business with a huge reputation for the quality of their construction, and his own personal reputation to maintain, which he seemed to take great pride in. Jed could see it from the way he had responded when Christie had mentioned that he had come under public scrutiny in the recent investigations into the attack on homeless people. Just the very mention of homeless people had set him off in that interview.

From the very beginning, when he and Christie had been analyzing the case, Jed had brought up that if Carrillo was behind the murders, he would likely have hired them out. That was where things got complicated, though it would also make things easier. If Carrillo was behind the murders, and had contracted them to someone else, then the voicemail and call would make sense. Of all three suspects, he was the one most likely to be able to pull off such a gig. He had the money, the connections, the motive... it all seemed to point to him.

Jed pulled up his bookmarked URLs and went back to the Discord server to see if anything had been posted since the last time he had been on the site. Since all the users in the server had anonymous usernames and the most random set of icons as their displays for their profile, no one would suspect him if he asked a question.

Everyone there was just as afraid of the server being discovered as they were of their identities being revealed. He wouldn't be surprised if some of the highest in command at Carrillo Contracting were on the server as well. He seemed to treat everyone poorly, so they were probably on here lamenting the same as everyone else.

Jed typed. *I know we agree that Carrillo is money hungry and power hungry and all, but do you really think he's involved with the murders that have been taking place recently?*

Jed held his breath as he pressed send. His username was just as anonymous, and his profile was just as untraceable as the other members of the servers were. He knew that he would not be discovered to be the one behind the question. It still made him a little anxious, though, and after double checking to see that the message had been sent, he closed down his computer. For now, he would continue working with what he had, and he would check to see if anyone had responded before he went to sleep.

Asking his workers whether they thought he had the potential to be a murderer, since their boss so readily displayed anger, aggression, and manipulation towards them, was Jed's bright idea for figuring out if he should seriously be considering Carrillo's involvement with a contract-killer.

On the other side of things, why would a contract-killer be hired to use knives to commit murders? That part didn't seem to make sense. Since the very beginning of the case, Jed had wondered why the killer had chosen to use a knife. Guns were very easy to come by in the city; as unfortunate as that reality was, it could not be ignored. Knives were tactile things and required contact with a victim to be weaponized effectively. That meant that the killer had consciously decided to get up close and personal with his victims in order to murder them, four times in a row. More than just the knives, why would any experienced, contracted killer risk being traced and discovered by calling the investigative therapist that was working on the case?

Then what Max had said to him came to mind. This killer was not afraid to attack older homeless men. In fact, it was only older homeless men that he had been attacking throughout his rampage in the past weeks, or compromised men like Ethan, who had been under the influence of Fentanyl. All easy to overpower. Jed's heart squeezed at the memory of what the voicemail said. *Maybe you should teach your clients how to fight so I can't overpower them so easily next time?* He took a deep breath.

Max's statement had been what had led Jed to realizing that the killer might not be attacking younger homeless men on purpose. That was part of his strategy.

His young client, a young homeless boy himself, had ever so casually pointed out a key component of what the investigative team knew about the killer so far. As far as they could see, he appeared to be afraid to attack younger men. That led them to inferring that he was a younger man himself. Overpowering and killing older, frail men would be much easier for a younger man than attacking outright, with a knife, younger, more volatile, homeless men.

That still did not answer the question of why the killer had decided to use a knife as his tool of choice. Was it he wanted to see his victims' faces up close while he hacked them to death? Was it some sort of satisfaction he got from blood splashing all over him as he committed the crime? Was it the screams that pleased him so much? Was it a preoccupation with how he chose to kill each victim—choosing to inflict stab wounds in specific areas? Had he studied his victims before executing the act? And why was he so fixated on marring the faces of the victims?

Jed's theory that he had shared with Christie about the suspect wanting to mar the faces of the homeless men he killed came back up. Was this supposed to be some sort of heroic, selfless, societal act? Was he trying to 'clean up the streets'?

That question led Jed back to the thought of the killer being contracted. In turn, he revisited the question of why the killer had chosen to use a knife to execute these murders. He stared down at the paper in front of him, rereading the scribbles he had hurriedly placed down as theories had run across his mind.

Christie was right. This case was a doozy. On top of all that, he still couldn't reconcile Ethan's death as part of the case. He did have stab wounds that could have been from the same killer they were trying to decipher, but there had been no dagger found at the crime scene. Was it that the murderer had found Ethan already drugged up and had gotten into a scuffle with him that resulted in Ethan's arm ending up broken? Had he failed to overpower Ethan—which would prove their theory that the killer was more easily able to overpower elderly, weaker victims? Jed sighed. If he thought about it long enough, it all made sense. But he still found that particular incident a bit odd.

With the call in the mix, it confirmed that the same killer had killed all the victims. He had just found Ethan's case a good opportunity to gloat to Jed about his failures as a therapist.

After more than another hour of trying to work through those two remaining thoughts that contradicted each other and prevented him from making further progress, Jed gave up. He was exhausted. He felt like he had looked over the crime scene photos for the hundredth time. All he wanted to do was have a late snack, take a well-deserved shower, and crawl into bed.

Frustration was building up inside him, and it made his muscles ache. As Jed stood and stretched his arms to the ceiling, twisting to the sides to relieve the aches in his back, his phone rang. It blared through the silent cabin, and he jerked before sighing into the ceiling. He was not in the best mood and wasn't sure he would be able to maintain an uplifting conversation with whoever it was that was calling him at this ungodly hour. In any case, he knew that it could only be one of two persons calling him—his two favorite women. That made him pick up the phone. It was his mom.

"Hi, Mom."

"Hi, baby!"

Jed smiled. "How have you been? I was planning to call you earlier today, but I got busy with the case. I'm sorry."

"That's okay, Jed. I've been working around the house, doing a little cleaning here and there, and I started working on my story today."

Jed nodded. "That's great news. How's it going so far?"

"It's going well, actually. I'm a bit surprised. It's my first time writing a mystery novel, and I thought it would be a bit more difficult to get into the heart of the mystery, and, you know, solving the crime, outlining the suspects… things like that."

"Well, you read a lot of mystery books to me as bedtime stories when I was younger, so I think you'll do fine."

Jed chuckled and his mom smiled on the other end of the line.

"I sure hope so. What did you have for dinner?"

"Um, well, today I made myself some fresh pizza. For the past few days, I've been having fresh caught fish—you know how I feel about fish when I'm at the lake."

"I know it well. It's the only time you eat fish that often."

They both laughed.

"Guilty as charged. It tastes—real—here. I don't know how to explain it. But there's something different about catching a fish right out of the water, walking ashore and tossing it into a frying pan right away. There's nothing quite like it."

"We can both agree to that."

Jed hummed. He thought he could see a bear in the distance, close to the shoreline, moving in the darkness. He was probably looking for a good place to nap. Jed couldn't blame him.

"Jed," his mother began.

He looked back to the table in front of him as his mom's voice interrupted his thoughts of sleep.

"How have you really been doing with this case? I know you went to the lake to get a break from everything and clear your mind so you could focus more on it. But how has solving it been? Anything solid yet?"

Jed sighed.

"Oh, do you not want to talk about it?" his mom asked.

"No, it's not that," Jed hurried to say. He didn't want to hurt his mom's feelings. "It's just that it's been very stressful—more stressful than usual. I think it's because it's so close to home for me. These victims were people that I could have... should have... worked with in addiction therapy to help them get their lives back together. One of them *was* a client of mine. So, to see them fall victim to murder... well, it's harder for me to separate myself from the case in order to look at it objectively."

Laurie nodded along, sipping on her cup of warm tea as she listened to Jed explain.

"I did make a good deal of progress today, however, but there's just one more thing that doesn't seem to want to crack so I can see what it's hiding beneath it. I keep going back and forth between two thoughts—one leads me to the other, and then that one leads me back to the other."

He sighed.

"There's nothing in between that I have to decipher, but it's just that I need to break down one of those thoughts so I can move forward, and I'm having trouble doing that."

Laurie offered her understanding. "I think I understand. Is it something like, 'If A is red, then B is blue,' but they're both not matching with those colors even though they should be?"

"Yes. Exactly like that. That's how it should be, but that's not how it is. And I'm not able to figure out why or which one of the concepts is the problem… which one needs to change."

"I think I get that. Are you planning to go to bed tonight and try again tomorrow morning?"

Jed looked at the clock in the hallway and grimaced. "Yes. That's the plan, for now. I've been at it since I woke up this morning, and it's almost midnight. I need to get some sleep. Maybe, in the morning, I'll be able to think a bit clearer and one of those thoughts will either make more sense or less sense. Either way, I'll be able to move forward with my processing."

"Hopefully, that's the case. You should have a snack before you go to bed."

Jed laughed. "Yes, Mom, I'm planning to have a snack before bed. I am kind of hungry right now. The last thing I ate was dinner at around six."

"Okay, great," Laurie chimed. "How have you and your lady friend been? Have you spoken to her since you got to the lake?"

"Yeah, I've spoken to her every day since I've been here. I had a call with her earlier. We discussed the case for a little while, some personal things for a little while, and then I got back to work."

"That's good. I just wanted to make sure that you hadn't completely isolated yourself. And that you were talking to somebody, even if it wasn't me. I know how you get when you hyper-focus on something. I don't want you to forget to check in with people because we won't know how you're doing, otherwise."

A grin spread across Jed's face as he thought of his mom's kindness. "Thanks, Mom. I've been checking in. Even if it's just a text message."

"Good. You're doing a great job. Don't forget that, okay? This case is probably harder than you're even making it seem. I can't imagine what it must be like to try to sit down and figure out four murders with three suspects and none of them seeming to make sense."

"Yep." Jed sighed. "It's been difficult. But I'm trying to keep pressing on because I know that there has to be something I'm either overlooking or just haven't figured out yet."

"You'll figure it out. I know you will. And I'm very proud of you for trying so hard and for making the progress you have been making. You know that, right?"

"Come on, Mom," Jed complained. "Don't make me start crying."

Laurie laughed. She looked out the window at the street-light at the end of her driveway and watched as a couple of cars rolled by. "It's important! I want you to know that I'm proud of you. I've always been proud of you, but I just felt like saying it tonight."

Jed pressed his fingers against the bridge of his nose, trying to regain control of his leaking eyes. "Thanks, Mom. I appreciate that."

"Of course. Now, go eat a snack. And then drink some water. And go to bed."

Jed laughed. "You sound like when I was a teenager."

"Because I'm still your mom!" Laurie exclaimed. "And call Christie before bed."

A laugh escaped Jed's lips. He had been planning to call her but had been going back and forth in his mind about whether he should. They had already spoken earlier that day, and he didn't want to disturb her if she had already fallen asleep.

"I will, Mom. I will."

Freshly showered and in his room, Jed looked down at his phone. He wasn't sure if he should bother to call. It was almost one in the morning. She had probably gone to sleep, and he didn't want to disturb her. But, despite all the spiraling thoughts in his mind, he wanted to talk to her—even if only to hear her voice for a few minutes. That's all he needed. He hesitated only a second longer before pressing the green call button. She picked up on the first ring.

"Hi, Jed."

"Good morning, Detective."

On the other end of the line, he heard her laugh a little. "You remind me of a guy friend I have. Always calling me 'kid' just to reinforce the friend zone. As if I was trying to get out of the friend zone with him in the first place."

Jed froze. "So, you interpret me calling you 'Detective' as me trying to put you in the friend zone?"

"Trying to? I thought I was in the friend zone."

Jed grinned. It was his turn to scratch his arm. "You weren't exactly in the friend zone."

"What zone was I in?"

"You're in the zone of colleague, currently."

"Oh! So, you don't even consider me your friend, huh?"

"No. That is not what I'm saying."

Christie swallowed the words she was about to say. His tone had changed to that deep, firm, masculine one he always used when he was trying to calm her down and regain control of the situation.

"You are my friend. But you're also my colleague. That's what I'm trying to say."

"Is that all you're trying to say?" She teased.

This would be the perfect time to say what he really wanted to say, Jed realized. But he didn't. That needed to wait until their plates were both clear.

"For now, yes. In any case, what are you doing up at this hour?" he asked, neatly diverting the topic away from what he knew she was going to ask next.

"I should be asking you that, Gray."

"I've been up working on the case. I've been trying to make sense of it all, trying to break apart what we know from what we don't know from what we think we know from what we think we don't know."

Christie laughed, and he smiled.

"I can understand that," she said. "I've been up doing some cleaning around the apartment. I couldn't sleep, so I just decided to get up."

"Do you always have trouble sleeping?" he asked, realizing that he didn't know much about her sleeping habits.

"Sometimes. Tonight, I've just been feeling a bit… heavy? I'm not even sure how to describe it."

"Oh," he said. "How come?"

"I'm not sure. I spent the afternoon journaling after I got home from work. I wanted to stop at the ice cream café, but for some reason I couldn't go. I wish you were here with me. Then I could get ice cream without feeling guilty that I'm doing 'one of our things' without you. When are you coming home?"

Something in his heart shivered. *When are you coming home?* That sounded like they were more than friends. Like they were… he didn't finish the thought.

"I'll be coming home soon. I want to come home by Friday afternoon, but I may come by Friday morning so I can meet with one of my clients in the afternoon."

Christie sighed, dramatically. "Okay, whatever."

Jed grinned. "You're not very good with expressing how you feel are you, Christie?"

She stared down at the phone. He'd used her name. Was it because of what she had just said? Was he trying to say that she was not in the friend zone?

"Um, not usually, no."

"Not to worry. We'll work on that."

Christie didn't know what to say.

"I'm just about to get ready for bed. Do you think you're ready to try again to sleep?" Jed asked.

"Yeah," she sighed and stretched. "It's been a couple of hours since I got up to start cleaning, and I'm feeling pretty sleepy."

"My voice is lulling you to sleep? Am I truly that boring? I'm insulted," Jed teased.

"No! That's not what I meant." She heard him start to laugh. "Oh, so you think this is funny, huh? That's fine. I'm going to bed now."

Jed grinned. She sounded just like a petty teenager. That was so cute.

"Come on," he cooed. "Don't go to bed mad at me. We're just playing, remember? You don't know how to play?"

"I do know how to play. I play to win, Gray."

Jed could sense the conversation coming to a close, but he wanted it to keep going. "Speaking of winning, how have you been faring with your own case analysis?"

"It's been okay. Not the way it usually goes. I haven't made as much progress as I would have wanted to by this stage. I don't know. I'm starting to wonder if I even went to school to earn this master's degree or if I just imagined it all. This case doesn't make much sense. I'm beginning to think it's me."

Jed laughed outright, throwing his head back and holding on to the side table for support. Christie smiled. At least he thought it was funny.

"Don't start doubting your capabilities just because a case is hard, Christie. I know you know better than that."

There was that firm tone again. It made her want to melt into her sheets. "Why do you use that tone with me?"

"What tone?"

"You know what I'm talking about."

"Yeah, I do, but I wanted to hear you say it anyway." He put his glass down on the side table and climbed into bed. "I use that tone because I want you to pay attention to what I'm saying and for you to know that I'm being serious."

Christie was quiet for a moment. "Is that one of your strategies for your clients?

"No."

"Wait, what?"

"It's not a client strategy. I developed that just for you."

"What?"

"What's the matter? Is it too... serious for you?"

Her voice hitched in her throat, and the word she was about to say turned into a cough. She wasn't sure she could keep talking to him if he continued to use that tone. The worst part of it was that she couldn't detect the slightest bit of teasing in his voice. The way she'd been shocked to find only serious, masculine energy in his gaze when she'd stumbled across the silk rope and handcuffs in his closet during the apartment search—it had made her knees get weak the way he'd looked at her.

"Cat got your tongue, Detective?"

"Something like that," she said.

Jed waited.

"It's not that it's too serious," she finally said. "I suppose it's just... different."

Jed hummed. "I take it none of your male friends talk to you the way I talk to you?"

"No, they don't. We have a more relaxed, kind of jovial, relationship all the time. Except when we argue, which is very rare."

"Good."

Christie stared at her phone.

"Goodnight, Detective."

Christie could not sleep. Much like other nights, she was wide awake, lost in thought. Tonight, she couldn't get Jed out of her mind. He was consuming her thoughts more and more every day. During the daytime, she put it down to wanting to solve the case—he was her partner, after all. But at night, she found herself wondering what the food he made tasted like. More often, she pondered how firm his bedposts were.

She flushed, and even though she was alone, covered her face with her hands. Christie had never before encountered a man she was this attracted to. She'd spent hours trying to work out what it was about him that made her want to give up her morals and ravage him.

It wasn't just the raw sex appeal, though God knew he was full of that. The way his sleeves were snug on his biceps and his shirts were snug around his chest. The way he looked down at her. His eyes. His hair. His hands. His lips. She wanted to scream.

Grabbing a pillow next to her, she used it to cover her face in the dark room, burning with shame and desire from her wayward thoughts. She remembered their first meeting at the restaurant, how shocked she had been to find that he was the only one wearing the shade of pink they'd agreed on over the call. When he'd stood to greet her, she'd thought her legs might give out. She wouldn't have recovered if she had embarrassed herself that night.

He was the kind of man women read about in novels and fantasized about at night, when they were alone—the kind of man that was so attractive you thought you were dreaming when you looked at him and melting when he was looking at you.

It would have been manageable if he had only been physically attractive. But he was incredibly masculine, yet attentive to everything she said, did, and thought. He was unraveling her strings, one by one, and she was helpless to stop him. She had been running from serious romantic relationships all her life. Now, with Jed, Christie didn't want to run.

CHAPTER 25

JED GROANED TO HIMSELF.

"This isn't working. This isn't making sense. I can't seem to get past these two rotating thoughts. It's like I'm stuck in a cyclone with no way to break through. What kind of logic trap is this?"

He banged his fist on the table, frustration getting the better of him.

The silence in the cabin did not answer back to him. He got up from the table, stretched, and did a quick jog on the spot. His workout routines for the past week had been painfully simple—mostly swimming, doing as many laps as he could manage back and forth across the little cove next to the cabin. Jed loved the water, and he'd made good use of the lake in all the capacities he could. Added to that were the frequent runs he went on down his favorite forest trail nearby. When he returned to the city and hit the gym again, he would have to take it easy on the weights until he got back into his normal routine.

He didn't regret his decision to come here. The lake was quiet and peaceful, and there were opportunities at every corner to engage with nature. This morning, before starting work, he'd gone for quite a long walk in the forest.

That was his second favorite part of visiting the lake—walking through the woods. There were so many different plants to look at, flowers blooming late as autumn ended, birds chirping. Sometimes, he even saw owls hunting in the evenings, trying to fill their babies up with as much food as they could find in the last weeks before they fledged.

Now, he was stuck at the table again, trying to make sense of what he was looking at. He had outlined the two contradicting thoughts on a fresh sheet of paper and had been staring at them for the past thirty minutes.

Is the murderer a contract-killer?

Has he been contracted by Carrillo to do his dirty work in order to clear the city of homeless men so that Carrillo can gain permission from the city council to begin construction?

Has the contract-killer been contracted by Lauren or Whitman?

Why does he choose to use a knife when guns are more commonly used in hits? Why does he kill his victims up-close instead of from a distance? Does he see himself as a sort of social hero? Does he think he is doing the city a favor?

The questions mocked Jed. He needed to focus on one question at a time.

Was the murderer a contract-killer? The only way to know that would be to make an inference based on the responses to his question in the Carrillo slander Discord server. Jed pulled up the web page, hoping to the heavens that someone had responded to his question. He was relying on it to get him out of this circular trap. He gasped at what he saw.

There were dozens of replies to his question. Twenty-five, to be exact. There were people having full on conversations in the comments, replying to each other as they tried to hash out what they thought. He grabbed a fresh sheet of paper and tallied the responses into the 'Yes', 'No', and 'Maybe' categories.

Of the twenty-five responses, twenty people said no, three people said yes, and two people weren't very sure. Jed was shocked. Twenty people had said no? Even though the same twenty people were around this man every day, dealing with his outbursts of anger, his rage, and his bullying? They still didn't think he had anything to do with the murders?

*I don't think he has anything to do with it. Don't get me wrong, the man's an *******. But I think he's a good guy at heart. He just got his execution all wrong. When he heard about the first murder, he was just as shaken up as we were. I don't think he has anything to do with it.*

Jed sighed aloud into the room once more, pulling on his hair. This had to be some kind of sick joke. He went back to his paper and looked at the two questions again. If the killer had not been contracted by Carrillo, that meant that the question was mostly off the table. By a vote of a majority in the tally of responses to his question, he no longer had to worry about trying to figure that out. That meant that question two was where his attention should be directed.

He needed to figure out why the killer had chosen to use a knife.

"Jed, this is huge!"

"Is it?" He smiled.

"Yes, it is. You've eliminated almost all the alleyways and half-plotted directions that this case had been going in, in just a few hours. That's incredible!"

"Yeah. I try my best, you know."

Christie laughed outright. "Stop trying to be humble. I'm really impressed. I'm currently pulling up the e-mail you just sent me. It all makes total sense, and you definitely hit the jackpot when you stumbled across that Discord server. I would have never thought to just ask them what they thought about Carrillo and his potential involvement in the case. That was definitely a win."

"Thanks. The new information from the workers doesn't clear him from the suspect list, but it definitely sheds some light on his character. Now it's kind of left me at another hard point. I have to figure out why the killer uses a knife when he commits murder. And funnily enough, that's actually just us needing to figure out what his motive is for these murders in the first place."

"Because instruments are usually tied to motives," Christie interjected.

"Right. The 'why' determines the 'how'. We have the 'how'. We just need to, somehow, work in reverse and figure out the 'why'."

"Alright," Christie said as she scrolled through the email. "Do you have any ideas so far?"

"One. The same one we spoke about at the start of it all. He uses a knife, but he doesn't just stab them to death and run. He stands there, over them, as they're bleeding to death and continues to inflict wounds on them—especially to their faces. I've noticed that their faces are the last place he goes for."

Christie shivered. "It's so gruesome."

"It is. Because by the time he works on their faces, he's already stabbed them to death. So, the person has long stopped breathing. It's overkill. But what does this mean to the killer?"

Christie replayed the crime scenes in her mind. There had often been eyeballs on the sidewalk, or a nose hanging onto the rest of the face by only a piece of skin where the dagger had cut through it. Her stomach turned.

"I think it's got to do with him not wanting us to recognize, or at least easily identify, the victims. And more than that, I think he's trying to send some sort of message by destroying their faces." Jed rubbed his forehead.

Christie tapped her pen against her desk. "Do you still think that it's him trying to tell us that we shouldn't even bother trying to figure out who these people are? That they're not important because they live on the streets?"

"That's exactly what I think it is. I think the killer is trying to tell us we shouldn't even be investigating these cases because these people are nobodies. Why else would he stand over them for minutes, at the scene of a crime after he's just murdered them, trying to mar their faces so terribly that we won't be able to see who they are?"

"Yeah, I see how that might be the case." Christie was staring at her phone where she had placed it on the desk in front of her.

"He's going out of his way to make sure that our jobs are difficult—but only when it comes to identifying who the victims are. If we go by that logic, that means that his 'why' has a lot to do with the 'how', in the sense that he chose the knife to make sure he could control how the victim's corpse looks after the fact. And then the 'why' plays into that, meaning that his motive could be that he's just trying to 'clean up the streets'."

Jed could hear Christie sigh through the phone before she said, "That's terrible."

"It is. I can't imagine what the crime scenes must have been like every time you walked up to them. Seeing the pictures on a screen after the evidence is collected has been gruesome enough. I wish you'd called me so I could have been there with you. If this happens again in the future, you always call me. Do you understand?"

"Yes."

"Good." Jed sighed. "The even more concerning thing is that none of the current suspects align with what we've just discussed. John's physical profile doesn't match the killer's profile, and he doesn't have the financial means to hire a contracted killer. Neither does Lauren, even though they both have motives and faulty alibis."

"That's true. But the person with the motive and the means has the crowd rooting for him, even though they all hate him."

"Yes. So, in terms of suspects, I'm beginning to think that this guy is an independent murderer that's not attached to any of the suspects we've already established. That would also play well with why he was so happy to call me and gloat about what he did with Ethan."

Christie slammed her pen onto the desk, huffing. "And we have no idea who he is because there's no crime scene DNA, and there's no way to identify him, except for that we know that he has blue or green eyes."

"And that he's arrogant as hell." Jed added, running his free hand across his face.

"So, despite the immense progress we've made," Christie said, "we have hit a dead end."

Jed didn't need to see her to know that she was shaking her head on the other side of the phone.

"For now, Detective. For now."

After hanging up and finally getting around to making lunch, even though it was almost two in the afternoon, Jed sang along to his favorite song. His own voice was a bit of company in the quiet cabin, and he thought about getting a pet as he worked on lunch. But what would he get? A cat? He didn't think he was much of a cat person. A dog? A dog was a big-time commitment, but at least he'd have someone that was happy to go wherever he went and have adventures.

His hands stilled over the stove. Loneliness wasn't something that Jed felt often, and realizing that he was feeling it now was a surprise, especially since he was at the lake, of all places, where he found the most peace.

He looked around, as though checking to see if he was still in the cabin. He was. Everything looked the same as it always did when he visited. The chairs and tables were the same, his bedroom was arranged the same, the lake was as cold and as beautiful as it always was; the forest was as alive as ever. And yet, something felt... missing.

It was Christie, he realized. Jed put the chicken into the oven and pressed his hands against his face. He missed her terribly. Since they'd started working together, he'd seen her almost every day. They spoke constantly. She'd become an important fixture in his life. Now that he'd been away for a few days, he was missing seeing her and talking, in-person, at the station. Working through the case together was something he had grown to look forward to, even though he'd been enjoying working semi-alone with the NYPD before their partnership had come along.

He clucked his tongue against his cheek, heading out onto the balcony with a glass of Lyre's. He stared into the cloudy sky for a minute before looking down at the drink in his hands.

"You're lying to yourself, Jed," he said aloud as he looked across the water. "Why am I lying to myself?"

He let the silence speak to him for a moment.

"Well, it's because I'm scared that if I admit to myself what I'm actually feeling, it'll show."

He listened to the words he'd just spoken echo around in his head. He imagined himself sitting in front of a therapist and tried to guess what the therapist would say to him. It was a great way to process his own feelings. *Jed, bottling up your feelings is unhealthy. Even if you do want to keep your feelings from interfering with your relationship, you do need to acknowledge that there are feelings there to begin with.*

He huffed at what the imaginary therapist had said and rolled his eyes. It was true. To hide feelings was to imply that there were feelings there to begin with.

"I have a crush on Christie. There. I said it."

Is that the whole truth, Jed? His smile turned into another roll of the eyes at the thought. He could tell himself that it was the whole truth, but he knew it was more than a crush. As work-focused as he had been his entire career, Christie's presence was pulling more and more of his attention to the idea of marriage and a family.

He squeezed his eyes shut and groaned aloud. What a woman. Thirty-four years, and he'd never met a woman that made him think of marriage this seriously before. Even though he had been in one serious relationship in the past, he'd always known in the back of his mind that they wouldn't have lasted. It was one of those situations where no matter how much you loved the person; you had to let them go. With Christie, letting go never entered his mind when he thought of taking their relationship further. He wanted to hold on forever—hold on to her hands, her waist, plant kisses all over her pretty face. And as pure as he tried to keep his thoughts of her so he wouldn't turn her into an object for his pleasure in his mind, there were times when the carnal urge to sink into her to the hilt filled his mind. His jaw tightened.

"Fine. It's more than a crush. I'm interested. Very interested. More than I can or should express. But I don't want it to show. I can't let it show."

His mind was silent. It seemed his imaginary therapist was satisfied with the response—with the truth. He chuckled to himself, and downing the last mouthful of his drink, he went back to his desk.

At ten pm, Jed still hadn't made much progress. He stared down at the paper in front of him. Knives. The killer was into knives. How would he use that to connect to a persona? He couldn't very well ask the NYPD to search every resident of

New York's house to figure out who had European daggers that cost four-hundred dollars each just casually lying around in their apartment.

They had established a motive for the killer, a clear 'why' that now connected to the 'how' and were confident in the case they'd made for why he chose to use knives instead of another weapon. They'd also come to the realization that the case was cold. None of the suspects they'd had their eyes on were strong contenders anymore. If they had missed the correct suspect all this time and had gotten to the point of interviews and analysis without ever having the right person on their radar, how were they to double-back and figure out who the right person was now? Jed needed some sort of miracle.

If he was honest with himself, he needed more than a miracle. He needed to call his mom.

CHAPTER 26

"HI, MOM."

"Hi, Jed. Is everything alright?"

"No. I need to talk to you about something."

"Okay, darling. What might that be?"

"I want to ask you about my addiction and rehab. I think I need to go back to that place to reconnect with what that was like. I'm hoping it will help me understand why the killer is attacking addicts and the homeless."

He heard his mom take a deep breath. "Are you sure you want to go back there?"

"I don't want to. But at this stage, I think I have to."

Laurie shuffled around, getting comfortable in her reclining chair by the fireplace. "Alright. I trust that intuition. Where do we start?"

"I suppose I need your listening ear while I verbally process."

"I can do that."

Jed nodded, letting the thoughts at the back of his mind come forward.

"Alright." He took one more sip of water. "So, I was born, and then everything started going downhill from there, as it so often does."

He chuckled, and so did Laurie. He always appreciated that she understood his sense of humor without a hitch.

"I got into sports, played lacrosse, soccer, baseball... I remember how much you and... Dad... had to run around every week to get me to all the practices and events I was part of."

The word 'dad' felt so foreign on his tongue. He wasn't sure he liked to use it to refer to his father anymore, but using his first name wouldn't feel right either.

Laurie smiled. "Ah yes, I remember. You were a very engaged, involved student. You wanted to play every sport there was, but there were only so many days in a week for you to go to practice!"

"Yeah. I was in way over my head. But it never felt overwhelming to me. It always just felt like fun because I enjoyed what I was doing so much."

"I'm very glad you enjoyed it. I think I could tell, too. You were always bubbling over with excitement after practice, even when you were bleeding down the side of your face from a nasty check. And when there were games, you were even more excited."

Jed winced at the memory of one particularly nasty check during a lacrosse game.

"I almost got injured multiple times in those games, but I would have played through it. It still surprises me that I never broke any bones playing lacrosse for as many years as I did.""Let's just be glad you didn't have any big injuries and walked away from all those games relatively unscathed."

Jed was quiet for a moment, remembering the good times.

A loving sigh echoed through the phone. "You were my whole world, Jed. I was so proud to be your mom. People asked me what my name was when I'd attend your games and I always said, 'I'm Jed's mom'. They aways laughed at that—thought it was sweet that I was so enthusiastic. But that's who I am—your mom."

Jed's jaw tightened. He couldn't start crying so soon into the conversation. They had barely scratched the surface of things.

Laurie continued. "Do you remember all the parties we hosted for you?"

"Yeah, I remember."

Jed smiled. Every year, his classmates looked forward to his birthday because they knew his mom would go all out for his party, and they'd all get invitations. His mom had enjoyed hosting a lot.

"Then the divorce happened," Jed remarked as he remembered how things had changed afterward.

Looking back at your past was such a trippy feeling, he mused. You were either shocked at how you could have done such things and felt lots of anger and shame, or you were struck by the underlying reasons and triggers that had led you down those dark roads and were filled with compassion. Jed thought he might be experiencing both of those feelings at the same time.

On one hand, the chain of events made total sense to him. Put someone else in his shoes, under the same circumstances, and the same things could have very well happened. It wasn't that he had been rebellious for no reason. That was just how he'd coped.

"Yes, then the divorce happened," Laurie confirmed. "What do you remember it being like?"

"I remember it was like one day there was peace and happiness, and the next minute there was destruction everywhere."

Jed stared unseeingly at the rug. Laurie quietly dabbed her eyes with her sleeve.

"One minute, he was watching me ride my bike in the yard and kicking soccer balls with me, and the next he was packing up and moving out for Christmas."

"Do you remember what happened between those points in time?"

Jed didn't. It all felt blurry, like the time had sped by. But the longer he thought about it, the more it all came rushing back.

"It started with the visits. The visits were terrible. He was trying to build a new family, as if ours had never existed. He wanted me to be best friends with his girlfriend's kids. They hated me. And she hated me, too. Whenever I tried to talk to him in private, she would barge in and interrupt, call me names, insult me... all kinds of things. She made it impossible for me to have a relationship with Dad. And he let her! He didn't do anything to stop her."

Jed paused, looking out the still-open door, out across the lake. Outside was dark. The stars were barely visible that night.

"He never defended me or stuck up for me. It's like he wasn't even there half the time. He just sat and let her rip me to pieces, even though he and I had just been talking and laughing together. It's like she had him brainwashed."

Laurie's heart was breaking. She hated to remember that Jed had gone through these things. She hated that his visitations had gotten so unbearable to where he'd ended up in the hospital from an overdose at fifteen. She hated that she hadn't realized how much he'd been hurting sooner than she had. That was the last time he saw his dad. "How did that make you feel?"

"Unvalued," Jed said. He let the memories continue to wash over him as he thought through what other adjectives could describe the emptiness he had felt. "Unvalued and unseen."

"I'm sorry your dad made you feel that way, Jed. I know it won't heal the pain, but I want you to know that I value you, and I love you, and I'm so proud of you."

It was a wonder that she could keep her voice so steady as she spoke, given that tears were running down her cheeks.

Jed stared out the door and had the bemused thought that his mother should have been a therapist as well.

"Thank you."

Laurie hummed in response. After a few moments, Jed continued.

"When they had officially tied the knot, it all got worse. It got to the point where I'd just pretend to not be there, so they'd avoid me as much as possible. When it wasn't possible, and they had to talk to me, I'd lie without thinking about it just to get out of the interaction. 'Yes, I'm fine'. 'No, I'm not hungry'. I'd do anything to get them to go back to ignoring me. Even starve."

Laurie wiped her cheeks again and took a drink of her water as Jed pressed on. "Then, I turned fifteen."

"You gave me quite a fright that year."

Jed smiled, more out of sadness than anything else. "I did, didn't I?"

"What drove you to that point? Do you remember? We've never really spoken about this in detail. I've never wanted to risk triggering you with the memory. As long as you spoke about it with your counselors, I was okay. But I always wondered."

He took a long drink of water. Now that he was thirty-four, and it had been almost two decades since it had happened, it was much easier to talk about it. It helped that he'd gotten an undergraduate degree in Psychology then a master's degree in mental health counseling; he'd worked through the emotional baggage.

"It was a long weekend. I was staying there from Wednesday to Saturday because you had to go out of town for work, and my aunt and uncle couldn't take me because they were on vacation. I was devastated. Staying there over the weekends had been hard enough. I could go a day, maybe a day and a half, so I didn't have to be micromanaged and bullied and wouldn't get in the way. But there was no way I'd make it from Wednesday until Sunday, avoiding real conflict. The longer you stay with someone, the more tired of you and annoyed with your presence they become. I wasn't welcome in the first place, but that weekend, I definitely overstayed my welcome."

Laurie's entire body was tense. She had asked for the details, but she wasn't sure she could bear them. She tried to focus on her breathing to stay calm as Jed continued.

"The kids. They'd been at my throat all week. Sometimes, on the weekends, they'd go visit their father, and I'd have less of a hard time dealing with them. But on weekdays, they were home. It was hell. They insulted me left and right, told me to kill myself because I didn't matter and said my father wouldn't notice, anyway. Nothing I did was good enough—my school was stupid, my sports were stupid, my friends were losers..."

Laurie's gasp interrupted Jed's sentence, and she clamped a hand over her mouth as she buried her head into her other hand. Jed paused.

"Mom, are you sure you want to hear this?"

On the other end of the line, she wrenched herself upright and swiped at her face quickly. "Yes. I want to hear what happened."

Jed sighed before he continued. "So, they told me to kill myself, and I just sort of… didn't respond. It was Friday. They'd been at me since Wednesday, and I was hungry. I hadn't eaten all day. So, later in the night, I wandered into the kitchen to see what I could find. There wasn't much. I grabbed an apple."

Laurie squeezed her eyes shut. She hadn't known that they'd been that bad. After all, Jed was his father, and they used to have a wonderful relationship.

"I saw some medicines on the counter, though. There were a couple of bottles. I looked through them. Most of them were low dosage painkillers and allergy medicine. But then I saw a bottle of blood thinners. That caught my eye."

Unable to help herself, a question burst through Laurie's lips. "Did you want to die? Or was it just that the boys had been using that statement to bully you?"

"Both. I thought I wanted to die. But knowing what I know now, I just didn't want to live like that anymore. I wanted peace and acceptance. Living that way wasn't worth it to me. All my sports friends at school were gossiping about my dad and his new wife—the perfect new family he chose over us… over me. Staying with him was torture. It was unbearable. When I saw the pills, I thought it was the perfect opportunity."

He got to his feet, taking the phone with him into the kitchen to rummage around for a snack. Remembering all the hunger at his father's house was sending his body into fight or flight, and he knew he needed to eat something to remind his body that he was safe. That wasn't his reality anymore. He found a pack of his favorite chips he had brought with him and had been saving for the right moment.

Now was the right time. He tossed one into his mouth and savored the crunch. Back at the table, he put his phone back down and started again right as his mom asked a question.

"Did you go to get some food because telling the story made you feel hungry?"

"Yes."

"Your nervous system is still healing," Laurie marveled. "I'm proud of you for recognizing that you needed something to munch on in the moment."

Jed smiled. "Thanks, Mom."

"You're always welcome."

The story overtook Jed's mind once more. "I took a handful of the pills and went to bed."

"I remember when you came home the next morning after telling me you couldn't sleep and wishing you'd been able to go stay with your aunt and uncle. Then you dropped that bomb on me out of... nowhere."

Her voice suddenly dipped when she said 'nowhere', and she swiped at her eyes.

"I feel bad just saying 'nowhere'. Because obviously, it was from somewhere. I just didn't see it."

Jed's chewing paused, his therapeutic training taking over. "Don't slip into self-blame, Mom. You didn't know the extent of it because I didn't want you to. I didn't want to add anything else to your plate. It had been bad enough that he had left us and abandoned your marriage and our family."

"Jed, I'm your mom. I should have noticed something was wrong. But I didn't, and it was because I was struggling to keep up with everything else going on in our lives. It's behind us now, but I still think about it all the time, wondering if there was anything I could have done to prevent you from trying to take your life."

His voice dropped into a soothing lull. "I don't think anything would have stopped me from attempting. I think it was an important milestone in my life. If I hadn't, I'd be a much different person today."

"That's one way to look at it."

Jed felt a pressure rise in his chest, a need to impress the next statement onto Laurie. "It's not your fault, Mom."

"Okay," she managed to say as she wiped her eyes.

"In any case, when I realized that I'd woken up the next morning, the crushing weight of disappointment almost took me under. I think that's why I brought it up to you. I had wanted it to happen overnight. But now that I was going home with you, I didn't want it to suddenly start working and then you had to watch it happen. I didn't want you to be the one that dealt with it."

"I am glad you mentioned it when you did. If you hadn't, things could have turned for the worse very quickly."

"Yeah."

They were silent for a few minutes, unspoken thoughts and memories floating between them. Jed was the one to break the silence.

"What happened on the phone? When you called him? Why did he want to talk to me?"

Laurie sighed heavily. "He wouldn't tell me anything. I called him from the ER to ask him to check the label of the bottle and tell me how many were left in it. You kept saying you only took a handful, but none of us knew what a handful meant. I told him what had happened and asked him to check and he started screaming at me. *'Where's Jed? I don't want to hear anything from you. I want to talk to Jed. Where's Jed?'* He didn't believe me and screamed that I was making the whole thing up. That's all he kept saying. I was so overwhelmed that I burst into tears. That's when the nurse took the phone and began talking to him."

"He's an ingrate."

"That was the only way we could get the information. What the prescription date was, how many pills were left in the bottle... and that's how we figured out what you meant by a handful."

"Yeah. It was just a handful."

Laurie looked at the phone incredulously. "Thirteen pills are *not* a handful!"

Jed laughed. "I'm just teasing. It was a lot. The only reason I didn't take the entire bottle was because I didn't want them to know what I used… when they found me the next morning."

Laurie shivered at that thought. What if the pills had worked? She would have gotten a call the next morning when she should be picking him up, saying they'd found him in his room, not breathing. She could barely breathe at the thought of it. She was so glad they hadn't worked. The knowledge that her fifteen-year-old baby thought suicide was his only option broke her heart.

"Then, there were all the blood tests and machines…" he said.

"And the waiting. The waiting was the hardest part. Because you were alive right then, but you could have been bleeding internally. And I would have had to watch you fade away. I was terrified."

Her voice broke as she spoke, and Jed squeezed his eyes closed.

Just like she had never heard his full story on what had happened that Friday night, he had never truly stopped to consider the gravity of what she must have felt as his mom, sitting by his bedside, watching nurses come and go, waiting to hear whether her son would be okay. He felt terrible.

"As I sat in the ER, and they were running all the tests on you, all I could think about was the phone call you had made to me before you went to bed telling me you hated it there and you couldn't wait until I got home. You told me you loved me. It was like I was getting punched in the stomach over and over again."

"I'm sorry, Mom. Even though I knew it must have been painful for you, I've never really considered just how painful that time must have been. It was hard on me, but it must have been especially difficult for you—watching me go through that at the hospital."

Jed paused for a moment. The story was only just beginning. He had gone on to put her through much worse in the next couple of years of his life. He felt shame creep up his neck.

"Then again, I only made it worse in the next couple of years, didn't I?"

"You can't blame yourself for your actions when you were high, Jed. You weren't in your right mind while you were so heavily intoxicated."

He winced as a few hazy memories came to the forefront of his mind. "No. I wasn't. But I definitely should have been."

"It's okay. You're better now, and that's all that matters."

Jed nodded with determination. "Better now and never going back."

Laurie nodded her agreement.

"After the hospital came counseling. Dad refused to sign the release papers for me to get the counseling, and the police and Child and Family Services got involved…"

"Yes. Your father refused to sign the paperwork, and since you were a minor, it didn't matter that we had divorced or that he wanted nothing to do with our family anymore. He was still required to sign. He was adamant that he wanted to talk to you first. After you'd just gone through that, I didn't want him anywhere near you. You refused to speak to him, and I would not force you to."

"Thank you for not letting him near me. It would only have deepened the wound. Though it hurt like hell in the moment, that was a good mom call. And thank you for getting the police and CFS involved in my case, even though it might have been… embarrassing. It's the reason I never hesitate to call in higher support and law enforcement whenever I have a case or client that needs it."

"Of course, Jed. You are worth far more than my pride in any situation. I knew you needed help, and I refused to let him stand in the way of that. I was so scared of losing custody of you if I tried to keep your father away from you. I saw how hard the visits with him were on you, but the courts forced the visits. I tried to believe that he would protect you. You were his son, after all. After the attempt on your life, I was ready to fight whoever I needed to so I could keep you safe. No one was going to put you in harm's way ever again!"

Jed nodded. After finishing the chips, he stared at the empty bag, reading the label and ingredients.

"Jed?"

He could almost hear the question before she asked it.

"Did the counseling help?"

He had been pondering that question right then as well—whether it had helped at all, since he'd ended up in the wrong crowd and doing drugs, anyway.

"I think it did." He sighed into the silent cabin. "It did. But at the time, I was so resistant to the process that I hindered my own progress, which later opened the door to me seeking that feeling of belonging and community with the wrong crowd."

"Resistant? I thought you enjoyed attending your sessions?"

"I did. But deep down, I didn't really want to be there. I didn't think it could really help me heal. I thought that what I needed were just some friends to keep me distracted from the pain of being abandoned... discarded like trash. I didn't think I was really worth it or even deserved to feel better. I felt that if my own father had thrown me away, why would anyone else care about me?"

He chuckled to himself. "Boy, was I wrong."

"Lesson learned, right?" Laurie asked with a grin.

"Very much so."

His brows pulled together for a moment.

"I suppose that's why I'm so insistent on clear communication, introspection, and emotional processing and regulation in all my relationships—especially in my relationship with Christie."

"Oh?"

"Yeah. That's something I've been trying to get her to be more aware of and teaching her how to do. Due to her career path, and the pressure that New York City has been piling onto her shoulders since we started working together, that'll be her anchor."

"That's good of you to do, Jed."

"I wish she realized that."

Laurie laughed at that. "I'm sure she does, darling. Just because she's a little resistant to the process doesn't mean she doesn't realize that it's helping her. The ways of women are confusing on the surface."

"Very confusing," Jed admitted to himself, smiling. "But I'll figure her out, eventually."

Laurie smiled and sighed wistfully. Jed narrowed his eyes at his phone.

"What's that satisfied sigh about?"

"An old lady can't just be happy and satisfied?" Laurie teased.

Jed laughed along with her.

"I'm glad we're so close. I think the divorce really brought us together even more as a team, you and I," Laurie said.

"I agree. I think that there's a lot to be admired for how our relationship progressed through those times. But when I was fifteen is when I really hit rock bottom."

"What triggered that decline?"

"I refused to talk about my relationship with Dad in counseling. So, I didn't work through the abandonment. I didn't have him anymore to lean on with sports or with... man stuff. So, my self-esteem tanked. It didn't help that I was a lanky, brown-haired teenager. Whenever the counselors tried to talk about my relationship with Dad, I would just shut down. There would be no progress after that."

Laurie laughed at his description of himself. "No! You were a very handsome boy."

"Of course you thought that, Mom. Those were my awkward teenage years. All the girls rejected me, and the guys didn't want to hang out with me. I wasn't cool enough anymore."

"Oh, no. My poor baby."

Jed grinned. "That's when I fell into the group of friends that introduced me to drugs. I was accepted there. They didn't make fun of me because my dad was no longer in the picture. They didn't care that my skin was red from acne. They didn't care that my life was a mess. They just wanted to have a good time. And I just wanted to be around people who wanted me to be around. The numbing effect I got from the drugs was a bonus at first. Then it became the driving force."

"Oh, dear."

Jed smiled ruefully. "The recipe for disaster."

"How did it start?"

"Someone handed me a cigarette. I didn't like it much, but they said it was the lowest level, so I should give it a shot. I did. Still didn't like it much, so I tried the green stuff. Now, that hit the spot. I'd smoke so much of it I'd either think I was flying or being dragged off by demons—no in between. Gradually, they introduced me to the other stuff. Meth, coke, f—"

He couldn't bring himself to say it. But he knew his mom would get the reference.

"I was so hurt and lost that I'd try anything they handed me, anything they fed me. They could have killed me if they wanted to, and I wouldn't have noticed. I was too deep in my sorrow to care."

"I'm glad they didn't want to hurt you that way."

"Me too. They were good friends, just... misguided. We all turned to the wrong things for the right reasons. But my involvement with them just made me more and more volatile. I started stealing money from you, vandalizing the house in fits of rage, lying like it was going out of style, inviting people over without you knowing. And then we started arguing."

Neither of them spoke. He and Laurie had seldom argued when he was a kid and had never argued since he'd chosen sobriety. But in that window of two years, between sixteen and eighteen, there were all out screaming matches between them—with Jed doing most of the screaming.

Laurie remembered how her life had changed over those years. She withdrew from family & friends. No one could understand what she was going through. Hell, she didn't even understand it! She was constantly terrified of what condition she would find Jed in when she got home from work—if he even came home. She went from home to work and back again. She had to lock up valuables. She felt like she was under house arrest, totally isolated and alone.

Jed had started stealing from her and selling the things from their home, damaging their house, breaking in through the windows after she took away his key because he and his friends could not be trusted to be there when she wasn't home.

Still, she hadn't given up on him. She was all that he had. She wouldn't have been able to live with herself if something had happened to him on the streets. Laurie would go days without knowing where he was, or when or if he would come home. She shuddered, remembering that feeling.

"I'm very proud of you for how far you've come in your recovery and how much passion you have for helping your clients."

As he listened to his mom, Jed remembered one particular argument where he'd screamed and screamed at her until she cowered in a corner, shaking and crying. She had only been trying to ask him where he had been the night before. He had been high on three drugs at once and had totally lost it.

It made his skin burn with shame when he remembered his behavior in those two years, and he'd apologized to her over and over again for it. The apologies couldn't erase what had happened, though. It was a mistake he had to own up to and ensure that it never happened again.

His poor, sweet mom had been totally out of her depth. She hadn't known anything about drugs or drug use, never known anyone who used or abused drugs. She didn't know what to do, who to turn to, or how to help him. Most of the time, Jed was hanging out in a drug house with his friends, or on his own, and getting caught in the middle of fights where men twice his age ended up dead. She would come get him, take him home, and he would be gone again by morning.

It was where he had learned to fight—to fight and win. In that short space of time, he'd learned how to survive on the streets. The only person who never faced or saw that side of him during those times was his mother. He'd never hit her, or even tried to. Jed wouldn't have been able to forgive himself if he had.

"Do you remember when I overdosed on GHB?"

"Like it was yesterday."

Jed could hear the immediate tears that filled her voice as she went on, "One day, at work, I just got a call saying that you had been found in a drug house, unresponsive. I rushed out of work. I could barely see the road to get to the hospital because I was crying so hard."

Jed sighed.

"Was that an… attempt?" Laurie asked. She wasn't sure if she wanted to hear the answer.

"It wasn't. That was purely accidental. I took too much. I don't have any memory of it, even today.

He heard her exhale. "I thought it was. When they told me you were fine, and they were going to discharge you, I begged them to admit you—just to keep you off the street. They refused and told me they had no medical grounds to admit you. You weren't considered a high enough risk. They said that you didn't want to be helped. I was inconsolable. And by the time we got home, you disappeared again."

Jed was quiet for a moment. It always made him emotional when he remembered how good his mom had been to him during that time. Now, reliving it start to finish was making it even more difficult for him not to cry.

"Even though that was discouraging, I still didn't give up. In fact, it made me try even harder to figure out what to do to help you. I took days off work and spent hours just researching addiction and what I could do to get you on the road to recovery. That's how I got you into the two court-appointed detox programs and the youth residential program for three months. But they failed," Laurie added.

Jed's ears burned with embarrassment. "I wasn't ready to let them work. That's when I lost house privileges."

"Yes. I told you that you couldn't be there unless I was there, and I took your key away. You were quick to anger, and honestly, I didn't trust you. I barely knew the person you had become."

That statement sliced Jed through his heart like a hot knife. The first tears fell down his cheeks.

"You were afraid of me," he whispered.

"I was."

He'd known she had been afraid of what he'd been capable of. But hearing his mom confess that she'd been physically terrified of him reopened a wound in his heart that he didn't know he still had.

"And then, on Christmas Eve, it all took a turn for the worse—and the better, at the same time," he continued.

Laurie agreed. "You didn't want to do our annual Christmas dinner with family and friends. You outright told me it was 'boring' and that you wanted to go hang out with your friends. By the time I got home, after midnight, and went in through the garage, you were banging on the front door. I don't know how long you had been waiting outside, and it was freezing cold. I looked out the window of the door and saw you. I barely recognized you. Your eyes were twice the normal size, and you were in a raging panic."

Jed winced as she told the story, memories of that night coming in flashes as she recounted the events.

"When I opened the door, you dove through and laid low on the floor, yelling at me to lock the door and not turn on the lights. I had no idea what was going on, and I've never felt such fear. I thought a thousand men were after you. Nothing you were saying made any sense. You walked around, hunched over, through the main floor for a while, slinking around in the shadows and avoiding turning on lights. You wouldn't go near the windows. Then, you went down into the pitch-black basement curled yourself into a ball on the floor."

Jed took a drink of the water he had just poured himself.

"I kept trying to ask you what was wrong. Then you finally started talking… *'They're after me. Someone's after me. There's four of them. They're in a black SUV. They went to the wrong house and went to the neighbors. The girl who lives alone with her kid, they shot her. They shot the baby. They want to shoot me. They're after me. She's dead. They're shooting everywhere.'"*

Laurie paused before pressing on. "You kept repeating yourself. Then, every now and again, you would go silent and ask me, *'Can you hear that?'* Like someone was walking around the house outside. All I could hear was the pounding of my heart in my ears."

A sigh escaped Laurie, as she swiped at her eyes as she shared the memory. "I called the police and told them what was happening, but it seemed to take forever for them to arrive. When they came, you refused to get out of the basement until I verified it was the police. There hadn't been any reports of gunshots anywhere in the area, and they drove around to make sure everything was secure. All was safe. At that point, I was totally confused. I just didn't understand."

She remembered staring at the two officers in her kitchen as they explained nothing was happening in the community and that Jed's story wasn't true. Two officers had come. One female and one male officer. The woman was mostly quiet. The man was less so, and not very compassionate either. He simply told Laurie that Jed was having a psychotic break from whatever drugs he had taken that day, and that this was all in his head. Jed remained very agitated while the police were there. Laurie barely recognized him—he was not the son she knew.

Laurie had been so stunned that she'd hardly known what to say or do. She'd felt like she could barely speak. Then, she tried to ask the officer what happened next. He had just shrugged as though this were an everyday occurrence for him and told her, *'Not much you can do. It's his choice and it doesn't look like he is going to change anytime soon'*.

For what had felt like the hundredth time in the past few years, Laurie was frightened of her son, and she was not sure she would be safe alone with him in this state. That night, watching Jed's eyes flick around the room and his neck turn like it was on a swivel, still on the lookout for his enemies even though the police had confirmed nobody was after him, Laurie listened to him beg her to sleep in the same room as him.

"That's when you started asking to sleep in the same room as me for the night. You were so scared. You told me you couldn't bear to be alone. You even asked me to let you lay on the floor like a dog—anything so you didn't have to sleep alone. I wanted to. But I couldn't. It ripped me to pieces, but I closed and locked my door, barred it with the dresser, and tried to go to sleep even though you were calling for me outside. You fell asleep quite quickly. You must have been exhausted."

Jed's t-shirt was soaked with tears. He didn't bother to try to stop the fast-moving flow of water as it rushed down his cheeks, but it was all he could do to keep from sobbing.

"It was that night that I made up my mind, for sure, that we weren't going to live that way anymore. In the morning, you seemed to have slept off most of the drug and its effects. It was Christmas morning, and there was only one detox center open. I remember calling every number I could find, searching for someone to help me. I begged them to hold a spot for you."

When Laurie had left her room that morning, she knew she needed to be strong for both of them. When Jed saw her walk into the living room, he had opened his mouth to speak, but she put up her hand, and he'd closed his mouth without making a sound.

"You have a choice to make today. I found one spot in a Detox facility that is being held for you this morning until ten-thirty am. I can take you there today, or you are on your own. You cannot stay in this house anymore in your state. I can't live like this anymore, and I don't think you will survive much longer."

Laurie sighed as she remembered her surprise when Jed had opened his mouth and nodded.

"I think that night was the turning point for you as well."

"It was," Jed admitted. "I was totally out of control in my body. I have never felt so helpless, fearful, disoriented, or angry—not before, not since. I never wanted to feel that way again. I felt like I was on the verge of death all night. It was awful."

His words were a whisper, and Laurie nodded.

"The detox facility was in a hard part of town, and I was so afraid to leave you there. But I had to choose between leaving you or watching you destroy yourself."

Jed thought that his mother had done well with her decision. "The detox was the start of my second chance. It was hard. The withdrawals were so painful—almost as painful as the high. Then you got me into a residential adult program because the youth one hadn't worked. That sure shook me up. I wasn't around kids my age or younger anymore that I could walk all over. I was eighteen and rubbing shoulders with men who had taken lives, set people on fire... done unspeakable things. I had to be careful. So many of them were in prison and were only in rehab to get time taken off of their sentences. I didn't want to be like them. And then I witnessed an overdose. He was out cold, had been for a while before I came across him. I started CPR, shouted for help, but it was too late. He was dead. Watching that play out from an outside perspective, especially when I'd been in hospital so many times for an overdose, was... life changing. I knew I needed to make changes or dying of an overdose would be my only future."

"And you've been clean ever since. Your sober date is Christmas Day," Laurie added, a huge smile breaking across her face.

Jed could hear it in her voice, and he smiled as well. "Yes. I have been clean ever since and will remain clean until the end of time."

"I hope that this conversation was helpful for you. Do you think it opened up some parts of the case that you couldn't see before?"

Jed nodded, finally drying his cheeks. "At first, I was scared that it wouldn't help the way I expected it would—that it would only reopen wounds and leave me high and dry."

"Now?"

"Now, I know what I need to do. I know with utmost certainty and urgency that I need to figure out what Max has been trying to tell me. He is on the streets the same way I was, at the same age I was. This conversation made me realize how much of the inner workings of my story are still unknown to you—like the conversations I had with my friends while we were high in the clouds, or the mischief we got into and plotted or saw coming from a mile away. There's a certain... vision... that you have when you're in that position, especially when you're younger, that you lose as you grow older. He's been trying to tell me something about the case, and I've been paying attention to everything but that. It's the same as when one of my older friends from that time got shot up because he ignored my little feeling of intuition that the rival gang he kept trying to steal drugs from was out to take him down."

Laurie listened, a sort of dread settling into her tummy as Jed revealed his perspective from being on the streets.

"It's almost two in the morning, Jed."

"I know, Mom. You should get some rest. I need to pack my things. I've decided I'm going back to the office tomorrow morning instead of tomorrow afternoon like I'd been planning. I sense I'm on the verge of a major breakthrough."

CHAPTER 27

A FEW HOURS LATER, Jed was showered, packed up, and trying not to let the tears overwhelm him. Friday had come quickly, and it was already time to leave. He'd gone for an extra-long combination morning run and stroll, taken his last swim for this visit to the lake, and had spent some time outside, listening to the sound of the birds as they called to each other. These were his final moments of peace, and they would be soon replaced by the noise of congested traffic and the never-ending hum of the city.

He climbed into the Jeep, took one last look at the view in front of him that spread across the lake and the forest that led up to the mountains, then started the engine. It was time to head back to normal life.

The good news was that he would see Christie soon, and he'd have the chance to speak to Max later this afternoon. He had missed both of them more than he had realized he would, and even though he was going back to the office in time to catch up on his weekly session with Max, he had been thinking about the boy since he left New York City. Christie, on the other hand... well, thoughts of her never left his mind.

Over the past few weeks, Max had dropped what Jed now considered to be three very important hints regarding the status of the killer who was still at large. As harmless as the questions themselves had been, and for as practically as he had answered them, in the larger context of their conversation at the time, Jed realized they were cryptic clues.

The first question had caught Jed off guard, but in the moment, he had put it down to Max's strange sense of curiosity that led him to ask personal questions—even, sometimes, questions that didn't seem to make sense. Since Max was anything but stupid, Jed always answered each question to the best of his ability, regardless of whether or not he fully understood the purpose behind it.

Max had simply said, *'Y'know Mr. G, they say we should keep our friends close but our enemies closer. Do you think they're onto something?'* The question had come after he and the boy had finished discussing his recent meeting with his mom. Max had conceded to give his mom a fair chance to redeem herself, since she had been so adamant in her initial reconnecting phone call with Max that she had been working on herself and had grown in their time apart. They had sat down over coffee on neutral grounds, and Max had made an attempt to have a conversation with her about their past.

As Max had been expecting, his mother did not want to talk about that. All she wanted to talk about was how much she had suffered since he had left and, in her words, 'ditched her'. The boy had been proud to report that he had implemented

Jed's strategies for regaining control of the conversation and had been more conscious of the narrative that was being written for him. He had not ditched her. He had left for his own emotional safety to pursue the truth of his father and their relationship. His mother had chosen to manipulate the situation, making herself the victim, and making Max out to be the villain. He had seen right through it. That had made Jed proud.

Jed hadn't understood the question right away and had taken it as literally as possible. So literally, in fact, that his response to Max had made the boy laugh. He had said, *'I've also heard the version where they say it's better to have an outright enemy than a friendly enemy. I suppose there are merits and drawbacks to both situations, but it's always advised to keep track of what your enemies are up to. After all, you can't defeat them or escape them if you have no clue what they are up to.'*

Max had burst so laughing. *'If you say so, Mr. G. If you say so.'*

The boy's sudden laughter had made Jed feel sheepish, at first. Had he misinterpreted the question? Had he butchered the opportunity to give deep, insightful wisdom? If he had, he knew Max would either ask again or pursue the answer differently. When the boy had just moved on, Jed had figured that he had answered the question correctly after all, and Max had just been unusually amused by his answer.

The next week, Max had brought up the same thread of enemies and friendships, but in an even more vague, unconnected way. *'You got friends, Mr. G? I don't ever hear you mention anyone.'* That had come in the middle of their conversation about his dad's new restaurant that he was opening near Jed's home. Max had hinted that he would be at the opening, and Jed had asked him if he had brought it up as a hint to get Jed to show up at the event. Of course, the clever boy hadn't answered the question directly but had posed a question of his own in response.

That was when he asked, *'You got friends, Mr. G?'* Naturally, Jed had answered yes, though he was a bit bewildered by the question. Max had dropped the second part of the bombshell. *'Keep 'em close, Mr. G. Keep 'em close.'*

Last week, Max had brought up something about knives. That was what had made Jed revisit their past conversations and realize that there was a common thread of seemingly disconnected questions from their usual narrative discussion. In the moment, with the first two questions, he had found them odd, but not odd enough to think that they were connected to the case.

It was the knives that got him thinking. Max had asked, *'Do you know anywhere where I could get some daggers to buy, Mr. G? I hear they're the new swing on the streets.'* Suddenly, acutely aware of the parallel to the case, Jed had responded with a 'no' as casually as he could. Max had chuckled to himself. *'Well,'* he'd continued, *'I hear there's a store that sells exotic daggers, that are collected from international places like, and it's near your building.'*

'Near my office?' Jed had asked.

He could hear the smile in the boy's voice when he finally answered. *'No. Y'know. Near your apartment.'*

As Jed cruised down the mostly empty country roads, heading back to the bustle of New York City, a thought struck him. Max had asked about daggers. Specifically, he had asked where he could get some daggers to buy, because he heard they were the new swing on the streets. That was one of the main things that Jed hadn't been able to crack while he had been at the cabin. He couldn't figure out how to factor in the knives and where the killer was getting them from. Max bringing up a place where you could get them, right in the city, under their noses, couldn't have been a coincidence. He had gone on to be as specific as to say that they were exotic daggers that were collected from international places. And that it wasn't near the building he worked, but his apartment.

Near your building... Jed knew that was supposed to connect to something else in his head. He knew Max was counting on him to telepathically connect to the secret message. *Near your building.* He had gone on to clarify that he did not mean Jed's office. That he was referring specifically to Jed's apartment complex. How did he know where he lived? Was that supposed to be relevant to the killer? Was Max implying that it was at this store nearby Jed's apartment that this killer was getting his knives from? That was the first place he was planning to stop at when he got back into the city.

It didn't unsettle him that Max knew where his building was. The boy was observant. Jed had noticed this when Max had casually mentioned that the three men who had attacked him were in the morgue on the same block as Jed's office. At that point, he and Max had never discussed where his office was located. When you were on the streets, you knew everything about the streets—and the younger you were, the more keen you had to be. *Near your building.* He was crossing the bridge into New York when a memory popped into his head.

Someone else had mentioned Jed's building, going as far as to refer to where Jed lived. *'I live around these parts. You live a couple blocks down from work, right?'* Jed began to remember, right then, how something inside him had tensed at the question—and not just at the question, but what it implied. Hugh had already known where he lived. How and why would he know where Jed lived without being told? Even if Hugh had seen him walking down that street after work, how did he know it was a couple of blocks away?

He had also mentioned that he lived around 'those parts', meaning on the other side of Manhattan from Jed. While Jed was stuck at a red light, he remembered how no matter what street the killer attacked his victim from, the CCTV footage always showed him heading toward the west—west of Manhattan, opposite from where Jed lived.

Maybe he was getting ahead of himself. Jed didn't have a genuine reason to suspect Hugh was a murderer. He thought back to their first conversation, where the man had brought up the murder that had taken place recently. If Jed remembered correctly, and he was sure he did, Hugh had said *'he had nowhere to run'*. How would he have known that the first victim had been trying to run? Jed tapped his finger against the wheel.

While watching the replays of the crime scene videos at least one hundred times for each murder over the past few days, trying to decipher the identity of the killer, Jed had made the observation that Allan had not only made it to his feet during the attack but had tried to run off in the opposite direction. The killer had intercepted him, however, and had switched the knife to his other hand, stabbing Allan from the left side so that he had no choice other than to run into the knife. How would Hugh have known that? Jed was getting a sick feeling. "Hey, Siri. Call Christie."

When the call connected, Christie didn't have time to speak before Jed demanded, "Christie. Where are you?"

"I'm at home. I'm off from work today. What's going on? Is everything okay?"

"Send me your location. There's something I need to discuss with you that can't wait. It absolutely cannot wait a second longer."

On the other end of the line, Christie rose to her feet and immediately headed for the shower. "I'll text it to you."

"Good. I'm already in Manhattan, so I'll be there soon."

He hung up just in time to click on the notification that popped up on his screen. Christie had sent the location. He programmed it into his GPS and made his way to her apartment. This wasn't his usual way of handling things. In normal circumstances, Jed wouldn't dare to demand her location or show up at her apartment uninvited. But these were far from normal circumstances.

All the things Jed had initially thought were completely normal things for Hugh to say were sounding sinister, like there was an underlying meaning behind every word.

'The homeless population is growing. I'm afraid it's getting a little out of hand.' Could that have been a confession of a motive for murder? Had Jed and Christie been right with their hunch that the murderer was killing people and marring their faces because he was trying to send a message to the city that these people weren't important and needed to be taken off of the street? Was he trying to be New York's hero, in some twisted way?

And what about Hugh's uncharacteristic silence right after Jed had mentioned the CCTV cameras that were all around the city? His comments had seemed normal on the surface, but Jed had read a bit of discomfort in his features. Initially, Jed had thought that he was just uncomfortable with the idea of being monitored by the government. I mean, who wasn't weirded out by that? Now, with all these other elements coming into play, Jed was starting to think that he was nervous about the cameras for another reason.

Hugh's demeanor when the CCTV had come up brought to mind the way the killer had turned toward the camera in the recording of the fourth murder. Maybe he hadn't been looking directly at the camera, but had just been looking to see if there was a camera on that street.

"Oh my God. Christie. I need to get to Christie. I can't keep all of this in my head for much longer," Jed mumbled to himself.

Jed recalled when Hugh had mentioned that he wasn't as efficient as Jed—that he was always at the office late, working. That meant he was always on the streets late, going home from work. And, if Hugh was at work late all the time, how would he know where Jed lived? How would he know it was a few blocks down and not clear across the city when all he could see from his window was that Jed had walked in that direction? Jed was growing more and more unsettled by the minute, and his hands were almost trembling as they gripped the steering wheel tightly, all his focus on making the last turn to drive into Christie's apartment's parking garage.

Was that what Max had meant when he kept talking about friends and enemies? Was that what he meant when he had warned Jed to keep an eye on them? Did Max know, or suspect, that Jed's friend was the murderer?

"Oh my God."

He mumbled the same phrase to himself, over and over, as he turned his engine off, opened the door, and jumped out of the Jeep. Jed had shot her a text to let her know he was about to take the elevator up, and she had sent him her floor number and apartment number. Though he was a bit dazed, he found the floor and the door easily. He took a deep breath before knocking. *Alright, Gray*, he thought to himself, *get it together.*

"Jed!"

The door opened, and there she was in all her glory. Christie was more beautiful than he remembered, and her smile made his breath stick in his throat. His eyes raked down over her, from her loosely curled hair to her white tank top and gray sweatpants. Before she could say anything else, his hands wound neatly under hers to circle her waist and pull her into his chest. For a heartbeat, they stood like that, without moving, until Christie slipped her hands up over his arms to wind them around his neck.

His heart trembled. She had never hugged him that way before. It was always the friendly, around-the-arms hug. The way she'd just trailed her fingers over his shoulders as she raised her arms was making his pants tighten, and he was glad he'd chosen to wear denim rather than sweats. Jed closed his eyes, focusing on thoughts of cold water, wrinkled prunes, and the spiky grass in New York City parks that made him itch.

When they finally separated, they still didn't speak. They stood, frozen, in the doorway, looking at each other, tensions flaring like electricity between them.

"It's good to see you," Christie said, breaking the silence.

Jed grinned. "It certainly is a pleasure to see you, Detective."

She shook her head at him and ushered him into her apartment. He glanced around the space as she pulled the door closed. It was a lot like his apartment, with floor-to-ceiling windows on one side of the room and an open-concept living, kitchen, and dining area. The kitchen was on the left side, the white oak cabinets and gas stove conveying an air of sophistication and simultaneous grit that made the space feel warm and beautiful—but like it was a good place to get down and dirty with some delectable cooking. The kitchen island had a waterfall of quartz down the side, and there was a woven fruit basket atop it holding bananas, oranges, and avocados.

Closer to the left side of the apartment, but still in the middle of the room, a white sectional couch and oval oak coffee table sat on top of a rustic pink, pale orange, and gray Persian handwoven rug. On the far left, an acrylic desk blended into the bustling skyline, with an acrylic chair to match. A few books were on top of the desk. Jed thought that must be where she had been when he had called late at night to talk about the case, and he had heard her scribbling down notes like she always did.

"You can make yourself comfortable on the couch," she said as she walked into the kitchen. "Can I get you anything?"

"Just yourself," Jed remarked, looking her up and down.

Her movement slowed where she was behind the kitchen island, and confusion covered her face. She had caught his casual look-over of her just then, and her heart was racing inside her chest. It made her feel faint to have him in her space the way he was, his brown hair and dark green muscle tee a stark contrast against the white material of the couch. His brown eyes joined the mix as he looked at her intently.

"What?"

A smile tugged at Jed's lips. He sank further into the soft white cloud that was her sofa and let his head fall back against the headrest, willing the weight of the case to fall off his shoulders.

"Just yourself," he repeated with ease. "Come sit next to me."

Christie did, after hesitating for a few seconds, and sank into the couch next to Jed. They sat in silence for a while, just breathing in and out, letting the stillness between them sizzle with unspoken words.

Jed looked over at Christie, who was twisting the gold Cartier band she always wore on her middle finger. "We should do this more often. It's very relaxing."

"What should we do more often?"

He smiled as he leaned his head back again and sighed a deep sigh of satisfaction.

"Just sit in each other's company, in silence. This is very relaxing."

"Interesting idea you've got for what 'relaxing' means, Gray."

"I'm always relaxed when I'm with you, Christie," he replied, easily.

Her eyes widened as she watched him breathe in and out, deeply and slowly, his eyes closed.

A grin formed on Jed's lips. "But adding a soft sofa and silence into the mix just really seals the deal."

She swallowed as she watched him swallow, his Adam's apple bobbing.

"I brought you something," he said, reaching into his pocket with his eyes still closed.

Christie looked over at him, a smiled tugging at her lips. "Did you now? Something to butter me up after ditching me all week, to go see your wife and kids?"

Jed chuckled. "The wife sends kind regards…"

"Ha ha ha," she droned, unimpressed.

That made him laugh, and he looked over at her as he handed her a small bag. She pulled it open, and her quiet gasp made the hours he'd spent searching for the perfect specimen worth it.

"A pink shell?"

He watched her pout a little as her eyes moistened and she clutched it to her chest. She'd mentioned in passing that her dad had always hunted for seashells for her whenever he went to the seaside or to a lake.

"Jed, thank you," she said, tears breaking her voice.

He reached for her again, pulling her into another quick hug. "Aw, it wasn't supposed to make you cry. It was supposed to make you happy."

"I'm crying because I'm happy."

He smiled. "Good."

Jed resisted the urge to kiss her on the forehead, on the nose, and on her glossy lips. Instead, he sat back on the sofa again and resigned himself to silence. *Breathe in, breathe out, breathe in, breathe out. Focus on your deep breathing, Jed*, he thought to himself.

To his surprise, Christie slid her way further over to him and leaned her head against his arm. He grinned. "Something on your mind, Detective?"

"Not really, no."

"Just in a cuddly mood?"

"Something like that," she replied.

"Something like that? Or just that?"

"Well, yes, I am in a cuddly mood. Except this isn't a cuddle. I'm just leaning against your arm."

Jed chucked. "Let me fix that."

Leaning down, he slipped an arm under her knees and lifted them so they were over his legs as he pulled her closer with the other arm around her back so she could lean directly against his chest.

"Is this better?" he asked into her hair.

She nodded her approval, and Jed smiled. He went back to leaning his head against the sofa, not wanting the moment to ever end. After a few minutes, though, he sighed heavily into the quietness and raised his head again.

"What's the matter?" Christie asked. "Not satisfied with this position?"

She was looking at him, their faces close enough for him to feel her breath on his lips. She watched his eyes darken at the question, realizing too late the insulation it held. She flushed.

"That's a dangerous question to ask, Detective. Unless you want me to hold you captive as my little spoon when I fall asleep, we need to talk about the case. I'm dangerously close to just… passing out right now."

Tingles raced through her at the thought of spooning with Jed, her back to his front, locked in an embrace as he slept. She cleared her throat. She wasn't sure if she should retreat to the other end of the sofa, but when his left hand came to rest on her calves where they lay across his knees, she relaxed into his side again.

"So. Let's rewind a bit. The last time we spoke, I'd shared my deductions, and we'd concluded that the case was cold."

Christie nodded.

"Well, Detective, the case has heated up very quickly."

Her eyes widened, and a smile spread across his cheeks. "You look like you're ready to jump up to go get your book and pen."

Christie's cheeks colored. "That was what crossed my mind, yes."

"Well go on."

She slipped her feet to the floor and walked to the other side of the room where her acrylic desk was pressed up against the glass. She extracted the book on the bottom of the pile into her hands without disturbing the rest and picked up a pen. He'd watched her hips sway all the way to the table and watched them sway as she walked back to sit next to him.

He looked over at her and patted his knee again, giving her the signal to put her feet back. She did, settling back into the nook at his side, opening her book to a fresh page.

"Here's what's changed. I had a long conversation with my mom, late into the hours of this morning, about something in my past that I thought would refresh my perspective on the homeless and those suffering with addiction on the streets of New York. I also hoped it would help me understand better why the killer would target the people that he's targeting. It was a lot of heavy lifting emotionally, but in the end, it helped me work through part of the case that I had overlooked before."

"What did you and your mom talk about?" Christie asked, looking up at him.

Jed tucked a strand of her hair behind her ear. His voice lower as he responded. "Nothing that I want to sully your pretty ears with."

He looked off into the distance for a few moments before continuing.

"After that talk, I knew with utmost certainty what I needed to do. There were some clues that a client of mine had been dropping during our addiction therapy sessions. You know I work with addicted people who are homeless, and of course, word on the street moves like wildfire. He is on the street at the same age that I was, with the same mindset I had, and my conversation with my mom about my experience made me realize just how much of the inner workings of my story was intertwined with what happened on the streets—the conversations I had with my friends when we were as high as high could be, or the mischief we got into, or the plans of our enemies that we saw coming from a mile away and could intercept. There's a certain level of... perception the street gives you that you slowly lose as you grow older. All of that is to say that I realized he has been trying to tell me something for the past few weeks about the case, and I've been paying attention to everything but that. Not on purpose, but I didn't ascribe the level of importance that I should have to what he had been trying to tell me."

"You used to be on the streets as a kid?"

"Oh, Detective," he said wistfully, "I used to be a lot more than just on the streets as a kid. That is a story for another time."

Christie nodded. Her pen was poised to write, and Jed smiled down at her.

"So, over the past few weeks, this client of mine has said a couple of things that I now realize were hints of sorts—clues, if you will—about the status of the killer. What made me take so long to realize that these were hints, or were even related to the case, was the way he asked the questions. This client of mine is very... peculiar. He never asks a direct question if he can avoid it, and he always prefers to get you to say something rather than saying anything himself. But, at the time, given the larger context of our conversations, the questions seemed harmless. It was in a later session, when he asked the third question, that I realized he was trying to say something more than just asking random questions, and I had to revisit the previous session's notes. It's a good thing I'm a pro at making client notes."

He said that part as he watched Christie scribble in her notebook, writing what he had just shared about his client's three hints.

"By the time we got to the third question," Jed continued, "that's when the questions themselves had taken on an air of mystery. His first question had caught me off guard, for sure, but at the moment, I had just put it down to this strange sense of curiosity that sometimes led him to ask uncomfortably personal questions. I never take those questions for granted or answer them lightly. Because, at some point, those questions could turn into the anchor points for a bigger exploration into something he's feeling, something he's thinking, or a belief system he has built for himself. The first question was, 'Y'know, Mr. G, they say we should keep our friends close but our enemies closer. Do you think they're on to something?'"

He paused so Christie could keep up with her notes and watched her pen fly across the page, adding in her own analysis as she went.

"That question, I thought, was random. He had asked that after we had finished discussing something related to his family. So, naturally, I thought he was asking me something coded about family relationships and whether or not to keep them. But, since I wasn't sure, I answered the question as literally as I could. I told him I've heard the version where they say it's better to have an outright enemy than a friendly enemy and that it was always a good idea to keep track of what your enemies are up to. After all, you can't defeat them or escape them if you have no clue what they are up to. He had found that particularly funny and had burst out laughing. Then, all he responded with was, *If you say so, Mr. G. If you say so.'*

At first, the laughter made me feel bad. I couldn't figure out if it was because I had missed the deeper meaning of his question or if he had just found what I said funny. Sometimes, it's hard to tell with him. The week after that, he asked another question along the same line of friendships and enemies. This time, it was even more vague and unrelated to what we had been talking about. He asked me, *'You got friends, Mr. G? I don't ever hear you mention anyone.'"*

"Obviously," Jed said, looking intently at Christie, who had looked up at him just then, "I said yes. Then he said the strangest thing. He said, *'Keep 'em close. Mr. G. Keep 'em close.'"*

Christy nodded along, her page filling up more and more by the minute.

"It was last week, in our most recent chat, that he brought up something that made me realize the other two questions were connected to the case. He brought up knives. He asked me, *'Do you know anywhere where I could get some daggers to* buy, Mr. G? I hear they're the new swing on the streets.' And he said it so casually, too—as though it was a perfectly normal thing to talk about with your addiction therapist.

Of course, I said no. I thought, for sure, that would have ended the matter, but he continued. That's when and where things get interesting. He said, 'Well, I hear there's a store that sells exotic daggers that are collected from international places, like, and it's near your building.' I asked if he meant near my office. By that stage, I could hear him smiling as he answered. He didn't mean my office. He meant my apartment."

Christie's eyes were wide as she stared at Jed. "So, your client has been trying to give you clues about the killer all this time?"

"That's how seems. It was the way he asked where he could buy them—as though he had known that we were trying to figure out where the daggers the killer was using were coming from. And it was the way he specifically mentioned that these were exotic, internationally collected daggers. While I was at the cabin, that was one thing I couldn't figure out how to reconcile. I couldn't figure out how to factor in the knives. Where the killer was getting them, and that my client just randomly brought up exactly where you could get them, right in the city, under our noses. It's definitely not a coincidence.

Then, that got me thinking even harder. *Near your building.* He had gone on to clarify that he did not mean my office—that he was referring specifically to my apartment complex. How did he know where I lived? Was that supposed to be relevant to the killer? Was he implying that it was at this store near my apartment that this killer was getting his knives?

It didn't unsettle me very much that my client somehow knew where my building was, but it had reminded me of someone else who had mentioned knowing where I live—a person who had made me uncomfortable right away. '*I live around these parts. You live a couple blocks down from work, right?'* My colleague at work had asked me that question, and the implication of the question had immediately made me feel unsettled. It implied that he had already known where I lived. At the same time, Hugh, my colleague, had also mentioned that he lived around 'those parts', meaning on the other side of Manhattan from me. While I was stuck in traffic at a red light, I remembered how, no matter what street the killer attacked his victim from, the CCTV footage always showed him heading towards the west."

Christie chimed in. "Oh. So, the direction of his home versus your home, and his subtle question and knowledge of where you live are playing together to create an uncomfortable situation when you factor in the direction the killer tends to come from and escape to."

Jed nodded. "It gets worse. In our very first conversation, he had brought up the murder that had happened over the weekend. He had said of the victim, '*he had nowhere to run'*. But there's no way he could have known that unless he had been there himself. I only noticed this detail while watching the replay of the crime scenes over and over again. Allan had tried to run away, but the killer had intercepted him and used his momentum against him in the end."

"So, he mentioned something in casual conversation that only case investigators, the victim, and the killer would know." Christie was starting to get visibly excited.

"Right. And we know he's not the victim, and he's not one of us. Another thing he'd said in that first conversation was, *'The homeless population is growing. I'm afraid it's getting a little out of hand'*. I think that could have been a confession of a motive for murder."

Christie's mouth hung open. "He could have accidentally or intentionally spilled his motive because he thought his tracks were covered."

Jed nodded. "At one point, after I mentioned the CCTV cameras that were all around the city, I could tell that Hugh hadn't know that. It made him deeply uncomfortable. At the time, I just thought that he was uncomfortable with the idea of being monitored by the government. Now, with all these other elements coming into play, I thought that he was nervous about this CCTV footage for another reason. Then, while I'd been thinking about that, it brought to mind the killer's fourth murder—when he turned to face the camera. I started wondering if, maybe, he hadn't meant to look directly at the camera but had been looking to see if there was a camera on that street."

Christie gasped. "Jed, I think you're onto something. We need to get an interview with him as soon as we can because this could take the case in a completely different direction than where we had been going before."

"I agree. And there are so many other small things that have happened in conversation that all point to him being the one behind these murders. I can't help but wonder if that was what my client was trying to hint at when he kept bringing up friendships and enemies. What if he was telling me to keep an eye on them because he knew a particular person was involved?"

"I don't even know what to say! There's so much to think about and so many angles to take."

Jed looked at the time. "I've got a meeting with this same client in half an hour, so I've got to get into the office. If I'm lucky, he'll casually drop another hint that will help us decide what to do next. The only thing I haven't made sense of so far is why Hugh would have called me to gloat about Ethan."

He slipped Christie's legs gently back to the floor and stood up, easing into a stretch.

"You, stay here," he instructed when he turned to her, "in case I get any news and need to rush back home to you."

Jed reached for his phone and keys and tucked them into his pocket. Her head was swimming, both from the information they'd just shared between them and his casual statement. *Rush back home to you.*

"But stay on guard, in case I get the kind of news that will make us have to run to the station."

Christie nodded and grinned, shutting her book and rising to follow him to the door.

"Either way, I'll see you again before the day ends. Standby, Detective."

"Aye aye, partner."

CHAPTER 28

JUST BEFORE FOUR PM, Jed was finally at his desk in his office. He'd stopped to get a hotdog before coming into work since he had missed lunch by talking over the case with Christie. Usually, by this time on Friday afternoons, he would have already spoken with at least two clients and would be waiting for Max to call so he could sign off work for the day. This Friday was a little different since he was just arriving, and it was well after three.

He wondered what the boy had been up to the past week. He wondered whether Max would offer him any kind of new insight into the case, or whether he would be ready to talk about how his mother's onslaught had made him feel. Maybe he would finally be ready to come see him in-office? All of those possibilities were in the cards. There was hardly anything off limits in conversation with Max. Last week, they'd gone as far as discussing sex.

Now that he had pieced Max's puzzle together and was on guard for anything else the boy could potentially share, Jed was sure that he had everything that he needed to confirm whether his hunch about who Max was referring to was correct or not.

At his core, Jed was anxious about his upcoming conversation with Max. That unease was compounded by his feelings for Christie that were swelling by the minute and the pressure he felt knowing that his mom was anxiously waiting for an update on the case. This case had come all the way home to his doorstep and unraveled itself in a mass of confusing turns, deceitful facades, and angry suspects. The target of the murders were people he worked with in his day-to-day career, that he shared the common experience of addiction and the desire to recover with. Now, the case had flipped on its head, and the primary suspect turned out to be someone he knew well. Or at least, someone he had thought he knew well.

On his way into the office a few minutes ago, Jed had been relieved to find the hallways empty and all the doors in the office closed. He wasn't sure whether or not Hugh was in, and if Jed was honest with himself, he had been dreading running into him. He just needed to be sure first.

Ring.

Jed looked at the clock across the room. It was exactly four pm.

"Hello?"

"Mr. G, what's up?"

Max seemed to be in an unusually pleasant mood today, and Jed stared at the phone.

"Hello, Maxwell," he answered. "How are you today?"

"I'm doing good, Mr. G. Did you check out that knife store I mentioned yet?"

Jed could hear the amusement in Max's tone. It bubbled over in the way he enunciated the word 'knife' and the way he, ever so casually, brought up the same question twice. Jed was on high alert.

"No, I haven't gotten the chance yet. I was out of town all week. I just got back in."

"Ah. You should check 'em out before they close this evening. You'll need one of 'em knives to tackle what's gonna go down on yer block later on."

Jed had been paying attention before, but now he all but launched himself upright in his chair, swinging his legs around and grabbing a nearby pen. Later on? What was Max getting at?

"Oh? What's gonna happen later on?" he asked as casually as he could.

"Oh, you know, there's this old guy on your stretch that people are getting tired of. He sleeps all day, all night. You know how old people are."

Jed's heart was pounding. "Let me guess. He's taking up too much real estate on the sidewalks?"

In the highest part of the old oak tree in Max's girlfriend's yard, a slow grin spread across his face. It seemed Mr. Gray was catching on to what he was trying to say. He'd been prowling around Jed's side of the city, scoping out his office building one night when he'd first noticed Hugh come out of the building and head home. He hadn't thought much of it until he saw Hugh and Jed walking together one afternoon, another time he'd been snooping around.

Max had been checking Jed out from afar to see whether he was right about him. From the start, when he'd first been recommended to Jed and had started his weekly calls, he'd gotten the impression that it was safe to confide in Jed. He'd ignored it until recently—until Jed had purchased a phone for him with his own money. Since then, Max had been scouting out Jed in secret. He'd observed him coming and going from his office to his home, trying to make sure he could trust him. He'd been thinking of starting in-person sessions with Jed.

Then, on the same night Hugh had murdered Larry, Max had been minding his own business in the back alleys of Manhattan when the scene had played out before his eyes. He hadn't moved, instead hunkering down and watching the whole thing happen. After Hugh had murdered the man, he had crossed the street and ripped his mask off. That was how he'd known it was him. He'd even seen the police cars when they arrived.

"Yeahhh," he answered. "The upstanding citizens can't walk in peace because of that junkie."

Max looked down at the blunt in his free hand, smoke curling upwards from the lit end. He knew what Mr. Gray would say if he knew he was smoking right then. He'd already given up most of the other harder drugs, but marijuana was his love. *You love it, I can understand that. But do you love it more than your own life?* He looked out over the city as far as his eyes could see and, sighing, let the blunt drop out of his hands, through the branches and leaves, and down to the ground.

"It's a real shame, though. Would hate to see him get kicked off the street because he ain't got nowhere to go."

Jed was making frantic notes. "Yeah. That would be a real shame. Too bad he can't defend himself."

"That be why I'm tellin' you about that there knife shop on your block. You could get one for him, like. So he can cut some food up tonight when he's cookin'. If you catch my drift, Mr. G?"

"Speaking of drifting, can you drive, Maxwell?" Jed asked, neatly switching the topic.

Max laughed and shook his head. "Man, I be drivin'. But I ain't got no papers."

Jed sighed, and it turned into a laugh halfway through when Max burst out laughing.

"Let's just move on."

Max laughed again, and Jed picked up his cellphone to shoot Christie a message.

Meet me at the station in ten minutes. We've got work to do.

"What?"

"You heard me. We need to organize a group of officers and set up a stakeout at the possible locations. We need to get moving. Now."

"Locations? There's more than one?"

"I checked out what Max said, and there's two old men on the same stretch as my apartment. One more closely matches the description he gave me, but it'll be better to stake out both, so our response time isn't delayed when the killer moves in."

Christie's eyes were pleading. "And you're this confident in what you were told?"

Jed was tightening the strap of his watch back around his wrist after just removing it to adjust the time. His eyes were determined, his expression was set, and his tone was firmer than Christie had ever heard it.

"I am as confident as if I had figured out this information myself. Does that satisfy your query, Detective?"

He looked down at her, watching her expression move between shock, disbelief, confusion, and finally, resignation. She nodded. Moving toward the door of her office and swinging it open, she called behind her.

"I'll be right back. Don't move."

When Christie came back into the room five minutes later, she was accompanied by a group of ten policemen. They all piled into her office, most of their arms crossed at the chest, their eyes studying Jed.

Christie took the lead, introducing them all, one by one, to Jed, then briefing the team on what was about to go down.

"We have reason to believe that there will be another attack on a homeless person at some time tonight on 58th St. There are two points at which we will need two teams of officers to stake out. Now," she said looking at their uniforms, "this is going to require some of you to be wearing plain clothes and some of you to remain in uniform. One of the plainclothes team will take a position at the restaurant across the street from one of the potential victims, and the other will take up a position in the bookstore across from the other potential victim," she pointed to a map, "along this stretch that we are focusing on. We are, of course, looking not just to thwart this murder attempt, but to capture the perpetrator and end his reign of terror."

Starting on her left side, she singled out five officers and called them forward.

"You guys are going to stake out at the bookstore next to Starbucks and directly across from the Hyatt apartments. The other five of you will stake out with Jed and I at the restaurant across from The Pink Café. Any questions?"

"Do we have a time? An ETA or anything of the sort?" asked the officer closest to Christie. Jed noticed his sharp features and blue eyes.

"No," Jed answered. The man's eyes flicked to him, away from Christie, who was rummaging through her drawer for the case notes. "What we have is a pattern of behavior. This killer has most often struck between the hours of nine pm and five am, so we'd be advised to buckle down for the night. Let's hope tonight he's in the mood to go home early."

They all nodded.

"You get to decide amongst yourselves which two of you will be in plain clothes and which three will remain in uniform," Christie said, as she made her way back around the desk to stand next to Jed.

"Dibs on plain," five of the men chimed at the same time.

The officer Jed had spoken to earlier rolled his eyes.

"Fine. I'll stay in uniform. The ladies prefer it that way, anyway."

The rest of the men laughed. The blue-eyed officer winked at Christie, catching Jed's attention.

"After you, Detective," Jed murmured to Christie when she looked up at him.

They set off. The first group of officers that would keep an eye on the homeless man across from the bookstore made their way one at a time to attract the least suspicion possible. The two plain-clothed officers took turns walking down the street and entering the store as though they were interested in making a purchase while the three remaining uniformed officers from that team took the roundabout route from the station and down a parallel street to take up their positions in the alleyway next to the store.

They crouched behind garbage skips and between mounds of rotting fruit and meat, eyes focused on the homeless man across the street, who was just starting to stir. It was just past dusk. After they had finished working through all the additional details of their mission—like the killer's profile and features, his gait, the direction he tended to enter the crime scene and other like details the officers would need to properly identify the suspect—the first group settled into the shadows of the alley.

A few blocks below them, Jed, Christie, and the two plain-clothed officers of the second team were sitting in the restaurant across from the popular Pink Café, ordering starters. Christie had complained under her breath of being hungry, and Jed had called for a waiter without hesitation. She stared at him.

"I thought I was whispering. Do you have amplifiers in your ears or something?"

He looked at her as he took a sip of the Lyre's in his glass. "I am always intentionally aware when I am around you."

She nodded, though her stomach coiled into knots—for different reasons than the nervous ones that were already there. Through the glass panes that separated them from the street, they could see an elderly man, clearly homeless, holding a cup in his hands.

Jed's heart twinged. As they'd passed the man on the opposite side of the street, they could hear him calling out for water. Water. He didn't have any water to drink. His voice had been feeble—only audible because the traffic on the street had been at a standstill because of the stoplight further down. Jed was sure he was the one Max had been referring to. He just knew it, deep down inside.

Outside, next to the restaurant, the three uniformed officers were crouched in varying positions in another alley, hiding, lying in wait for the killer to make his move.

"The restaurant closes at eleven. The bookstore closes at ten," Christie whispered to Jed.

Jed nodded. "It's just after eight thirty. Let's hope the killer pulls his stunt by then."

Jed looked out to the streets again. The crowds had dispersed, and there was only the occasional passerby hurrying to either get home or get to dinner with friends. This side of town, the one his apartment was on, was a little less congested during the nights than central Manhattan, and Jed loved it.

During his apartment hunt, he had spent a few weeks scoping out the neighborhoods he wanted to search in. The sparse night crowds hadn't been lost on Jed as he investigated, sometimes in this very restaurant, having dinner and scouting the area. Now, he was in this restaurant again, digesting yet another dinner, his eyes fixed on the old man across the street, who seemed to have given up his pleas for water and had laid down.

It was nine-fifteen when Christie grabbed his arm, her eyes wide as she stared out the window behind him. He put his drink down and turned to look, thankful the restaurant had dim lighting, and saw that the old man had moved a little further down the street, where the businesses were long closed. Jed figured he had moved away so that he could get some rest without the noise that the patrons of the restaurant made when they were entering and exiting.

In the darkness, his eyes picked out the silhouette of a man, dressed in all black, hands stuffed in his pockets, a hoodie over his head. The static from the P25 reached Jed's ears, and he grabbed it where it had been attached to his hip. The officer confirmed what he and Christie had been thinking.

"We have a man approaching that matches the suspect's visual description. Keeping him in sight."

His heart was pounding as he raised the radio to his lips.

"We have a visual of the suspect as well."

Jed rose to his feet and made his way to the window, peering out of it with Christie fast on his heels. They watched the figure walk a block down until he was close enough to touch the homeless man. It played out just like it had the first time Jed had watched the footage of the first murder.

The man veered off his path, and his left hand came free from his pocket. The blade of a gleaming knife shone through the air.

"Suspect is the killer. Move out."

Jed barely felt the ground beneath his feet as he swung the door open and rushed out after the three officers who were running toward the scene, weapons drawn. It was as though time had slowed—like he could see everything all at once playing out before him.

One officer tackled the knife-swinging man, who hadn't seemed to notice the seven people speeding toward him. The two toppled to the ground, and so did the dagger, its blade sheathed in blood.

Christie was calling an ambulance as handcuffs were being clicked shut, and Jed rushed over to the groaning man on the ground. His hands trembled as the man writhed in pain, and as he pored over his shaking body, he found one wound on the lower left of his abdomen. Jed applied pressure while the officers called in to the station, and the one that had tackled the killer pulled him to his feet, ripping the mask off his face.

Jed's eyes made contact with Hugh's blue ones. They looked green under the yellow streetlight, and Jed's heart lurched, sank, and broke all at the same time. He'd been right. *Max* had been right. Hugh had been behind all these murders. Eyes level with Jed's, Hugh grinned the way he always did, his arms taut behind him where the officer was holding him. The familiarity of the smile made Jed feel ill.

The sound of sirens filled the New York air as Christie dropped to his side to speak to the old man, who was still groaning. At least groaning meant he was alive. Jed turned to look back up the street. The blue and red lights of the NYPD and the red ones of the coming ambulance lit up the night. Sirens were blaring. Onlookers were gathering around. For a moment, Jed squeezed his eyes shut, trying to ground himself in the present.

"Hi. I'm Detective Christie Jamison, with the New York Police Department. We're gonna get you to the hospital, okay? And we're gonna get you some water, too."

The groaning man could only manage to nod, and the burden in Jed's heart lightened for a moment when he heard Christie mention water. She'd heard his pleading cries earlier, too. As though to check once more if he was seeing correctly, to check if his mind was conjuring up images, Jed looked over at Hugh again, who was already looking at him.

"Jed, are you okay?"

He turned back to Christie. His eyes were moist, and he forced a smile.

"Congrats, Detective. We did it."

CHAPTER 29

AT THE STATION, JED and Christie stood and stared at each other in silence in the dark of Christie's office. She was rummaging around for the case folder, and when she found it and turned back to Jed, she found him staring out the window, eyes glazed.

"Are you okay, Gray?"

"Doing just fine, Detective."

"I think that's the first time you've lied to me. You must really not be handling this well."

Jed's jaw tightened, and he still stared out the window. Silence stretched between them when he didn't respond. Christie sighed and walked over to him. She hesitated only a moment before raising her arms and wrapping them around his neck to pull him into a hug.

His hands came up to hold her waist right away, and he tugged her even closer, enveloping her against his body.

"And I think that's the first time you've initiated physical contact, Detective. You must really be feeling sorry for me."

Christie sighed right by his ear, and Jed closed his eyes, letting the security of the hug wash over him. The way this

woman made butterflies erupt inside his chest and simultane-
ously grounded him every time she was near him was out of
this world. It was getting harder and harder for him to keep
all his feelings compressed.

"The occasion calls for it," she said.

He only hummed in response, and her eyes widened. "Well,
not that there was never an occasion for it before, but I—"

"I understand what you meant, Detective."

She sighed again, and he chuckled a little, the vibration
rumbling through her where their chests pressed together.

A thought occurred to Jed. "Though it makes me wonder
whether you've been afraid to touch me all this time."

Christie swallowed as Jed pulled back, keeping his grip on
her waist firm so he could look down at her in the dark while
their bodies were still in an embrace.

"And it makes me wonder whether you deciding to hug
me for the first time in the dark is you trying to tell me
something," he whispered, his lips slightly parted.

His eyes were on hers, and her lips followed suit. His eyes
dropped to them as he released her.

"C'mon, Detective. Let's get this interview wrapped up so
we can both catch a break."

In the investigative room, three armed officers were standing around Hugh, who was sitting handcuffed, in the interviewee's chair. Christie dropped the folder on the table.

"Let's cut straight to the chase, shall we?"

Jed was standing behind Christie, arms folded, in the same stance he had taken when they'd interviewed Carrillo. Hugh hardly acknowledged Christie. He was staring right at Jed.

"So, Mr. Larson…"

"I'll spare you the pleasantries, *Detective*," Hugh spat, his nasty glare now leveled at Christie. "I killed them because, *like I said* to Jed over here, they were getting out of hand. The state refuses to do something about the problem and treats those scumbags like they deserve any kind of sympathy for their disgusting addictions. Who the fuck cares? *Nobody*. I did the cleanup myself."

Hugh huffed. "The housing crisis is totally out of control. Developers are taking over the affordable housing and pushing more and more vulnerable people onto the streets. The system is bursting at the seams! These people have nowhere to turn, have lost hope, and turn to drugs to escape their realities. I was bringing the crisis to everyone's attention! It was on the news, on the front page of the newspapers, trending online. People can't ignore it anymore! If it took a few faceless drug addicts to get the message out, it was worth it!"

Christie didn't flinch at the tirade, and neither did Jed. But he felt himself die a little inside as Hugh expressed what he truly thought of the homeless and addicted. He felt like someone had punctured his heart. Jed had been one of those addicted people, wreaking havoc on the streets of New York, and he was so happy his mom had fought for him. Hugh was berating the very existence of some of the same people he worked with in his everyday job.

Christie was all control, all ice. "You sound mighty proud of yourself, Mr. Larson. You think you did a good job?"

Hugh grinned. "Sure as fuck, I did. I took out the most annoying ones, too—the ones that take up too much space in the neighborhoods people live in. Residents of this state deserve to walk home without having to fear old druggies who might try to rob them of their valuables. The only loss here are those beautiful artisan daggers that I used. Those were a nod to my ancestry and great taste.

I knew every one of them. They came to see me as a counselor, but I couldn't help them. They were too far gone. We are stuck in the middle, trying desperately to help these people with no aid from the government—which is only focused on helping the rich get richer on the back of the poor! People need to know what is going on and wake up to the reality around them!"

Jed's brows furrowed at that, and two of the officers that stood behind Hugh looked over at each other, equally puzzled. Jed thought for a moment.

With a voice that was both deadly firm and calm, Jed said, "Let me get this straight... you failed to help them because you're a mental case that's a fucking scar on the face of humanity, and somehow, you've convinced yourself to focus on their vulnerabilities instead of your failings as a counselor and murder four innocent people?"

Hugh looked surprised at Jed's outburst, but the look was replaced by a smile. "You mean three murders? You interrupted my fourth."

Christie interjected, "It's interesting that you would say three, Mr. Larson, because there are four murders in this case, and—"

"What?" he asked, interrupting Christie as though he was hearing that detail for the first time. "I killed the first one, Allan—the poor, lumbering idiot never stood a chance. Then Warren near Starbucks—he was the hardest to take down. He had life in him, I'll give him that, but I gave it to him like there was no tomorrow. And then, there was Larry."

Hugh's expression was one of bewilderment that Jed was reading as genuine. But this was a serial killer they were dealing with, and if he hadn't killed Ethan, who had?

Hugh's gaze turned to Jed as he continued. "Larry was the third, and after I learned about those stupid cameras, I messed him up good and well, so even if he was the last one I managed to get, my point would be clear. And you all messed up the fourth one. I ruined their faces because it didn't matter who they were. To most people in this city, those homeless people blend into the shadows and go unnoticed as we go about our lives, anyway."

Hugh's expression darkened suddenly, and Jed watched a potent mixture of anger and disgust fill his features. "As for Charles tonight, I only managed to give him one good stab before whoever tackled me took me down. I don't know how I didn't hear you all coming. The wind must have been blowing in the wrong direction. If you hadn't *interrupted* me, I'd have killed him and all the others on my list, too. But I guess my downfall was that I shouldn't have been bothered to be friends with *you*. I didn't think you'd catch on. It's not like I was dropping tons of hints. How did you figure it out, anyway?"

Something hot surged inside Jed's chest when Hugh directed that question at him, and he recognized it as the protectiveness of Max. Christie cut in before Jed could give the leering man a piece of his mind.

"That is for us to know and for you to find out in court. Enjoy your stay in your cell, Mr. Larson."

CHAPTER 30

BACK IN CHRISTIE'S OFFICE, Jed sank into the chair across from her desk and let the quiet soothe his mind as best it could. As he opened his mouth to speak, there was a knock on the door, and it swung open before Christie could even respond.

"Great job tonight, Detective."

It was the blue-eyed officer who had winked at Christie earlier, before they had staked out at the restaurant and bookshop. Jed had learned that his name was Jason. The man had completely ignored his presence and was directing his megawatt smile at Christie.

She gave him a sweet smile back and nodded. "Thanks, Jason. You guys were right on the ball with response times."

Jason smiled again.

"But it's all thanks to Jed's sleuthing throughout the case," Christie continued, looking over at Jed, whose eyes were already fixed on her.

Jason looked over at Jed, as though noticing him for the first time.

"Yeah, that was on point the way you predicted how it would turn out. Great work, guys. I'm off to celebrate with some drinks with the team. Wanna come, Detective?"

Jason winked at Christie again, and Jed's jaw tightened until his teeth hurt. Christie smiled politely, but shook her head no.

"We've got some wrapping up to do for the case, so I'll have to join you guys another time. Thanks for the invite."

Jason shrugged and waved as he retreated and closed the door, and they could hear him calling down the hallway to the rest of the officers. Jed rose to his feet without speaking, and with two strides to the door, bolted it shut from the inside before returning to his seat, his eyes once more fixed on Christie.

"Everything alright, Gray?"

It was quiet for a long moment before Jed eventually made himself respond.

"Everything's just fine, Detective."

Christie frowned. "That's the second time you've lied to me since I've met you. Are you not a good liar, or are you trying to make it easy so I can tell?"

Jed raised a brow. Christie sighed and got up, walking around the desk to sit on the end, facing Jed.

"Should I be worried that you haven't said anything about the fact that Hugh only confessed to three murders and left out Ethan?"

Jed closed his eyes. Something about Ethan's case hadn't been sitting right with him from the beginning. When he'd connected Max's hints back to Hugh, the voicemail had felt like a gut punch. Why would Hugh have stooped as low as he had to say Ethan's murder was Jed's fault? Now that Hugh had confessed to the three other murders and not Ethan's, the feeling of empty sadness that he'd felt when he'd first learned Ethan had been killed was back, and more intense. Jed couldn't reconcile it. Who had killed Ethan? Who had left him that nasty voice message?

"Should I be worried that you bolted the door and shut us in my office at eleven o' clock at night?"

Jed watched her features carefully, trying to discern whether she was asking him subtly to unlock the door. If she was trying to let him know, she felt unsafe.

"Should I be concerned that you didn't speak, not even once, when Jason popped in?" she continued. "You didn' even look at him."

Jed kept his eyes level with hers and watched her eyes ru down over his chest to his lap for a split second. She look back up to his eyes.

"Should I be concerned that you're trying to process los who you thought was a friend and the fact that your cl was right all along?"

Christie sighed when he didn't respond to that ques either.

"You're not usually this quiet, Jed. I'm worried. Say s e-thing. Anything."

Christie watched his jaw tighten yet again, the way it had when Jason had first entered the room, when he'd called her 'detective' and invited her to have a drink with him.

What Jed wanted to say was *You're mine, and I'll get charged for the assault of an officer if Jason doesn't back off.* But she wasn't his. And that was pissing him off more than anything else that had happened today. He wanted to focus on the case and process through the events like he should, but he couldn't stop hearing Jason's voice in his head, calling Christie 'detective' the way he did. Jed couldn't let himself speak when he was this riled up.

Christie's expression grew sadder the longer he bit his tongue, and she got to her feet. "May I give you a hug?"

Christie watched him stand and do a light stretch before he did the 'come here' motion with his fingers. Her knees turned to Jell-O. She walked into his arms and wound hers around his neck, and her body pressed against him soothed the jealous fire burning inside him for a moment.

"If I'm honest, Detective," he whispered into her ear as he tightened his arms around her until she almost couldn't breathe, "I think I've become a bit territorial when it comes to you. I despised hearing him call you 'detective'. That's *our* thing."

Christie flushed a shade of pink she had never flushed before and was sure she would explode from his voice so near to her ear whispering the way he was. She was thankful he couldn't see her cheeks, but she still hid her face in his neck.

"So, you were jealous?" she asked.

"Painfully so."

Her breath caught in her throat, and her thighs were on fire. Jed whispered again, and this time it was her heart that was on fire.

"I'm selfish. I want you to myself."

Jed continues to search for Ethan's killer while he is thrown into another case that will test his partnership with Christie. Read the next book in the series: **Flavors of Gray** https://bi t.ly/JedGray2.

***

Want to learn why Jed was chosen for this partnership with Christie over any of the other qualified therapists? Claim your FREE copy of **Origins of Gray** https://dl.bookfunnel.com/q

ikjjxz4u7and learn more about how Jed came to know Ethan. Or you can go the Jodi's website: <u>jodiwalter.com</u> to get the link to download it when you join her newsletter.

***

Honest reviews of my books help bring them to the attention of other readers, who are more likely to read something from a new-to-them author if it has more reviews. Reviews are the lifeblood of little authors like me. I would be grateful if you can find the time to leave a review. Thank you!

Here is the universal link to this book to leave a review: https://bit.ly/JedGray1

Or you can scan this QR code with your phone to take you to the universal book page:

ACKNOWLEDGEMENTS

I am grateful for the ongoing support and inspiration from my family and friends. Without them, I would not have had the courage or confidence to conquer all that I have so far. It is comforting to know that they are alongside me as I dare to continue on the amazing adventure we call life! I can't wait to see what we can all do next! Even though writing can be daunting and overwhelming, if my stories help to inspire one person to go for one of their dreams, it has been totally worth it!

ABOUT THE AUTHOR

Jodi Walter was born and raised in the Western Prairies of Canada. She spent her childhood enjoying nature and animals on the family farm. She continues to volunteer with animal rescues and has adopted two rescue dogs that she shares her home with today.

Jodi went through some difficult times in her early thirties when her marriage broke down and she became a single mom of a fantastic young son. After picking herself back up and succeeding in whatever challenge she faced, she became a firm believer that "we are never put in any situation we can not handle".

Her newest endeavour is to write mystery thriller stories for you to enjoy. Delving into her subconscious, she creates characters she hopes will connect with you. Jodi has experienced a profound amount of catharsis by putting her pen to paper and releasing her characters into the world.

Jodi's website: jodiwalter.com or https://thirteen-pages-b txdiq.mailerpage.io/

Jodi's Facebook: https://www.facebook.com/jodiwalterau thor

www.ingramcontent.com/pod-product-compliance
Lightning Source LLC
Chambersburg PA
CBHW021133260626
47169CB00005B/1589